Dirk van den Boom

Betrayal

DIRK VAN DEN BOOM

THE EMPEROR'S MEN

BETRAYAL

1

Once they entered the large encampment that housed the Western Army, Rheinberg got a first impression of the size and power of the Roman Empire. Gratian was able to lead 25,000 legionaries into battle, strengthened by auxiliary troops and a small entourage. Here in the camp, which the Emperor had set up nearly two weeks ago, something resembling a small town has developed inside the picket fences that the soldiers had rammed into the ground as a demarcation. The trek of the German infantry, guided by the roaring truck, was witnessed with silence by the masses of the Roman soldiers. The approximately 160 infantrymen looked like a very small, very lost column that marched through the wide path toward the giant tent of the Emperor, at any time in danger of being crushed by the overwhelming number of surrounding Roman soldiers.

Rheinberg almost developed claustrophobic anxiety at the thought. He pushed the emotion aside with care, focused on riding next to Aurelius Africanus and the two tribunes, progressing somewhat gracefully on top of his horse. From the corner of his eye, he scrutinized the glances of Roman soldiers. He hoped he didn't look too bad.

When they had reached the tent of the Emperor in about two hundred yards, the column stopped. From here on, only Africanus and Rheinberg were allowed to proceed. They dismounted from their horses, which were led away by members of the imperial bodyguard. After they had walked to the large linen canopy, four guardsmen who stood in front eyed them suspiciously from under their gleaming helmets. Finally, a curtain was thrown to the side, and an old, bearded man in full armor stepped out. Africanus and Rheinberg stopped before him.

"I'm Arbogast, General of the Emperor," the muscular man with a weathered face said. "My Lord ordered me to lead you. You are Trierarch Africanus?"

The officer confirmed this and presented the letter Renna had given him. Arbogast accepted it but stuck the paper carelessly into his belt. Then he fixed his gaze on Rheinberg. "And you are the leader of the strangers, of whom we have heard many fantastic tales?"

Rheinberg tried to smile, but the old warhorse didn't seem to notice. "I hope they have been nice tales, and nothing too negative."

"People talk a lot," replied Arbogast. "I hear you're German."

Rheinberg hesitated. Arbogast's name suggested that it was one of the numerous German officers in the Roman army. A predecessor of the legendary Stilicho, who would be a great man and a great failure in the not too distant future. Or maybe not anymore.

"I do come from the area, but –"

Arbogast uttered a sentence in a hard, completely incomprehensible-sounding language. Rheinberg was sure that it was one of the numerous German dialects. The Germans were still centuries away from any resemblance of unity.

"I don't understand you, General."

"You are not a German," said Arbogast.

"I'll explain it to the Emperor," Rheinberg dodged.

This seemed to satisfy the general, for he turned abruptly. "So follow me."

The interior of the tent was more like a hall. Thick carpets were laid out on the floor and dampened the steps. Close to the tent walls were guards who watched the visitors with attentive eyes. Furniture was distributed seemingly at random, and a rear part of the large room was separated by curtains, most likely this was the private area of the Emperor. Clamped up between two support posts of the imperial tent was a large, colorful and very artistic map of the Roman Empire. Before it, a mighty marble table stood that was completely overloaded with documents, maps, and other material. Next to the table, two men waited. One of them Rheinberg recognized immediately: He was young, barely more than 20 years

6

old, and he wore a richly embroidered toga under a purple cloak. It could only be Gratian, the Emperor of Western Rome. The look from the eyes of the young Emperor seemed awake and curious and Rheinberg regarded that as a good omen. The other man was much older, safely around his 50ies and just like Arbogast wearing full armor. He had to be a military in high position.

From the corner of his eye, Rheinberg saw Africanus settle on his knees. He immediately followed his example. No sooner had their knee touches the ground than he heard the soft voice of the Emperor.

"Arise. Later we have time for formalities. Arbogast, these are our guests?"

"It seems, my Emperor."

"Then offer them seats."

Servants appeared from the background and pushed chairs to the front. Out of nowhere, wine carafes and bowls with simple food appeared on the small table placed next to them. Arbogast, who appeared not to be too enthusiastic about the extent of hospitality, grunted and made a welcoming gesture, once Rheinberg and Africanus had risen.

"You have already met my faithful General Arbogast." The Emperor presented him again. "This is Malobaudes, King of the Franks and another highly respected counselor in military as well as civil matters."

Rheinberg gestured to the older man with a slight bow, which he silently took note of. The captain felt insecure. He had once attended an audience with Emperor Wilhelm II, along with 28 other young naval officers. It had been a very brief encounter, but the courtly ceremony had been reduced to the bare essentials for the Emperor's favorite soldiers. Wilhelm had appeared in a navy uniform and tried to treat its guests more like comrades and less like subjects. If Rheinberg remembered correctly, it all went like a bad operetta, although the spectacle surely had impressed at least some of his fellow officers. But there was a difference between Wilhelm and Gratian: While one dreamed of the war and the military, with its ceremonies, its pomp and splendor worshiped, the other, since

7

his youth, had led an endless war for the safety of his realm, lived more in field camps than in imperial residences, and was under the constant expectation of his people to oppose any threat. As much as the imperial West and the Eastern Empire were dominated in time of peace by courtly ceremonies of almost oriental proportions, so every Roman emperor also had to be a pragmatist and learn to do without these things if it was necessary. Marcus Aurelius, the famous philosopher-emperor, had spent the last years of his reign only on military campaigns, and this had no doubt contributed to his stoic beliefs. So young as Gratian might be, he had been influenced by life as a commander for a long time.

Africanus took it then to introduce himself as well as Rheinberg. They had both agreed that at the beginning the trierarch would be the one that would describe the past history of the arrival of the *Saarbrücken*, since the Emperor more easily would believe one of his soldiers. Africanus held his description short, closely following the facts and refraining from unnecessary embellishments. He also gave no judgment on the character traits of the new arrivals in order not to be suspected of wanting to influence the Emperor and his assessment unduly.

Gratian's face was expressionless, as he listened to the lecture. He was a picture of concentrated attention, and it was not discernible if he judged the accounts of the trierarch as credible. Arbogast's features, however, darkened with each progressing minute. The veteran seemed to hold little regard for this story, though Rheinberg could not see why – maybe he considered Africanus or himself as not trustworthy, the first probably seen as unduly influenced. Rheinberg had to always keep in mind that magic and sorcery in this era was regarded as something absolutely real, and a corresponding charge was done very quickly and would lead to a trial and a mostly deadly judgment.

When Africanus finished, there was no immediate reaction of the Emperor. Arbogast snorted but didn't express his opinion before Gratian spoke.

The Emperor turned his attention to Rheinberg. "It seems like you can perform miracles."

8

"No miracles, Your Majesty. I have some technical means that are unknown to you. But I'm human, mortal, and would be struck down by your generals here, if we should take up the sword against each other."

Arbogast's expression led to the conclusion that the general didn't consider this possibility as something bad.

"If I have understood Africanus correctly, you claim to have traveled through time."

"Yes, Emperor. But not on purpose. We don't have this power."

"So others have taken care of this?"

"Others or one other. We do not know."

"With what intention?"

"We do not know."

"And what are your plans now?"

Rheinberg took a deep breath. "My Emperor, we are castaways, if you will. We are looking for a home."

"My empire?"

"That would be convenient."

"What can you offer us?"

"Our technical achievements and knowledge."

"What do you ask for?"

"Security."

Gratian frowned. "Security? Who could be more secure than you with your mighty ship?"

"This will last only for a short time. Like any machine, ours will only work if properly maintained. For this, we need a base, raw materials, workers. Our security would melt away fast without all this."

"So why don't I allow you to melt away and collect what's left afterwards?"

Rheinberg nodded. "You can. Probably we would try to escape and ask someone else to support us. Your ships cannot stop us. The Persians may possibly have more interest."

Gratian's eyes narrowed, and Arbogast seemed to be alarmed by these words. "You threaten us?" the Emperor said.

"I want to survive. I would very much prefer to do it in your empire. I can help you to save it."

"Save it?"

"There's a lot we can do. An important historical development has begun, only to be presaged by the Goths. The empire is facing an abyss, especially the West, and you yourself will face death in a short time."

Gratian exchanged a look with Arbogast. "You can see into the future, can you?"

"I know the past, because I come from the future."

"And you want to share your knowledge with us?"

"In exchange for security."

Gratian sat back and looked pensive at the tent roof. Arbogast could no longer restrain himself now. "We need a proof of your good will," he growled.

"We have brought down the pirates," said Rheinberg.

The General made a derogatory gesture. "You attacked a couple of sailing ships and captured a criminal. Fine. I mean a real challenge."

"What are you thinking?"

"You say that the Goths were just the beginning?"

"They are harbingers."

"Harbingers of what?"

"Numerous other peoples who will flock to the borders of the empire and ultimately crush the West in less than a hundred years," said Rheinberg.

"And you know what we can do about it?" Arbogast said.

"I have some ideas."

"Show us what you can do now. You know how it looks in the East?"

"Valens fell, the Goths plunder everywhere, and two-thirds of the eastern army is dead."

Arbogast hesitated. "Two-thirds."

"About 22,000 deaths," affirmed Rheinberg. "Only one supreme commander has survived."

"Which one?"

"Flavius Victor."

"Sebastianus is dead?" Gratian seemed to be hooked.

Rheinberg nodded. He had reread everything just before he had come here. Each of his "predictions" had to be right.

"Good. Then show your superiority and the power of your knowledge and fight against the Goths!" Arbogast demanded.

"I will."

Stunned silence followed Rheinberg's outspoken and quick response.

"With your ... how many men?"

"One hundred and sixty."

"But the Goths are –"

"Maybe 20,000 or 30,000. Who knows."

"This is absurd. You're a phony."

"Come with me."

Arbogast opened his mouth and closed it again immediately. When he saw an amused smile on Gratian's lips, he was at once more embarrassed than angry.

"Yes, Arbogast. Accompany him. Take a unit of legionaries, but also horses and carts with you and then it goes to the East. I wish you to travel over land; I don't want to provoke any great stir through the miracle ship. In addition, the strangers should get used to our soldiers and vice versa. Unite with Flavius Victor, and maybe you can discern if something is to be achieved against the Goths."

"You make me the general of the East?"

"No, this will be Theodosius. I decided it yesterday. The son of the old general, a Roman of high blood. I have already sent a messenger to Spain. He will meet me here as fast as he can."

Gratian's attention was back on Rheinberg. He agreed with the commands of the Emperor. To travel over the land, as an extended trust-building measure, was not a stupid idea in order to fight mistrust and fear. It took time, but they were not really in a hurry. Theodosius had spent years fighting the Goths, and it would surely not take that much now.

"Theodosius is in your past?" Gratian asked.

"He became emperor of the East."

Gratian didn't seem surprised. "A good emperor?"

"Could have been worse," Rheinberg said cautiously. "But there were also better ones."

The Emperor waited for an explanation, but Rheinberg decided to stick to it for now.

"But a good commander," asked Gratian.

"A thoroughly capable leader," Rheinberg admitted. "But he didn't manage to defeat the Goths."

"What is the result? The East lost?"

"No. He will offer the Goths the status of *Foederatii* and allows their king to rule. They will not be subjects of the empire but may settle within its borders, and they will not accept orders by the Roman administration, only being required to accept counsel."

Gratian didn't seem very happy about this answer. "That seems risky," he muttered.

"Very risky," Rheinberg agreed. "And it constituted a precedent. It leads indirectly to the dissolution of the empire, especially in the West, because your followers will take the same, simple and convenient solution in other cases."

Arbogast looked thoughtful. Malobaudes, who had not said a word, nodded. As Frankish king, he could very well appreciate what kind of reasoning led to the solution Rheinberg mentioned. Gratian also seemed to recognize the importance of such a development almost intuitively.

"You'll have to tell me more about this, Rheinberg," Gratian finally said.

"I'm at your disposal. But maybe you and the revered Arbogast are interested in a demonstration of what we want to impress the Goths with?"

Arbogast's eyes glittered. "A demonstration? Indeed."

"A good idea," said Gratian. "What do you need?"

"Targets. And an open field."

"Malobaudes ..."

"I will provide everything," the general replied immediately.

"Then may I invite you all to attend a small display of our prowess!" Rheinberg said with satisfaction.

The men rose.

On the way out, Rheinberg told Malobaudes what Becker had described in their joint preparation. The general seemed a little confused at first but promised to get to it at once. As they all stood in the sun in the late morning and only the Frank hurried to give his staff orders, Rheinberg waved Becker. After a sign by Gratian, he was admitted to the small group.

"That's Legate Becker, commander of my small cohort."

Becker bowed deeply.

"He'll demonstrate the power of his weapons. The Emperor has consented to the presentation. It is all prepared."

Becker smiled and asked to be allowed to withdraw, which was granted. No sooner had he reached his men than he shouted commands, and the infantrymen jumped up to unload three machine guns from the truck. Gratian and Arbogast looked at the vehicle with undisguised interest.

"I invite you and your guardsmen to come along to the site of the demonstration in our car," Rheinberg offered spontaneously. "Your guardsmen can accompany us so they can punish me if anything happens. Take it as another presentation of our technical achievements."

Arbogast tried to dissuade his Emperor of a quick decision, but Gratian had already given his consent with barely concealed enthusiasm. The general had no choice but to shout to a centurion, who immediately came trotting up with two dozen guardsmen.

"Here we go!" Rheinberg helped both Gratian and Arbogast into the cab, before he took his seat behind the wheel. Then he heard the guards entering the emptied truck bed behind him, while one German helped them to put the narrow benches down and secure them. They were surely squinting suspiciously at the now orphaned MG on the roof above their emperor.

Rheinberg started the engine. The rattling and shaking of the heavy diesel shook the car and Rheinberg noticed that the fingers of the Emperor involuntarily clutched in the barren upholstery of his seat. He decided to drive very, very slowly.

"Where to, dear General?"

Arbogast looked pale through the windshield and it took him a while to finally show Rheinberg the way.

Rheinberg released the handbrake. The truck rolled on softly. In a careful curve, the captain moved the vehicle slowly around until it bumped over the uneven, just mashed "main street" of the camp. From the corner of his eye, Rheinberg saw that they were followed by a troop of cavalry. On this terrain, he would never be able to escape them, and Rheinberg didn't even think of trying.

The truck rumbled through the main gate where the guards didn't know whether to stare at their emperor in the cab or bow down in a hurry. Under the direction of short instructions by Arbogast, they reached a field in front of the camp where the car came to a halt.

Rheinberg turned off the engine and looked invitingly at Gratian.

"Well, Your Majesty?"

The Emperor looked a bit pale around the nose, but otherwise he was in good spirits. The speed could not have impressed him, as each horse could compete. The fact, however, that the car had been into in motion without a draft animal ...

"And you are sure that it wasn't magic?" Arbogast asked.

"Magic that is so loud and stinks?" replied Rheinberg. "Come, I will show you something!"

The men climbed out and Rheinberg opened the hood. Gratian and Arbogast and stared blankly into it.

"This is a machine that we call a car-engine. It drives the wheels of the car by burning alcohol."

"Burn alcohol?"

"At least something like that," Rheinberg admitted. "No magic anyway. Invented by people, built by people, and it needs human hands to repair it and keep it working."

Gratian touched a hot cylinder gently with his fingertips. "Can we build it? I mean, let's assume I present you the best craftsmen of my empire, and give you all the materials that you desire – could those people build it?"

"No."

"Why not?" Gratian asked.

"We lack the tools to build the right tools that are necessary to develop the engine. But we can build a similar, simpler machine that also can drive a car or a boat. We call this a steam engine."

"In it also burns alcohol?"

"Wood. Or coal. It works with steam."

"Steam?"

Rheinberg nodded.

"And my people could build one?"

"From bronze, yes. We could instruct them. Afterwards, they'd no longer need our help, and can do it alone. Your galleys would not depend on weather anymore and would dominate the seas with a higher speed. No pirate and no enemy would dare challenge you."

"The Mediterranean is ours, and who wants the rest?" snorted Arbogast, still full of doubts.

"Once the Vandals conquer North Africa and thereby the granary of the empire, you will judge differently."

The general and Gratian looked at each other. "When shall these things happen?" asked the Emperor.

"It starts in fifty years and ends not even ten years later."

Again, the two men exchanged glances. They knew the catastrophic economic consequences of such a blow.

Arbogast cleared his throat. "Your demonstration, Rheinberg."

"Certainly, sir."

The legionaries of the encampment had now joined the onlookers. Men had built targets of high variety, lots of old wood, straw dolls, exercise machines, boxes and all kinds of other garbage, sometimes low, sometimes piled high, and all on a straight line of maybe 200 meters in length. Becker had left his men in the camp, suspiciously observed by Roman guardsmen, and brought only nine of his soldiers: three per machine gun. They took position next to each other, each about ten feet apart, and put their mighty guns on three legs.

Becker joined Rheinberg. "Over there are also some trees, in a good range."

"We deforest this place" whispered Rheinberg. "Today, we don't skimp on ammo. We only have this one chance. It must be very, very impressive work."

"Impressive, yes," Becker said with a grin. He rejoined his men who had completed their preparations. Rheinberg pondered for a moment to explain the Emperor what to expect in detail, but then decided against it.

"Your Majesty, you now see the capabilities of the most powerful guns that we carry with us. They will destroy, in a very short time, all the targets your men have generously built. In addition, we should consider that little group of trees over there."

"Consider?" echoed Arbogast.

"It is pretty loud," Rheinberg continued his explanation. "Do not frighten. We begin when you give the command, Emperor!"

Gratian nodded measuredly. Rheinberg could hardly blame him. "Then begin!"

Rheinberg gave Becker a sign. The captain barked a command. The guns fired.

The MG 08 with its more than 70 cm-long barrel was a formidable weapon. It had a caliber of 8 mm and was fed with a cartridge belt, which could be easily replaced. A belt grabbed 250 cartridges that could fire the gun with a cadence of 500 or 600 rounds per minute. With an effective range of fire of nearly two and a half kilometers against ground targets, the reference to the near end of the group of trees had been anything but showing off. It was a heavy weapon that required a mount to set it up and straighten. Ideal to sprinkle a whole battlefield from a secure, elevated position.

Rheinberg had exactly that in mind when it was time to confront the Goths.

The guns' sudden, unmediated chatter echoed across the plain, and Gratian flinched visibly. Almost simultaneously, the target dissolved into shredded wood, and chips and bigger wood parts flew through the air, as the three MGs methodically swung from left to right. It took less than thirty seconds, and nothing remained of the man-sized targets except rubble and scraps. For a small moment, calm descended over the field, then the shooters had new targets, and again the staccato of bursts shook joints and marrow. The distant tree group consisted of six low-grown cedars. An invisible fist shot through branches and trunks, and as the three machine guns merged their fire on the trees, the dry plants shattered under the whirlwind of destruction.

Then the guns were silent.

Everyone stared in silence at the stumps and debris. For a moment, some wood particles flew around lazy in the summer air, and at last the view was free to the countryside beyond.

Rheinberg let the image impress for a moment, then waved Becker. "Who of your men can disassemble the machine gun fastest?"

"Corporal Lehmann is the man you are asking for."

"Then may I ask."

Becker turned and yelled.

"Your Majesty, if you order for a table, I show you that even in this case no magic is involved."

Gratian and Arbogast looked pale and shaken. Malobaudes shook his head incessantly. Finally, the Emperor nodded.

Zealous servants brought a sturdy wooden table from the camp, made their way through the staring Legionaries under which an incredulous, gripped murmur had spread.

Lehmann arrived and started with his gun, heaved it on the table at the behest of Becker. They waited a short time to give the heated weapon the opportunity to cool slightly. With flying fingers the soldier began to disassemble the mechanism. After three minutes, the machine gun was broken down into its essential components, and the Emperor and his two generals bent over it.

"You see, noble gentlemen, that this is a mechanical construction," said Rheinberg. "It is surely superior to weapons your craftsmen can produce, yet ultimately it is only a logical development out of weapons which are not unknown to you."

Gratian ran his fingers over the now cooled metal parts and nodded. "It is true," he muttered. "This is not magic, but superior craftsmanship."

He looked up. "Arbogast, predict for me what we can do with these weapons on a battlefield chosen by us? What's in it for 20,000 Goths if we have three good positions from which the field can be controlled? We would commence a bloodbath, without having to bring one of our men in danger!"

The officer might be an ungracious and suspicious man, but this demonstration hadn't missed its effect on him. "Yes, my Emperor. We would have to use our legions only as decoys to bring the enemy to the right position."

"For the remaining troops of the East, this should be enough," Rheinberg said. Gratian and Arbogast crossed their looks in silent agreement. The Emperor straightened up and observed the shredded targets. "Trierarch Rheinberg, I'd prefer you to become a friend of the Roman Empire and not our enemy."

"My preference as well."

"Then we should go back to my tent and discuss the details."

Gratian turned away, headed toward the camp, deliberately bypassing the truck. His guards hastened to bring him a horse. Becker, Rheinberg, Arbogast and Malobaudes looked after him.

"Very well," growled the German general. "But I'll keep an eye on you, I promise."

"I look forward to your counsel," Rheinberg said with a smile.

The man snorted and stomped back to his master.

"Forgive my comrade," said Malobaudes and stroked his stomach with satisfaction. "He'll not cause any problem. The only real goal he has is to serve his Emperor."

Rheinberg nodded thoughtfully. When he persuaded the grumpy old man he would also convince the Emperor, of that he was now certain.

2

The *mulio* – the mule guide – hadn't asked many questions. Trade in the Roman Empire was sparse enough because of falling production, and those who had surpluses hoarded them. More and more producers were focused on their own needs and only sold the required weapons for the army to the state and food for the maintenance of urban centers that otherwise would cause great unrest, especially in Rome itself. And so was the overland trade, once one of the lifelines of the Empire, oppressed by the levy of government regulation, the harassment of the ever-expanding bureaucracy, and the lack of products. The carts were only half-filled. When the young woman had put two gold pieces in his hand, which had apparently not been stretched by lower metals, he had willingly offered a place in the cart. Her companion, a young man who clearly felt uncomfortable in his new and rather fresh patched tunic, silently stood by. Both young people each carried a large bundle, and they were dressed for a long trip but looked a little too neat for frequent travelers. The fingernails of the young woman had been carefully manicured, as it was noticed by the *mulio* immediately, and although her companion didn't look as if physical work was completely alien to him, he didn't seem to be a day laborer or craftsman.

But two gold coins were two gold coins, and as long as the travelers behaved quietly and made no trouble, he wouldn't bother.

The column of four donkey carts started one early morning from Ravenna. The roads were good, but the donkeys slow, and the traffic impressive. Northern Italy was still one of the economic and political centers of the empire, and this was reflected in the density of the population and the extensive transportation systems between the many urban settlements in this region.

Around noon, when the sun was high in the sky, the foothills of Ravenna had just disappeared from their sight. Their first stop took place in Milan, another important city. From there, they would make it to the east, moving along the shoreline, make station in Sirmium and ultimately end in Constantinople. The foreman had dismissed as scaremongering rumors that the Goths would dominate the flat land of the east. If this was indeed his earnest opinion or just an attempt to convince himself that nothing was wrong, neither Julia nor Volkert could surmise. Volkert knew what was happening in the east of the empire, but he was sure that the situation would have calmed down as soon as the slow carts had traveled the long and arduous way up to Sirmium.

The ride was slow and monotonous. The driver of the cart, on which Julia and Volkert had found space, was a taciturn old man who sat with bent back behind the donkeys and – except for an occasional smacking – made no sound. Sometimes he dismounted and walked beside the animals, patted their heads and clucked. The donkeys seemed to accept this as confirmation of their good services; at least they made no apparent trouble. Volkert had the impression to see a good team.

So he and Julia had only to sit back on the cart and talk. Julia had made it her task to supplement Volkert's rather crumbly knowledge of Latin and Greek, and she went to work with a certain zeal. As practice material, they had nothing else than just their lives, and they asked each other questions and described what they had experienced in their respective eras. Julia didn't like much of what Volkert reported, and with a large frown took note that the position of women in society many hundreds of years in the future hadn't really improved. She showed little interest in his portrayals of technical achievements but was much more in the medical advances and, interestingly, in political structures. As Volkert tried to explain the function of the *Reichstag*, she had few problems understanding this – the Roman Republic was still quite strongly anchored in the historical consciousness of the Romans, and her father was a senator. The descriptions of the political situation, the emergence of social democracy and its rejection of the monarchy, found some sympathy with her, because ultimately there was a historical counterpart in the struggle between plebeians and aristocrats in her own history, although certainly in a different guise. It seemed to disappoint her that not much had changed. Apparently she had nurtured the hope that the people of the future were more advanced on many more issues than in her time, but the descriptions of the international tensions and wars apparently reminded her very much of the history of the empire and their own present.

After they had talked all morning about these things, they discussed other issues. Volkert understood how the privileges of a senator's daughter had at the same time cramped Julia's life. A golden cage despite two loving parents. For Julia, this trip was more than just an act of defiance to the rejection of her lover by her parents, it was a very essential liberation. Basically, she said bitterly on one occasion, she should have been born a man, because the life of a woman in Rome was restricted beyond measure. Both talked at length about their families, and Volkert remembering that he would probably never see his parents and siblings again made him sad and silent for several minutes. It spoke for Julia that she recognized it immediately, and instead to press the issue, she just took him in her arms, while he considered wistful memories.

When evening came, they reached one of the many hostels on the side of the street. It was a sprawling, low-rise building with stables, consisted of a large common room and an adjoining building with accommodation in different price classes – dormitories with simple straw bags as couches for the less well-off, single rooms with proper furniture for the more affluent traveler. Volkert and Julia would be theoretically able to afford a slightly better accommodation with the gold carried by the senator's daughter but had decided not to attract attention. So they pushed together two straw mattresses and after a rather frugal supper lied down exhausted on their uncomfortable sleeping place. The hall was filled to only one-third, and the travelers were spaced as far as they could. The nightly snoring, sneezing and coughing wasn't new to Volkert, as the sleeping halls of his navy-training had a similar noise-level, so he quickly fell into a deep sleep. Julia, however, quite accustomed to a little more privacy and a more luxurious night's sleep, wavered between disgust, fear and nervousness back and forth. Finally, she wrapped her arms around Volkert's body and pressed against him. Covered with their roughly woven blankets, one could hardly make out the contours of her body in the dark. Playfully Julia let her hand slide down Volkert's chest, slipped over his abdomen in direction of ...

Julia giggled.

"Mentula tua iubet, amatur!"[1] she whispered in Volkert's ear. He opened his eyes, and although he hadn't quite understood what Julia had said, the massaging movements of her delicate fingers circling around the top of his penis needed no further explanation. He suppressed a groan, as he wanted to avoid unnecessary attention to their actions, but it was hard, and the harder it became, the more intense Julia's massage.

Her lips pressed on his, demanding, dominant. He himself started to squeeze the young woman who plied him incessantly below. A sigh from her lips reached his ear, then a whisper, *"Immanis mentula it!"*

Whatever that might mean – Volkert wasn't able to focus on vocabulary – it definitely had to do with his hard penis, which pressed almost painfully against his now much too tight pants. His own hands explored Julia's body, held the firm breasts of the young woman who let out a strangled moan and replied his caresses fiercely.

Then, with slow movements, Julia pushed her body over his. With a hand clamped firmly around his shaft, she fumbled it out of his pants, and then she squeezed his cock tight against her pussy. The rough hair scratching at the tip of his penis, and then she enveloped him with warm, wet tightness.

"Lente impelle," Julia whispered hoarsely. This Volkert understood. Push slowly! He didn't ask twice, forgot his surroundings. He didn't care who heard or saw what happened, as he was overcome with unprecedented passion, the delicious combination of desire and love he had never encountered in his life before. He felt his

---

[1] "The cock commands, love is made."

penis pushing deeply forward into Julia's body and started gently with circling movements, demanding her hip to respond until all self-control became an illusion. With a weakly suppressed, hot gasp, he poured into the young woman, felt her hands clawing at his neck and Thomas was, for this happy moment, not of this world.

Slowly his vision cleared, and despite the darkness, he saw dimly the smiling, sweat-drenched face of Julia. He knew he would have to endure longer in the future, but he saw no blame in the eyes of his lover, but only a deep, contented expression of shared happiness.

On the neighboring bed there was a dirty giggle and a man's voice said, *"Filius salex, quod tu mulierorum diutuisto!"*[2]

Volkert became deeply red. Less because he understood but rather because Julia looked embarrassed.

"What did he say?" asked Volkert just to be sure. Julia nodded and smiled and told him. The young man decided not to react. At another time he would reveal his lover that this had just been the very first sex in his life.

Julia pulled away. Their sleeping place was sticky and sweaty, but they didn't care. And had the senator's daughter still suffered from insomnia, now it didn't take long before the weariness overcame her. Her sleep was deep and only a loud noise would wake her up.

Well after midnight some more than just unusual sounds brought them out of their sleep. Oil lamps lit the dormitory and loud curses echoed through the room.

"Cacator!"[3] shouted an older man, than a foot nudged and forced him to turn around. Julia opened her eyes and pressed herself against Volkert, who sat up sleepily.

Four legionaries in full armor had entered the dormitory. They were led by a fat man in civilian tunic, carrying a heavy bag at his belt, from which a clicking sound came anytime he moved.

"Men!" His voice echoed through the hall. Meanwhile, he had the undivided attention of all guests. In many faces Volkert acknowledged fear. He had no idea what was going on.

---

[2]"Horny son, with how many women have you done it properly?"
[3]"Asshole!"

"Men of Rome!" said the fat man in his remarkably penetrating voice. "The Emperor calls you up! The Empire is exposed to serious threats! Valens, our Divine Emperor of the East, has fallen against the marauding hordes of Gothic barbarians! A shame, Romans, that affects us all! A shame that can be extinguished only by the blood of the barbarians on our swords! Men of Rome! I give you now the opportunity to rush to help your Emperor and fulfill your duty to the Empire!"

The fat guy paused and looked around. Despite the dim lighting, it looked like he scrutinized each and everyone of those present. Volkert also felt unpleasantly examined by him, especially since he now had a good idea of what was going on.

The man in the tunic was here to recruit new meat for the Roman army. At his belt hung a bag of gold to pay each volunteer the entry money, if anyone would accept the man's offer. Volkert knew this kind of men, as he had met some of them in Germany not too long ago … just then … The ensign was trying not to muddle up the various levels of time but finally failed. In any case, the basic skills and methods of recruiters seemed to have not changed over the centuries.

"Gold for everyone who writes his name!" the voice boomed now. "Regular wages, land and property by the end of the service period. Anyone here who still has no Roman citizenship? You'll get it at the end and even earlier for your children. Glory and honor – and riches – if the enemy army is defeated and once its treasures are up for distribution. For those who want to become more than a simple soldier, many paths are open. Double pay for good craftsmen. For a blacksmith, even thrice the amount! For those who have proven themselves, rise in the ranks. Hasn't our divine Diocletian himself risen from a simple soldier to become an emperor? Highest honors and offices for the successful! Honored back in your villages, exempt from all taxes and duties! There is no better life, and there is no greater adventure!"

The man's voice was doubtlessly a well-tuned instrument. He joined pathos with facts, looked convincing, amusing, serious, ironic and honest, depending on what was currently required. The man mastered his business, and Volkert was sure that he would receive a corresponding amount of gold for each volunteer successfully recruited.

But no one in the dormitory seemed too impressed. At least not in the way as the fat guy would have liked. There was the fear in the faces of the woken, as they sat silent in their beds and avoided direct eye contact and did everything not to draw attention to themselves.

The recruiter sighed and gave a nod to the four legionaries. Volkert tensed, but the soldiers did nothing more than to march down the aisle between the resting places and look around. Then they turned and stood with a composed face behind the uninvolved civilian.

"Very well," he finally grunted. "But when the barbarians are in your house, take your wives and daughters to rape them, pillage your belongings, burn your property, and abduct you into slavery, don't beg the Emperor for help, because then it's your own fault, as you left the Empire down in its hour of need."

Surprisingly nimble, the man turned on his heel and left the room. The soldiers followed him. With them went the lights. Darkness returned to the hostel, relieved whispers filled the room for a short time, until all laid down again and the ubiquitous snoring returned.

Julia had cuddled with Volkert and stared for minutes with restless eyes into the darkness. Then also her eyelids fell, and she returned to sleep.

She jumped up again as rough hands grabbed her and pushed her to the side. She screamed involuntarily, pressing the thin blanket on her body. Screams, shouts, roars were heard in the hall when a group of grim-looking legionaries trudged through the space, isolated men, pulled them up, reviewed them briefly and then drove them together in the middle of the room.

"Damn," Volkert shouted in German, as a mountain of a man grabbed him and put him on his feet. Ignoring his protests, he was flung against the group of now seven or eight men who were held in check by three legionaries with spears. Wide-eyed, Julia watched the spectacle. There could be no doubt about what was going on.

After the peaceful and voluntary recruitment attempt had failed, they had resorted to other means. The men here, as far as the short examination judged them useful, were recruited by force.

Julia had heard of it, and as they were far removed from the reality of her existence, she had viewed the stories as regrettable and rationalized the need to provide the armed forces with the necessary personnel. But now she was flooded by the chaos of horror and growing despair. She tried to hold back the tears when she saw Volkert's helpless glances. The legionaries had the "recruits" now roughly tied and began to lash the cords together with another long rope. There was no chance of escape.

"So!" The voice of the fat permeated the room. "I have good news for you, men, you shall serve the Empire and your Emperor. Maybe not entirely voluntary, but that doesn't matter a lot." A bleating laughter that had nothing to do with the rhetorical brilliance of his first appearance came with the jab. "Just to let one thing be clear: Whether voluntarily or not, you are henceforth soldiers of the emperor. That means 25 years of service and all the wonderful amenities that I have promised you. And of course the laws: On desertion follows death. Who helps deserters, also dies."

The nagging look of the man seemed to fix each on the recruits. "That's clear? Shall I repeat it? Who runs away, will be executed! Whoever will help or hide you, dies as well! I hope no one develops any ideas. Arrange yourself with your destiny, and you can probably make something of it. Fight us, and you won't be happy anymore in your life. Once the training is over, write your letters and get in touch with your family. Once you've completed a certain period of service, you may even marry. Anything goes, no problem. Whoever is already married, reports to his decurion, and if you keep up well, you might receive visits."

Volkert threw Julia a long, hard look. In it was a silent but very intense message. She immediately understood and nodded. It almost seemed as if the young man could even smile now.

Whatever had just happened, it was certainly one of the most appalling proposals of marriage in human history.

"And now we leave!"

A legionary pulled on the rope, and the recruits, still dazed by the overwhelming events, followed more or less willingly. The occasional encouragement of the soldiers finally got the column to move, and as fast as the nightmare had begun, it was over.

Remaining was the chaos of rumpled straw bags, bewildered travelers, a terrified-looking innkeeper who ran around desperately and helplessly, not knowing what to say or do.

And a silently weeping Julia.

3

"Rheinberg was right."

"I hear that phrase too often."

Gratian threw Arbogast a mildly reproving glance. The grumpy general bowed his head in apparent submissiveness, but he couldn't hide his true feelings from the Emperor.

Richomer refrained from any comment. He had just arrived in camp when Rheinberg and Becker had already finished their demonstration, but he had received vivid reports especially by those comrades who had witnessed the spectacle up close. The Emperor seemed to be inclined to accept the strange trierarch and the not less strange legate or tribune, and that was sufficient for him. Arbogast, however, with his habit to stir things up against the foreigners, had apparently no intention to change this behavior.

"Anyway, it's true," Richomer confirmed. "An estimated 22,000 dead, 8,000 survivors, a number of them wounded. Of the 8,000 around 2,000 are officers and NCOs, less than 6,000 normal legionaries. We therefore have eight legions, but each of them with more than the required number of officers. Flavius Victor took over the supreme command, and the troops are still gathering at Adrianople. This is not a good staging area, because the Goths still hold on in the area."

Richomer leaned over the large map of the Eastern Empire, which was spread out on the huge marble table in Gratian's tent. On it, one could place more easily little figures as symbols for units and cities than on the stretched version in the background of the tent. "Flavius proposes Thessaloniki as a rallying point for a new army."

"The idea isn't bad. But do we want to wait in peace to give the new general-to-be the chance to organize himself in the east?" Malobaudes asked. "The arrival of Rheinberg has changed the situation. The trierarch is of the opinion that there is no reason for a long wait and an excess of caution. He suggests the Tribune Becker sends his men at once to Thessaloniki to unite there with the survivors and to use the remaining legions as bait. No new army. We use the old one."

Richomer looked from Malobaudes to Arbogast and back.

"As what?"

"As bait, as I said. They should pretend to be looking for another battle. Fritigern should feel attracted, because if he was successful against 30,000, he will probably be able to beat even 8,000."

"He's absolutely right," muttered Arbogast.

"In fact, the legions have to keep a prepared battlefield and act seemingly ready but then withdraw from any attack and leave the ground in order to give the miraculous weapons of Becker the chance to teach the barbarians a lesson that they will never forget."

Richomer looked at the map again, as if by studying it he could understand fully what Malobaudes had just told him.

"But I get this correctly – this Becker hasn't even as much as a full cohort with him, yes?"

"He says he doesn't even need all of his men. It requires no more than a good position to align his shooters so that they have a clear shot but remain in cover. He doesn't expect many losses but wants to use our men as his bodyguard for protection, should some stray Goths break through. For that they should still be capable enough, or are they, Richomer?"

"Morale has fallen," the officer considered. "But I believe that I simply don't understand properly what these men can do with their weapons. Anyway, this attack is yours to command, my Emperor; I'll do anything to support this man Becker."

"Good," said Gratian, who had previously followed the discussion silently. "I will also send Arbogast; he should take command from Flavius Victor, who is still injured. A few legionaries I can send as well, but I need to march westward again as soon as possible, because the borders are not safe if I don't take care of them."

"What about Theodosius?" Arbogast inquired. "He's still the candidate to become commander of the East?"

"He is. He will make his way to the East as soon as the message has reached him. If Becker fails, he'll hopefully pursue the war with vigor. If Becker is successful, we'll have to worry about a lot of quite new ideas in many areas afterwards."

"I think so, too!"

All heads turned around. In the entrance of the tent stood a figure, dressed in simple traveling clothes. He needed no introduction and no legitimacy. Each of rank knew the man with his crooked face.

Gratian rose. "Ambrosius!"

"My Emperor!"

"What a surprise and delight!"

"I am welcome?"

"You are always welcome! Elevius, a seat for the bishop. Bring wine and something to eat. You must be exhausted!"

"I'm tired, but I'm fine."

Nevertheless, the bishop gladly accepted the offered seat and sat down with a sigh. He took several deep gulps of wine, which was handed to him, and stretched out his legs. Richomer and Arbogast exchanged glances full of perplexity. What had moved the bishop of Milan to make the arduous journey up to Sirmium? It was not too bold to assume that this had to do with the arrival of Rheinberg and Becker. But the officers kept their counsel for themselves. This was a matter between Ambrosius and Gratian, and although the Emperor was formally the more powerful, everyone knew that the young man worshiped the energetic clergyman and had repeatedly sought his advice in the past.

"The long road from Ravenna to here – you surely haven't come just to bless my fight against the Goths."

Ambrosius hid a smile. Gratian was maybe pious, and quite easy to influence, but he wasn't an idiot. "You're of course correct in your assumption, my Emperor. Urgent business brings me here. It's about those strangers who have appeared in Ravenna and have, it seems, left a lasting impression on senators as well as the common people."

Gratian leaned back. "Senators, the common people – and myself."

Ambrosius hardly seemed surprised. "They are here, I've seen them. I heard stories of miraculous weapons."

"I intend to send them against the Goths, so that they can prove their value to us."

"Well, maybe a wise decision. The situation in the East is tense, and the death of your uncle a most unfortunate development."

Arbogast frowned. "Your enthusiasm seems to be limited, Your Eminence."

"It is."

"Why?"

"I don't care if the strangers fight against the Goths, and I'm quite happy if they win against the barbarians and establish security in the East."

"You don't care?" asked Arbogast.

"Well, it's not so important to me. There are other things that cause me concern. On the way here, I have received messengers from Ravenna. Liberius has done some research on my request. One of his closest confidants has had interesting information, as he himself had established contact with the strangers and developed some trust ... and we learned much about them and their friends in the city."

"Can I interpret this correctly," Gratian now said, with barely disguised distaste in his voice, "you initiated inquiries in Ravenna, behind my back, and that has included the military officials of my army? Senators of the empire probably also?"

"It was inevitable," the bishop justified his actions. "Many senators are involved."

"I have conferred with Symmachus and Michellus. Their arguments as well as their intentions appear to me without blame," Gratian said. For hours he had talked with the two men, both individually and together. He knew who Symmachus was, and he knew what Ambrosius thought of the famous senator – very little would be an understatement. Sometimes, the Emperor had the impression that Ambrosius regarded the highly educated and rhetorically trained Senator as a direct threat, a living indictment of his theory that salvation by faith in Christ and a faithful life is the only possible way. Symmachus liked neither Christ nor did he strive for any salvation, but no one would put the immaculate integrity of his public life and his honorable disposition in question – Gratian certainly not, despite being obliged to the teachings of the Church. Symmachus, as it seemed, lacked this fanatical gleam in his eyes, and he developed his arguments probably with the aim of intellectual understanding but rarely with the simple goal of persuasion. Perhaps it was this small difference which ultimately accounted too much.

"Michellus is a man of great wisdom," Ambrosius admitted. "But he seems to me that he suffers from the fatal influence of Symmachus."

"And what exactly is this unfortunate influence?" Arbogast said.

"His insistence on certain outmoded restraints and laws that are in urgent need of revision."

"How about the excessive tolerance in regard to the Arians, who call the shots in the churches of the East, and who we seek to liberate from the yoke of the Goths?" Arbogast said. "Or even laws like the one edict of the great Constantine, the first who freed Christianity from its shackles and helped develop the influence it enjoys today?"

Ambrosius stared at Arbogast with recognizable indignation. "General, this is a philosophical debate. Why do you complain?"

"I've learned that philosophical debates tend to be discussed on the backs of the soldiers at a certain point."

"This is outrageous!" exclaimed the bishop.

Arbogast sighed. "Your Eminence, my army consists of Christians, Trinitarians as Arians, followers of Mithras, the faithful of Mars and Jupiter, Osiris, and ah, I don't know how many other gods. What you request is ideally suited to split the army and to open a crack through the whole empire, and that won't help us currently."

Ambrosius rose. "So it's true! The insinuations of Rheinberg fell on fertile ground!"

"Rheinberg has nothing to do with common sense," the general replied acidly.

"I know what kind of theses the leader of the strangers spreads," Ambrosius insisted. "Preserving the edict and even expand it! To

32

not fight the Arian heresy! As if that wasn't enough, what else do I hear? To increase the revenue of the empire it is necessary to rescind the tax advantages of ecclesiastical property and the servants of the Church? What a blasphemous approach is that?"

Gratian threw Arbogast a confused look. "Has Rheinberg suggested that?"

"Not to me."

Ambrosius looked from one to the other, sat back, his eyes fixed on an imaginary point in front of him. He noted that he almost made a fatal error.

"Well," he said in a quiet voice. "Then nothing is lost. What I have just explained to you is what has been reported to me from Ravenna. You have not yet been privy to Rheinberg's plans, probably in order not to scare you, only to gain your trust, and then when you no longer can do without him he will come up with these absurd proposals. I warn you, noble majesty – and you too, General! There is more perfidy and corruption in those foreign visitors as their outer appearance might imply! Be on your guard, and don't become easily impressed by the sweet words of this stranger."

"His deeds should impress me," Gratian replied unmoved. Still, there was now some doubt in his eyes.

Ambrosius controlled himself to not too obviously show his triumph. He had arrived in time. Now could he still wield his own influence against the heretical nonsense of foreign demons. But he had to do proceed full of caution. The situation of the empire was desperately enough for Gratian to cling to any hope, and it seemed indeed to be the case that the strangers could mitigate the Gothic threat. "My Emperor – let the strangers fight against the Goths. They may succeed where Valens has failed. But then, my Lord, then you have to be vigilant."

"I'm always vigilant," muttered Gratian, and his expression didn't indicate whether he considered this a virtue or a burden.

"Of course," Ambrosius was quick to confirm. "But this is about more than just political power and the containment of a military threat. It is ultimately about the salvation of the whole Roman people! Here no risk can be too great to ensure that the during approaching end of days Rome is ready for the judgment of the Lord."

Gratian nodded. "That is true, bishop, and I would be the last to contradict you there. I will consider your words. In any case, you will be pleased that I have the younger Theodosius appointed as general of the East. I have already sent for him."

Ambrosius' face brightened.

"Theodosius? A wise man, full of honor as well as of true faith. A Roman who will make the empire proud, especially after the highly unfortunate incident with his father. A very excellent choice, my Emperor!"

Gratian smiled quite pleased. "Thank you, Your Eminence. I'm glad that my decision has your blessing."

"It surely has."

Gratian looked around.

"We still have some military matters to discuss, my friend. You are certainly tired from the long trip and have need of rest. Let the conversation continue at another time."

Ambrosius knew when he was accepted, and when his continued presence would be distracting. He rose and left the tent with a bow.

Arbogast stared after him. "A pious man," he said.

Gratian looked at Richomer. Everyone in the tent knew that the officer was an Arian. But there was absolutely no emotional response, and it wasn't apparent if the words of the bishop had hurt him or not.

"Pious, yes, but he confuses politics and religion to an extent which threatens to limit his judgment," said Gratian now. "He sees danger where there is none, and the positive potential is beyond his grasp."

"So you'll not listen to him?"

Gratian looked at Arbogast with raised eyebrows. "Not at all. I will absolutely listen to him. He represents a great power in the empire, a power on which I am dependent. I believe in God and his Son, Jesus Christ. I believe that the Arians are in error and the Trinitarian belief represents the true doctrine. I also think that we have tolerated the old cults and other religions for too long, and have been too generous ... In addition, I believe that the empire is in peril. I think that the idea of Constantine to make Christianity the unifying bond that holds everything together has ultimately failed. I believe that I need people like Symmachus and Richomer if I want to consolidate the empire. I believe that I am emperor of Rome and that brings certain obligations with it and I may not have the freedom to indulge my personal preference too much." He measured the officers with a long glance. "I also believe that there are historical trends one can't ignore. What Rheinberg told me about my fate – to be betrayed and killed by an usurper – I have often read in the history of my predecessors. I would like to avoid this fate. For that I must do certain things and will allow others, and not all of it will be approved by Ambrosius." His eyes narrowed. "When one is confronted with a shameful death in the not too distant future it changes the perspective on one's own life and one starts to set different priorities. And the first priority is a victory in the East." Gratian turned to Arbogast. "You will leave in two days with a selected unit and Becker's men. Allow him tactical and strategic command, but don't take any personal risk. Report to me regularly. I'll stay for a while in Sirmium, but then I'll go to Ravenna, look at this marvelous ship. For some time now I have considered the idea of making this city my residence, perhaps this is a good opportunity."

Arbogast stood and bowed. "It will happen as you command, Augustus!"

4

"Something's not in order," von Klasewitz murmured. Since the night Volkert had disappeared, the first officer had picked a bad mood. When he learned that the ensign didn't go alone, but most probably disappeared with a certain senator's daughter, his mood had deteriorated further. Neither Köhler nor Behrens could blame him; both regarded the love-drunk decision of the ensign to desert as dangerous, thoughtless and ultimately plain stupid, although Köhler was ready to give the impetuosity of youth some room, or, as he described it, the "effect of bodily juices." Von Klasewitz boiled from within until today, when the *Saarbrücken* did finally arrive back to Ravenna under the command of Joergensen. The fact that their guards persistently refused to let them back on the ship, although this had been the agreement, was evaluated by the hostages rather different – Köhler and Behrens agreed that it was the consequence of some political change in Ravenna while von Klasewitz was the conviction that Rheinberg had made a stupid mistake and therefore the wind turned. Whatever might be the facts, something was definitely different.

But no one wanted to talk to them about it.

For von Klasewitz, this was particularly frustrating. Following the invitation of Petronius, he was introduced to a part of the higher society, which pleased him very well. The church services that he had visited had been both familiar as well as strange. But the nobleman was highly impressed in any case. What had fascinated most was this deep religious conviction in regard to the approaching judgment day, which seemed to be expected almost immediately, maybe even longed for with burning force. It was this fervor that he himself had missed often, and this feeling had touched a chord in him that he hadn't known to exist before. This feeling evolved following discussions, especially with Petronius, but also other church leaders, representatives of urban curia, with senators of the Christian faction. There was the corruption that prevailed in the Roman Empire, described with great eloquence and very vividly, the sins that undermined the empire, the schisms and apostasies that ripped it apart. Von Klasewitz knew quite well that no judgment day was at hand, just as he knew quite well what was going to happen to West Rome in a few decades. And just as Rheinberg he saw the need to prevent this, only – and that it was more clear to him with every passing day – the steps he'd take would vary heavily from what the captain suggested. Neither false tolerance of aberrant opinions was the solution nor cooperation with lowly barbarians and wild tribes, but only the cleansing power of true faith and a strong guiding hand, a new patriotism implanted in the empire – if necessary even by force and against all possible resistance.

Petronius met him a lot, as others spoke to him. They welcomed him and opened his eyes more and more for the erroneous assumptions Rheinberg was obviously determined to follow. It was necessary to do something about that, and probably with even greater determination and also at the risk of ...

Yes, von Klasewitz was convinced of what he had learned and experienced, and so much that he didn't exclude the possibility to remove Rheinberg from his post anymore. And now that the captain was in Sirmium, trying to gain the ear of the Emperor, and Becker, his faithful loyal assistant, had accompanied him there, the *Saarbrücken* was commanded by the colorless second officer and within reach in Ravenna. And right now whoever was in charge didn't want to let him out; he and the other hostages had been more or less cut off from the outside world.

The restlessness that pervaded von Klasewitz and his urgent need to seize the moment, unconsciously influenced the other hostages. Had they known what kind of thoughts the first officer vented, the other two would certainly not have been of the opinion that the constant moving about of von Klasewitz in the sprawling villa rather had something amusing. No, that thought would've been to the very last.

"Something's going on," Behrens said. He waved to the soldiers under his command. They had no guns with them, but they were strong guys who had been selected by Becker not least because they had proved themselves in endless brawls. Köhler and he carried pistols with three magazines. It wasn't much, but hopefully enough, if there should be trouble.

For the NCOs, trouble had been in the air since Volkert was gone.

Now it was clearly heard: chants, songs, the voice of a gathering crowd. All this took place across more than man-high walls, but the sounds were hard to misinterpret.

"A mob," muttered Köhler and threw Behrens a meaningful look. Both groped on their uniform shirts, under which they had hidden their weapons. Von Klasewitz looked at them half disapprovingly, half fearfully, but said nothing.

Something rattled. Someone yelled, very close, very loud.

"We should ..." But von Klasewitz didn't get to express his plans as suddenly a door slammed open. Two legionaries of the city guard burst in, and both with their swords drawn.

"Quick," said one breathing heavily. "We can't stay long. The back door."

"Who is causing the commotion?" the officer asked.

"Priests. Angry priests. Many of them, and common people. They want us to deliver you."

Von Klasewitz was pale. "Deliver to whom?"

"To them. Quickly, the back door!"

No one asked any more questions because again there was a loud clatter and crash, screams of pain and then the sound of a struggle. The comrades of the legionaries seemed to try everything possible to stop the protesters storming inside, but it could only be a matter of a few minutes until they entered the villa.

The legionaries and the hostages rushed to the back of the villa, where two slaves were already waiting excitedly at a little door, probably a kind of delivery entrance. The men were served with clothes that would make them look unsuspicious. Also, the legionaries now hid their blades. A quick glance through the half-opened door, then the command to follow them.

The hostages were on the small alley. Everything seemed quiet. "Follow us!"

They hurried along the narrow path to the next intersection. Von Klasewitz carefully looked to the right, saw the crowd of protesters as they poured into the villa. Screaming, chanting priests, incomprehensible at most, but also incited onlookers who seemed to take some pleasure from the spectacle. No one understood what this was about and how it started, and the Roman soldiers seemed to have no interest to answer their questions.

They moved away in the opposite direction. The noise of beaten and battered furniture doors quickly became quiet as a column legionaries marched to the house, all with a grim face, and it was probably better if they were not in the vicinity of what was happening now.

Then a call from a side street. "That's them! The devils! The demons! They have escaped!"

Köhler began to suspect what kind of arguments had incited the priests. And he began to realize what was about to happen – because he was sure that their enemies would certainly not deal squeamishly with devils and demons.

"Faster! To the port!" Köhler shouted. He showed the way. The legionaries wanted to go somewhere else, but the NCO didn't have time for diversions. The garrison of the harbor-troops was too far away and it was better to go the direct route to the *Saarbrücken*. There they could be sure that the mob couldn't penetrate the iron walls easily.

"There! The demons! They want return to the ship of hell!"

The news seemed to spread in a flash. More and more city residents poured into the open, partly curious, partly willing to participate in the hunt. The priests, still preoccupied in setting the mansion on fire, were now pouring into the streets and rushed to follow the call. The column of legionaries was rinsed aside, the fanatical and incited men threw themselves against their weapons, as they sought an early end as a martyr. The soldiers had apparently been ordered to make only moderately use of the blades, more as threats and banging them on their shields.

That wasn't enough. The thin chain of legionaries quickly broke, and scattered soldiers were lost in the mob.

"This way," Köhler cried, the handle of the gun firmly clasped under the cowl. It was a 04 Parabellum pistol with a magazine for eight cartridges. Its effective range was only about 50 meters, but Köhler was good with the pistol and Behrens was selected because there was nothing in the German gun cabinet he couldn't handle masterfully. The Army soldier had placed himself at the end of the group and tried to keep von Klasewitz in the middle.

"Leave it!" the officer shouted. "I can very well take care of myself!"

The soldiers looked pleadingly at Behrens, who just shrugged. The sergeant had never been of the opinion that one should prevent an officer's suicide.

They ran on an open square, crowded with merchants, beggars and customers. Here the spreading unrest apparently hadn't been noticed much. A few curious looks were all that the hooded refugees received. The Germans were slow and tried hiding in the crowd, but their temporary luck didn't last long.

"There! Make way! Clear the way!"

The screams echoed across the square. People turned around, saw bareheaded priests in their robes run from the streets, wildly swinging wooden crosses in their fists. The crowd parted and it became clear who the men chased, and the passers-by tried as quickly as possible to create distance between themselves and the Germans.

"Run!" Köhler gasped. "This way!"

He ran down an alley, and at the end he did make out the glint of the sea. The others followed him blindly. As they stumbled down the steep path, the angry howling of their hunters in the back, they finally arrived at the port. Köhler wasn't mistaken. There, at the old pier, was the *Saarbrücken*, carefully tied up and separated from the rest of the harbor by a guard of about thirty soldiers.

"We can make it!" Köhler panted, who, in contrast to Behrens and his men, had neglected his cardio training for several years. Von Klasewitz also was red in the face and gasping for air, and even if he had intended to contradict anything the NCO intended, he was hardly able to utter a word under his hard breath.

"Then forward!" the sergeant growled, and the men started a final sprint. The legionaries were aware of the uproar, and the guards on board the cruiser had become aware as well.

The legionaries were in formation, as the mass of priests soaked the port facility and rushed screaming to the *Saarbrücken*, that symbol of everything that had sparked their anger. The Germans threw away their disguise, and the port guards allowed them to stumble through their ranks. Then they climbed up the gangway, where Joergensen was waiting with a worried expression on his face.

"What the hell –" Joergensen began.

"I wouldn't talk about hell at this time," said the NCO, still breathing hard. "May I humbly suggest that the *Saarbrücken* detaches and drifts into the harbor? Our friends of the legion can't ward them off for long."

Joergensen looked questioningly at von Klasewitz, who was leaning with bulging eyes and panting to a metal wall.

"Yes," the first officer groaned, "throw the ropes."

It wasn't delayed. When the first wave of priest crashed into the shields of the legionaries, the sailors had already released the ropes. A good twenty men with long poles began to press the *Saarbrücken* away from the pier. Köhler saw Dahms rushing on deck, looking around wildly. He turned to von Klasewitz, "Should I order steam? The engine is cold!"

"Yes," gasped the nobleman. "Steam. Cannot hurt."

"It will take time."

"Steam," Klasewitz coughed with a definite undertone.

Dahms wasted no time with a repetition of the command and disappeared below deck. The combined efforts of the sailors were finally successful. The *Saarbrücken* moved very slowly away from the wharf, the gangway was withdrawn and the connections gone.

The first priests, uttering cries, broke through the ranks of the guards, literally overran the soldiers, and rushed to the drifting *Saarbrücken*. Two particularly zealous ones jumped on, soaring with swirling arms and legs through the air and slammed with such force against the railing that one could hear the cracking of the breaking bone. They were vigorously attacked by the sailors, and two of them fell screaming into the water.

"Get them out!" Klasewitz commanded.

Two sailors tore shoes from their feet and jumped; others grabbed two lifebuoys and threw them into the water. It took a few minutes, then the powerful men climbed back on board with the limp bodies of the wounded, where Neumann's assistant was already waiting for them. Stripped of the robes, their broken ribs and limbs showed. One of the priests was unconscious, the other wailing cries of pain.

Their angry crowd of brothers didn't try to do the same. The cruiser had separated a good three to four meters from the quay wall, and the dirty water between the stone and the railing seemed to be quite a deterrent for the furious zealots.

Unfortunately, they quickly decided to look for another way. Led by the more intelligent, they ran along the quay wall and stormed a number of fishing boats moored there. The owners of the vehicles didn't defend themselves; some jumped sideways from the onrushing crowd to avoid being ripped apart by them.

"Renna's men are coming!" Joergensen shouted. In fact, the heavy steps of more legionaries who had reached the harbor was clearly audible. Reinforcement for the more or less overwhelmed comrades lying on the ground who had to watch the hustle and bustle of the mobs helplessly.

The priests didn't care. Motivated by the loud screams of their ringleaders, they manned the boats and tried to move them. Few seemed to have experience with seafaring, but when Renna's men finally starting to engage away the protesters, after all half a dozen small sailing and rowing boats had already left the pier and moved with well over 60 priests on board toward the *Saarbrücken*.

"We need to avoid a fight," Köhler urged. "They are totally fanatical. But if we have to defend ourselves ..."

"We cannot use the guns," the second officer objected. "The attackers are too close, the angle of inclination is too low. We have to gain distance."

"The machines are cold, you have heard Dahms," said von Klasewitz. "We shouldn't kill any of them. They are men of the church, probably misguided in their beliefs through demagoguery. We can't harm them."

Köhler looked down at the slowly approaching boats. "They have no real weapons," he said soberly. "And they have nothing with which they could climb up the railing. If I may make the suggestion, we let them just come and drum their fists against the steel as long as they want."

Von Klasewitz looked surprised at Köhler, as if he could not comprehend that the NCO could actually have a clever idea, but the officer immediately recognized the elegance of Köhler's proposal.

"Pull the men from the railing, we don't want to unnecessarily provoke the priests!" Joergensen commanded.

Quick execution of his order followed. When the first two fishing boats scraped with their hulls against the *Saarbrücken*, the officers looked at the spectacle from the bridge, where they had quite a nice view. They heard the furious clamor of the attackers, as they noted in their despair that there was no way for them to climb up on the smooth metal hull of the cruiser. The clamor grew louder as the other boats approached and the desperate attackers apparently started yelling at each other for the stupidity of their plan. It took about ten minutes, then even the most fanatical of them had realized that all this came to nothing. When, finally, the cruiser began to tremble and Dahms had brought the machine in motion, they gave up. They didn't know that the *Saarbrücken* still wouldn't be able to move for some time, because it took a long while until the machines were ready. Uttering threats, the fanatics rowed the boats back to the pier where they were received by Renna's men. With relief, the Germans realized that the Roman authorities had regained full control of the port facilities. Although a considerable crowd had gathered, there didn't seem to be any intention of violent action against the more than 200 armed men. The trellis of spears brought into position by which the legionaries held everyone in check certainly encouraged a good degree of restraint at this point.

"I think we can return," von Klasewitz finally said, and Joergensen immediately gave the corresponding commands. To bring the drifting *Saarbrücken* back to the pier wasn't a particularly easy task, though, and required some maneuvering and a good measure of manpower.

Von Klasewitz seemed lost in thought for some minutes, but then he apparently had made a decision.

"Joergensen, I want a meeting of all the officers in the mess hall," he said. "This incident has shown us how precarious our situation is at the moment. It is necessary to make some decisions."

"Yes – but Captain Rheinberg has enjoined us to judge these people according to the time they live in, and we shouldn't –"

"Captain Rheinberg has made his decisions, and this led him to the court of the Emperor," von Klasewitz interrupted sharply. "And he's not here. I'm in charge, and I command now. This incidence must not be repeated, it endangers the safety of ship and crew. There we surely agree, right?"

"Of course."

"Very well. All this wouldn't have happened if Rheinberg would have taken time to consider the prevalent religious feelings. But all is not lost yet, and we can correct this error. So, all officers in the mess hall. I guess I'll have to talk to the Roman commander now, but then we should draw our own conclusions from this disaster!"

Von Klasewitz stalked off the bridge. Joergensen looked thoughtfully after the first officer. He exchanged a quick glance with Langenhagen, who hadn't said a word.

"What is he up to?" the lieutenant murmured finally.

"I really don't know," was the answer of his comrade. "But somehow I don't like the tone of it. Leading up to something."

"Can we send a message to the captain?"

"What good would that do? Sure, we can do that, but until we have an answer it might take weeks. No, we wait, what Klasewitz intends, and then we'll see if it's insane or merely annoying."

"Officially he is still a hostage."

Joergensen grinned weakly. "I don't think the Romans want him any longer. In addition, the *Saarbrücken* has returned, and he would've come back anyway in the course of the day – though perhaps not quite at this speed ..."

5

On foot, on horses, in donkey carts and a truck, around 200 German
soldiers, 500 Roman legionaries – a strange procession. The men
groaned, especially when marching became strenuous, and there
was evidence that the legionaries were quite able to outpace their
German comrades. Things turned even more depressing once the
infantrymen were put on horses. Aside from the few who were able
to ride, and those fewer who were blessed with a natural talent, this
evolved into a disaster. But Becker was at least as merciless as a
sullen Roman centurion, and Arbogast seemed to find this approach
likeable. The German officer saw benefits in the exercise, not least
because by this the Romans and time travelers had developed a
bond that would otherwise hardly come about. Although the Roman
cavalry made their jokes about the German comrades, the shared
hardship and the fact that the Roman officers as well as the German
shouted their orders alike, regardless of their origin, certainly did
its own. It helped also to show those Romans who have been
intimidated by the weapon demonstration that the time travelers
didn't otherwise possess any superpowers.

They followed a Roman military road south, which would eventually take them to the Via Egnatia, the lifeline of the Eastern Empire.
Roman military roads were quite different from modern streets and
didn't follow the diversity of the countryside, like leading around
hills and mountains and meandering along rivers. Roman military
roads were a beautiful symbol of how Rome had governed over the
centuries and became strong against all odds: They stood straight
and followed miles without any change in direction, ignoring hills and
rivers and forests and swamps – all sorts of obstacles were cleared by
generations of tireless road builders out of the way through digging,
bridges, drainage and any other available means. Roman military

roads led directly to the target, and their determination was inherent in their structure. Non-military travelers were very happy to use them as well, but they served primarily the sole purpose to bring Roman troops quickly and effectively from one place to the next. And the mode of transportation was above all marching, marching and marching.

Not that this has been completely foreign for Becker and his men. They were foot soldiers, and as soon as a man wore the uniform of the emperor, he marched. But this was obvious: the further away from Sirmium, the greater the admiration of the Germans for the perseverance and discipline with which the Roman legionaries marched. A well-trained and well-rested legionary could cover 20 Roman miles a day, as Becker and his men were informed, the rough equivalent of 30 kilometers. In former times, legions, however, have been larger and somewhat unwieldy units, and only the reforms of the late Emperor Diocletian had made them relatively smaller troops.

Becker rode at the head of the column, along with Arbogast and the legate of the legion, an officer named Marcus Tullius Secratus. He was a taciturn young man who had recently been promoted to that rank, and at least Arbogast seemed to think highly of him, because he himself had chosen him and his men specifically for this task.

Africanus, who wasn't too happy to continue his service at land and not at sea, had received his emperor's thanks and the subsequent order to continue to remain with Rheinberg as a kind of liaison officer, a promotion he had accepted with mixed feelings. Becker was forced to come to terms with his new comrade. Perhaps this was also the quite a wholesome jump into the cold water and to simply test their new collaboration. The true probation but would be their first joint campaign. Deeds were usually more convincing than words. Becker assumed that their own losses and injuries during a military engagement would keep within very narrow limits. He always had been of the opinion that it was his job to help the enemy to die for his country, instead of having the honor himself. With the Goths, he had to admit, it was a bit more problematic, since they had lost their home and were actually set out to find a new one.

The march to the east brought more things to light than Becker actually would have expected. The longer the two units marched or rode, the more the officers mixed. And although the infantry of Rome and the German Empire was divided by many centuries, the common soldier recognized despite all the problems of understanding that they shared the lot of all infantrymen: sore feet, too heavy a bundle on one's back, irritated officers, too short breaks, too little wine and too little sleep. Becker saw it with joy, while Arbogast seemed to regard it rather with suspicion: But from this shared experience mutual understanding and friendship developed. And in the evening, when the camp was established, the dice were brought forth, and the Germans were just as quick to understand the game as the Romans were eager to learn how to play *Skat*. And the commonly enjoyed ration of wine – so bad that swill might be – helped to establish a mutual agreement between the men. Finally, there were Roman decurios and optios and German sergeants who patrolled the campfires together with a stern face, scrutinizing the soldiers, probably unanimous in their inner lament about a rebellious recruits, inexperienced braggarts and incorrigible drunks. Here, too, quickly a silent understanding developed that was based on the common belief that without commissioned officers the army would only be of little value, but also that most officers wouldn't even find their ass without help after darkfall.

So many things fell into place, and Becker was extremely happy about it.

When they reached Greece after several days of marching, they received a messenger send by Flavius Victor, who still resided in Thessaloniki according to their latest information. He appeared to come to the conclusion to better stay in Thessaloniki instead of traveling to Sirmium and probably had to trust that Richomer, who had joined them on their trip, would do and say the right thing. Becker had quickly developed a particularly good rapport with the squat, sometimes quite sarcastic German cavalry officer. Richomer was about his age, and his views on the losing battle against the Goths and the basic military problems of the empire coincided largely with those who Becker and Rheinberg had been hotly debating all night long. Becker was more and more of the opinion that the Roman Empire in the West didn't fail because no one had recognized the problems and weaknesses, but because many wrong decisions had been made at the wrong time and with misguided priorities. This was evident in the tragic death of Valens, even if he had otherwise not been an impressive emperor; his religious policy had remained fairly tolerant and had thus incurred the wrath of the Western church hierarchy. The fact that Rheinberg wanted to discuss all these things was also the reason that he had remained in the camp of the Emperor. He had discussed with Becker to move the *Saarbrücken* once the exact collection point for the troops was known. Now he had to know that the new army was formed in Thessaloniki, which was easy to reach for the cruiser.

Becker hoped he would be able to provide Theodosius, the new commanders of the East, with a *fait accompli*. The fewer the chances for the talented Spaniard to prove himself, the higher the probability that Gratian wouldn't elevate him to the Emperor of the East.

The messenger of Flavius Victor brought quite welcome news as Richomer had sent him several messages to alert him to the Germans' arrival. The information about the historical developments proved to be reasonably reliable, although the intervention of the Germans began to leave their mark: Instead of waiting for the arrival of Theodosius, Arbogast had given orders to avoid the Goths and to reform the remaining troops in the vicinity of Thessaloniki. That did also happen in reality, according to Rheinberg, but only much later. The Goths themselves had left the area around Adrianople and were now invading Greece, a long, disorganized trek that rampaged through the country and deliberately evaded major cities, since the Gothic leadership knew well that they only could overcome significant fortifications by treachery and nothings else. So far, no traitor had been found, therefore the invaders had to focus on rural areas. Since this had an impact on the supply situation of the cities, it was already bad enough.

According to plan, the two Roman units and the German infantry-men were by now on their way toward the Thessaloniki venue.

In the evening, Becker, Arbogast, Richomer and Secratus sat around the campfire to discuss the strategy.

"I need a battlefield to which we can lure the Goths," Becker started. "We should already convey our ideas to Victor so that he can mentally prepare."

"What kind of battlefield exactly? And what role should the legions play?" Secratus wanted to know.

"Decoys. Take no offense, but we cannot send the demoralized remnants of the eastern army into a real battle. They should pretend to offer a fight and then retreat to a prepared position. This position will subsequently allow my men to fight the mass of the Gothic warriors with our weapons from elevated positions. Or we will make digging trenches, and after the legionaries have reached safety, we open fire from there. More likely, since we meet at a city well-fortified, we find proper positions in the fortifica-tions."

"Trenches?"

Becker took a parchment and began to draw the principle of a trench onto the sheet. "These positions provide optimum coverage for my men and are at the same time a good position for our attack. It would, of course, be fatal if the Goths storm the trenches, therefore we will need your legions as a shield. But I assume that it will not happen. If we position the MGs tactically, especially on the walls of the city, the Goths will suffer hundreds, even thousands of deaths in a very short time and will be completely demoralized. It's not our goal to exterminate the enemy but to allow us to dictate a peace on Roman conditions."

Arbogast nodded. "So it is. If Fritigern and Alaric see that their men are taken by an invisible force, they must accept an offer of talks. I have authority to negotiate for the Emperor as Theodosius won't arrive in time. We want clear conditions: The Goths get the promised settlement area, but there will be no status as allies; they have to submit to Roman rule completely. We need the Goths for what is coming."

He threw Becker to a meaningful look. Rheinberg and the captain had drawn a haunting and realistic picture in regard to the impending invasion of the Huns and the attacks of the Vandals and other tribes. The empire had to prepare, and it also had to be able to exist without the machine guns of the Germans, because the ammunition would probably already be in short supply after this battle against the Goths.

"So an area that looks like a good battleground for the Goths. It can be a bit steep in their favor. I need hills or cliffs overlooking the terrain within two to three Roman miles – or I just need the city walls. There I will position our machine guns. There must be no obstacles in the line of fire; we need a completely free field for all MGs. We must be able to fire over the heads of the retreating legions."

Richomer frowned, as the tactical concepts, foreign to him, began to form in his mind. "I don't know the area particularly well; I've been operating almost exclusively in the West. We must rely on Victor's expertise. Nevertheless, as far as I know, the whole area is consistently hilly in Greece. There are valleys and plains, but I am very confident that we will find a position that meets your needs, Legate Becker."

Becker stifled a reaction to the title by which Richomer addressed him. A legate was normally a legion commander and the subordinate officers of his were tribunes. These were mostly very young men who had entered the service from the nobility or knighthood. Men in Becker's age usually had long since left this rank behind if successful. They normally held the office of a *Dux* and were responsible for an entire province. That he had been addressed with the rank of legate was connected to the fact that the Roman comrades felt the need to classify everyone correctly. Moreover, Rheinberg had introduced him with that rank, and therefore he had to accept it.

Sooner or later, they had to fit into the Roman military structure if they were to be integrated into the empire. Becker was not quite sure which rank corresponded to that of Rheinberg. Trierarch Africanus might be a ship commander, but Becker had gotten the impression that he was regarded by many fellow officers as not more than a sergeant. Probably Rheinberg would be made navarch, somewhere between squadron commander and admiral. Köhler would surely become a centurion. Becker smiled. Centurion Köhler, that had something. Or were they called differently in the navy? There were moments when Becker was very grateful for being a simple infantryman.

"Well, we're waiting for the helpful hints of Victor," he agreed. "But we should write down our ideas and send them ahead by messenger. Swift action is needed. Each day on which the Goths continue marauding through the country will weaken the empire and increase the suffering of the population."

Everything was written down quickly, and soon a messenger rode from the camp at night toward Thessaloniki. He would still take a few days until he'd reach the city, and then they possibly had to act quickly. Of course, there was another reason why Becker urged haste: He wanted to unite his men as soon as possible with the *Saarbrücken*. Despite the good cooperation with the Romans, he felt a little lost and helpless in the middle of the Roman East, and the metal walls of the cruiser had given him a greater sense of security than he wanted to admit. The cruiser was home, and before their position in the empire did not really strengthen and their legal status was clear it would remain so.

As Becker went to sleep and dozed off after a few minutes, the likeness of his fiancé crept in his consciousness. He had banished her face in recent weeks, aware of the memory, and in self-protection, because there were so many other issues to consider. Even now her image flickered for only a short time before his inner eye. The awareness of being removed from her by many hundreds of years, an unbridgeable time, weighed heavily on him. Feeling helpless was not his nature. To accept the inevitable had always been one of his strengths. Yet he had imagined for a moment what it would have been like if he had not made this very strange journey through time. He probably would be somewhere in Africa after the outbreak of the war, probably struck down in time by British colonial troops or incensed natives. And even if they would have returned to Germany, he would have quickly found himself again in another battle. Unlike

Rheinberg, who had eagerly awaited the approaching war to be formally declared and was firmly convinced of the victory of the German Empire on all fronts, Becker had not shared both his passion and conviction.

No, he probably wouldn't be able to return to his fiancée. For a moment he thought about it, considered if that was a comforting thought or not, and was asleep.

6

The shackles for the recruits were only removed within the encampment. The partly younger, partly older men already looked around, some scared, some apathetic. They were marched through the night until they finally arrived in this camp. It seemed to be only a temporary reception center for mustering and assessment. After that, a good-humored guard had told them during the march, they would be spread over legions that had urgent staffing needs, where they would also receive training for their role as warriors of Rome. Due to the growing shortage of personnel, the training had been shortened and often enough it happened that troops of unprepared legionaries had to go to an unexpected fight – which in turn automatically and very quickly led to sudden staff shortages again. A well-trained, well-equipped and well-run legionary was still superior to any known attacker. However, this combination became increasingly less common, and Volkert noted with bitterness that the for this time supposedly alien concept of "cannon fodder" could in fact be applied to the recruits gathered here.

With red-rimmed eyes and covered in dust, the brave fighters stood in the central square in the middle of the camp, observed by a number of attentive legionaries. In some cases Volkert could read hints of compassion in their faces, and it was likely that one or the other of them had been pressed into service, too. The bulk of the staff replenishment was provided by the soldiers' families, for the son of a legionary was legally obliged also to become a soldier, regardless of inclination and talent. The job of a soldier was not entirely unattractive, because in some respects the wordy recruiter had certainly spoken the truth. Whoever proved himself and survived could, in fact, leave the armed forces with a higher social status than he had at the time at which he had entered into it. Veterans still enjoyed privileges. Nevertheless, the enthusiasm to join the armed forces apparently had subsided with time.

A gray-bearded centurion stood in front of the hopeless bunch. He chewed on something and ran his hand over his unshaven chin. Then he spat on the floor and cleared his throat. "Greetings, legionairies."

Silence answered him, but that didn't seem to bother him.

"My name is Lucius Latinus. Welcome to the legion. You are now warriors of the Emperor, and I am your god. This honor will earn you a decent signing bonus, which might hopefully soften your disappointment about the somewhat unconventional way of recruiting."

The centurion explained the procedure once more, leaving no doubt that he wasn't too interested in the whole thing on a personal level. Volkert felt his attention wander, and very quickly the face of Julia appeared before his mind's eye. The painful longing for the young woman mingled with despair about his current situation, and for a moment it seemed to him as if his heart would burst. A deep despondency fell upon him, and he quarreled with fate. With all his power he desired a miracle that would free him from this predicament. But not for a moment he thought that all this was the fault of Julia's daring plan. The senator's daughter wasn't responsible for the difficult situation of the empire and the blatant injustices that came with it. Volkert knew that Captain Rheinberg was convinced that it had been, among others, these injustices that had ultimately contributed to the demise of the empire. He wanted to use his influence to rectify some of these basic grievances. But for Volkert this would come too late in any case. The young man already envisioned himself lying in his blood on some foreign battlefield, forgotten by the world, and only mourned by a girl he'd never see again.

Volkert lowered his head so no one saw the tears in his eye. Overwhelmed by self-pity, he saw no chance to change anything in his fate.

"You there!"

Volkert hastily wiped the moisture from his eyes.

The centurion suddenly stood in front of him. "How old are you, boy?"

The man smelled as if he had not bathed for days. Volkert was trying to gather air through the mouth and not to show his disgust.

"I'm 22, Centurion."

"What is your profession?"

Volkert thought quickly. Which part of his knowledge could he use to pretend having a profession recognizable in this age and time? He remembered only his long sailing trip on the North Sea which he had made with his father, during which his love of the sea has been awakened.

"I'm a fisherman."

"You're wrong. You are a Legionary."

Volkert pressed his lips on each other, but there was no reproach visible in the face of the fierce centurion.

"Understand that rather quickly, my boy," the man continued with surprisingly soft voice. "It makes things easier. For everyone of you, there is a place in the legion, believe me. If you're lucky, you'll be placed in one of the garrisons and sit on your butt for years, watching the farmers plowing their fields and help their daughters to discover their interest for men in uniform."

The man's almost conciliatory tone surprised Volkert somewhat. He took courage and answered. "I have a bride."

The centurion nodded sympathetically. "There are writers and against a few small coins messengers who are ready to deliver letters. If your bride is ready to follow you, then she can join the train to the camp."

"She certainly followed me," Volkert said, feeling exactly the security he expressed. Julia would have put the wheels in motion to find out where they had taken him, there was no doubt.

"Then wait until your transfer is clear and give her your recruitment bonus so she can join you. Once the training is over, you possibly will be given clearance to leave the camp quite soon. You are not allowed to marry yet, but everything else your centurion will not be interested in, if you give him no reason to complain in important matters. If your bride is faithful to you, there is a way.

And the empire will give you the opportunity to earn even more if a battle has been won. You two could have it worse." The centurion put an arm on Volkert's shoulder. "Believe me, I am also sorry how we have to make howling youths into legionaries. I would also prefer it if the recruits would come voluntarily into service, because of fame or at least only because they hope to get rich through all kind of looting. I didn't make the time we live in, though. Pull yourself together."

Abruptly, the man turned, and Volkert felt that bitter stench of that man didn't matter anymore.

Volkert lowered his head again. He no longer felt quite so miserable as a few minutes ago. At this place and at this time – and by this man – he probably enjoyed at least a brief moment of understanding and compassion. It proved to him that there could still be soldiers who, in a time of permanent war and great cruelties, had retained some humanity and had not completely degenerated into animals. It didn't make his situation any better, but it gave him some hope, and the honest words of the centurion had at least shown him that perhaps all was not yet lost.

Volkert stretched, as the column of the recruits was called to come to the *medicus* to be examined. He was healthy, muscular, well-trained. He would be taken, there was no doubt about that.

Volkert's gaze wandered to the edge of the camp, where he could make out the rows of tents. The certainty that Julia was out there somewhere helped him through these difficult moments as much as the compassionate words of the old veteran. There was hope. And if he only nourished it, a way to muddle through would be found.

"Forward!" the centurion commanded.

And forward he went.

7

"Gentlemen, some serious mistakes have been made, and we have to correct them as quickly as possible."

Joergensen, Langenhagen and Dahms exchanged meaningful glances, as von Klasewitz positioned himself at the head end of the table and began his lecture. It had taken longer than expected until the officers had gathered here. This had been because von Klasewitz had received unexpected visits twice after the cruiser had been moored back. First Navarch Renna had appeared. He had apologized with many words about the "incompetence" of his numerically much inferior port guards, at least that was what the others had picked up from the subdued conversation. A quite important decision was leaked – namely, that Renna had been appointed military prefect and been granted the military command of northern Italy. Everyone knew that this promotion had something to do with the *Saarbrücken*. Renna himself seemed to regard this sudden honor with mixed feelings, but of course he was not in a position to question the decisions of the Emperor even remotely.

The conversation had ultimately been relatively short, because the three officers knew very well that Renna had slowly begun to share Rheinberg's doubts about von Klasewitz's skills.

A short time later, Petronius had appeared.

Köhler had reported to the other officers about the very strange conversation they had with the envoy of Bishop Liberius, so that they were briefed fully. The meeting with Petronius, who had established a relationship with von Klasewitz which was obviously based on mutual understanding, lasted nearly three hours. It was followed by a triumphant announcement by von Klasewitz that there would be no further attacks from the clergy – interestingly, a guaranty that Renna had obviously not wanted to make, perhaps because he doubted his ability to deliver.

"We are lucky to have both the opportunity and the insight necessary to rectify said wrongs, and I'm sure that you are as happy about it as I."

If von Klasewitz had expected to evoke visible agreement with these words, his expectation wasn't readily met. Only Ensign Tennberg, after Volkert's desertion the only remaining cadet aboard the *Saarbrücken*, seemed to find extremely important to keep an open mind in regard to von Klasewitz's slightly nebulous hints.

"Captain Rheinberg has already clarified his strategy to us, and in many areas, I, of course, agree with him," von Klasewitz said. "Nevertheless, the captain is not immune to misperceptions and the events of today have very clearly shown where those can lead and have led to." Von Klasewitz glanced around, looking for approval, but met again only patience and serenity. Given the fact that he had not said anything of substance, this wasn't surprising, but it seemed to rankle him, because his face turned somewhat acidic as he continued. "Gentlemen, a fundamental principle the captain has postulated for us in our approach to the Roman Empire has been complete neutrality when confronted with religious differences. Actually, Rheinberg wants to apply this principle to a higher political level as well; at least that's how I understood his hints before his departure to Sirmium."

Von Klasewitz cleared his throat.

"Anyway, in this historical phase we encounter, I consider it dangerous to pursue such a policy," he continued. "In the German Empire, a well-established political system, characterized by a high degree of patriotism and love for the fatherland and imbued with loyalty to the excellent personality of our Emperor, one might be inclined to allow some tolerance in these matters. And indeed, it would have been a step backwards to antagonize Catholics and Protestants, who are also found in peaceful harmony with each other on this ship. Even in regard to Jews, one may accept a degree of tolerance."

Von Klasewitz's expression showed quite clearly what he really thought of this kind of tolerance. Dahms threw another look at Joergensen, and he obviously didn't fancy the undertone. His fiancée, separated from him through the ages, was of Jewish heritage, and that was certainly one of the reasons why the required dispensation for marriage had not been issued until shortly before the trip of the *Saarbrücken*. Still, no one interrupted the first officer, who had continued unabashed, though Joergensen still looked like he wanted to throttle the nobleman immediately.

"But here we are in another era! Here the Church is not so stable and resting in itself, as in our time! Heresies and apostasies are ubiquitous, and the struggle to adhere to the true doctrine everywhere has not ended! The state couldn't be neutral in this – and rightly so. The coming emperor that our dear captain seeks to prevent is called by Christian historiography 'the Great' gentlemen! He has driven the heresy of Arianism and the paganism of ancient cults with fire and sword from the Roman Empire, preserving the unity of the Church, and thus laid the foundation for our venerable Western tradition! And all this is under the guidance of one who is now venerated by Catholics as a saint and father of the church, Ambrosius of Milan! Who are we – who is Captain Rheinberg? – that we want to counter this inevitable historical development, this necessary catharsis, this pressing, cleansing flood of events? And what is the consequence if we even try? We noticed it today. Priests have tried to use force against us, and they have the orthodox population of Ravenna on their side! Dumb luck saved us from the worst! Next time, I fear that we will not get away unharmed! And this reveals the sensitivity of this major error in Rheinberg's assessment of the situation!"

Even his critics would concede that von Klasewitz could be quite convincing once he gathered some rhetorical momentum. The flushed cheeks and the twinkle in his eyes showed that he was in awe of his own words.

"And so, gentlemen," he continued, "our path is clearly marked. In this historical conflict, we must not go against but with the flow and the flow goes clearly in one direction: to the Trinitarian doctrine against heresies such as Arianism and of course also against all other pagan cults which may once have been relevant in the past, but now belong to the junkyard of history."

The first officer paused and looked around. On the faces before him was a remarkable range of emotions. Some men seemed to have become thoughtful by his eloquence, some had taken the argument at least momentarily, others seemed to remain indifferent. Joergensen, Langenhagen and Dahms were largely appalled, and their eyes spoke volumes. From their perspective, von Klasewitz wanted to play with the fire, he wanted to promote a conflict that could not only lead to civil war but also to the profound weakening of the Roman Empire, as Rheinberg had warned strongly against.

"What exactly do you propose?", asked Dahms.

"Thanks for a good question," replied von Klasewitz. "In fact, I already have a plan. First, we must make it clear to the local clergy that there is no doubt where exactly our loyalties lie, and that is true regardless of what the new military prefect says about it. We need to demonstrate our devotion, prove that we are not only all true Christians but that we also know what the Trinity really means and how it is to be evaluated. I thought of a blessing ceremony with the Archbishop of Ravenna, attended by all the officers, and a renewal of baptism for all on board."

"More than half of men are Protestants," Langenhagen reminded him.

Von Klasewitz looked irritated at the man. "These are minor details that we really don't need to rub the nose of the local Christians with."

At least at this point his critics could only agree with him. It would replace one conflict only by another if one would talk too easily about Luther's theses and the subsequent schism. Nevertheless, von Klasewitz, apparently a renewed Catholic, whose seemingly deep faith had formerly been quite unknown to anyone present, was clearly not ready to take any existing religious feelings of the crew into serious consideration.

Von Klasewitz apparently expected more questions and comments.

Joergensen was finally the one who spoke. "Your reasoning has certainly some appeal," he said, trying to restrain himself. "But such a fundamental decision is something we have to discuss with the Captain. We cannot do anything of importance without his consent, especially not such an important change of strategy."

"Captain Rheinberg isn't here," von Klasewitz stated. "The attack by the angry mob today should have impressed on you that time is running out."

"Didn't Petronius promise to keep the people under control?"

"Oh, I'm sure he will do his utmost," the first officer replied evasively. "But how great is his influence? I cannot tell. Do you?"

"No," admitted the second officer. "But when I think about Petronius and thus the Archbishop's moderating effect on the fanatical elements, and when I see likewise that Renna has authorized us an additional department of harbor guards, I see really good conditions created to wait for the return of the Captain. We should expedite the matter, surely. We should immediately send him a message."

"No!" von Klasewitz snapped. "The Captain is entrusted with highly sensitive negotiations at the Imperial Court! Any disruption can have fatal consequences! We must deal with this problem ourselves."

Joergensen shook his head. "With all due respect ..."

"You don't seem to agree to my ability to assess the situation properly," interrupted the nobleman.

"This is not an assessment of your abilities," Dahms chipped in. "It is about the fact that you want to make a fundamental decision of great military and political significance. I also have a feeling that we should not ignore the Captain in this matter. We have heard clear instructions of him, especially regarding the fact that we should not interfere."

"These orders are based on outdated information," von Klasewitz said icily. "The latest developments could not have been foreseen by him!"

"I have the impression that the Captain has imposed restraint on us exactly because he was afraid of these and similar incidents," Dahms said.

"What do you want to accuse me of?" asked the nobleman. "Insubordination?"

Dahms raised his eyebrows. "I did nothing of that sort. What I want to say is that we have clear instructions, and we have no authority to simple override them, especially since there is no immediate emergency. If the riots occur again, we set sail and wait in front of the coast for the Captain's return. Renna will surely agree with this course of action."

"Have you talked to the prefect on this issue?" Joergensen added immediately, grateful for that keyword. "I'm sure that we should seek his counsel!"

"Oh yes?" von Klasewitz's face showed his increased displeasure. "Now I will also discuss with the local authorities? Who should I ask in addition? The Oracle of Delphi?"

"The counsel of Petronius for you was quite extensive," Dahms said dryly.

"Don't be cheeky, Mr. Engineer!" von Klasewitz snapped. "I have convened this meeting not to play *Reichstag*! I'm the commanding officer and I insist –"

"That the standing orders of the legitimate captain are to be respected and followed and that he is informed of any changes immediately and without delay." Dahms was equally icy now, but backed by greater self-control.

The initial enthusiasm for Klasewitz's plans had subsided. Some of those who were moved by his words at first now seemed to remember their duties. Only Tennberg glanced annoyed at Dahms.

Von Klasewitz looked around, read the rejection in the majority of the faces. He gritted his teeth, suppressed the undoubtedly harsh reply already on his lips and lowered his head in apparent agreement. "Well," he rasped. "I see that I cannot achieve much with my reasoning. Your blind loyalty to outdated commands and a captain who has left us alone with the problems will have its repercussions. But good. Tomorrow we send a message to the East with a report about the events of the day. And until Rheinberg condescends to answer it, we feed the cocks and push ourselves into a corner, hoping that the righteous wrath of the indignant mass won't haunt us again in this city."

Von Klasewitz's description of the Captain bordered on insult, and if Rheinberg had been here, he would have stopped these utterings immediately. But now the other officers were just glad that any danger was averted, as von Klasewitz seemed to give up his plan for the meantime.

The meeting of the officers ended in stony silence. When the men left the room, von Klasewitz disappeared with Tennberg, grumbling in the darkness of nightfall. Joergensen and Dahms looked after them. They felt that slowly a wedge threatened to be driven into the crew of the *Saarbrücken*. They knew that von Klasewitz had his friends on board, NCOs and men who expected an advantage or shared some of his sharper views. It was to be feared that the gap in the officer corps of the cruiser would extend downward. That was the last thing they needed.

"I hope Rheinberg comes back soon," said the second.

"Yes. And we should talk to Köhler," the engineer added.

They set out immediately to do so.

8

"I don't get it, Judge."

"Me too."

Fritigern sat on his horse and glanced at the long line of covered wagons and carts pulled along the hilly area. Small groups of warriors galloped along the whole route, to warn of surprise attacks by the Romans if any would occur. But so far no one had disturbed the mile long trek, and if it was true what he had just been told by his breathless scouts, nobody would soon.

"It's a little unexpected," Godegisel said now, rubbing his chin. "Yes, a consolidation of the Roman forces was inevitable, but not as fast and not under the command of Victor. I thought that Gratian would send a new general – a candidate for the Eastern throne, especially now that everyone thinks Valens is dead."

The gaze of the young nobleman fell involuntarily on the big cart, which was surrounded by eight riders from Fritigern's personal guard. The cart was bulkier than the others, and seemed very stable, and in its interior sat chained like a dog aforementioned Valens, staring blankly.

"Valens is as good as dead," muttered Fritigern. "He speaks only gibberish and has few bright moments. An undignified spectacle. Even if we should return him, he will hardly be able to claim the throne again. We need to do something so that he will survive a meeting with a Roman envoy reasonably sane. Then I shouldn't care what becomes of him."

"But what have the Romans done? They assemble the remains of their eastern army at Thessaloniki. Good. Do they want to attack us with that rabble?"

"I don't know. But it wouldn't happen if they were without a plan. We must be doubly alert and send out more scouts than before.

But it is clear that we have to face the threat somehow. I would like to destroy the remaining troops of the East, especially now, where they have not been able to add new recruits to compensate for the losses. At the same time, we must try to establish an official contact with the Romans."

"Will Gratian send troops?"

Fritigern waved to some passing warriors, before he turned back to the young man. "Possible, but unlikely. Although we'd have a lot on our hands with Gratian's troops, the risk is too great for the little emperor: we could destroy his men, while the Alemanni march in the West, like many of the other German tribes. They'd overrun the garrisons with the certainty that no army could oppose them anymore. No, Gratian's too much his father's son to take completely unpredictable military risks. He is looking for another solution."

"Yes – send a general, give him some gold, maybe a few good officers and the order to evade us and build up the troops again, a request which can take years to accomplish. But then it wouldn't start by pulling the remnants of the eastern army in front of us already. He must know that we notice that. This smells like a trap."

Fritigern sighed. "That may be – but what kind of a trap will that be if he doesn't have any men to let it snap?"

"A secret alliance with one of our allies?" Godegisel mused.

"It's possible. But unlikely. Traitors could quickly become the betrayed. The risk would be very high for both sides. No, I think it is due to an act of desperation, some political problems that build up at the court of Gratian or in Constantinople. Something we cannot know."

"You want to continue to let Alaric go to Constantinople?"

Fritigern nodded immediately. "An excellent idea. The old man is highly regarded, and he is at the end of his life. The respect he enjoys he can't translate into real political power without help; he needs me. But he is a wonderful ambassador, and the Romans will receive him with honor, because no matter what Gratian's up to, he will not be averse to negotiations. But I still need a Roman envoy to see Valens and at least briefly talk to him. Or something else."

"Valens is crazy," Godegisel replied curtly.

Fritigern didn't answer. On the cart rumbling past their current location a tall young woman, not even 20 years old and with straw-blonde hair sat on the front seat. Her rather ragged clothes couldn't hide the very obvious charms of her body.

Fritigern frowned thoughtfully. "I have an idea on how we can possibly rid Valens of his delusion – at least for a certain time."

Godegisel looked at him quizzically. The Judge pointed to the cart and the figure of the young woman who slowly moved away from them.

"Do you know her?" Fritigern said.

"Yes."

"I need to know her, too. Bring her to me."

"Judge, I am not your –"

"Not for me, my son," Fritigern interrupted the protest. He now smiled dreamily. "Not for me, Godegisel. It is a gift for the Emperor."

9

"Work faster. Even faster. You there – dig deeper! Do you want attacking barbarians to simply tip over the stockade and massacre you? Or do you want that damn wall to protect us? We build no fucking village here, we build a military camp! Hey, you! What is this? Did I order a break, scumbag?"

The shouting found no end. Volkert didn't dare rest the shovel to wipe the sweat from his forehead. His whole body was wet from the work. Over the tunic, he wore a matching breastplate, the helmet of a legionary on his head, and tied to his belt the sword, the main weapon of the Roman soldier. It was warm, late summer, but at no time had the roaring centurion allowed them to take off any piece of equipment. One must always be prepared to follow the call to battle, he said, especially if you build a camp in enemy territory. Volkert controlled himself not to tell him that during the latest battle against the Alemanni, Gratian had been the last emperor to lead Roman forces across the Rhine. From now on they would be wholly on the defensive and rather have the problem that the enemy, no matter which one, would take the fight into the empire.

He kept it to himself.

The Roman forces didn't much resemble the elite legions that had once built the empire, Volkert thought. The military reforms of Diocletian had the old system replaced by a more flexible structure with smaller units. The once 5,000-strong legion had been reduced to 1,500 soldiers. A distinction was made between the border troops, who were often no more than militias, and the mobile strike forces, the best trained units, the main army that went on campaigns with the emperor. What remained was hard training and discipline. But the glorious past of the Roman legionary was long gone.

The training for Volkert and the other involuntary recruits had begun shortly after the speech of the centurion, and as an instructor the gruff veteran Latinus had presented himself as much as a relentless grinder as Volkert had feared. They had received equipment, some still adored with dried blood spots collected from a battlefield, taken from the dead body of a comrade. They had not started training with weapons but with important basics. They learned how to pack one's bundle and what had to be included – from food to firewood to important details such as a sewing kit. And then they started with two central training units: marching in formation and building of a field camp.

The marching wasn't any problem for Volkert. He had done quite a lot of it in his life and knew what was up. As soon as he reasonably understood the barked commands of the centurions, the drill had not been a fundamental challenge for him. But when they had practiced battle tactics and had to form the turtle with a phalanx of shields, the pain in his upper arms had almost been unbearable at some point. When he had to lower his shield, he had to learn that in the Roman army very traditional practices of instilling discipline were popular. These were other times, but Volkert had to adjust to the fact that whipping was lavishly applied particularly in cases of recalcitrance, and in the worst case entire units could be decimated – that is, every tenth legionary was selected by lot and beaten to death.

But the worst thing was his current task. Setting up camp sounded relatively harmless but was obviously murderous work. Erecting the palisade, digging the necessary excavation, cutting down of trees, cutting the piles, balancing and fixing, building the tents – and all this after a well prepared plan in which one activity must go hand in hand with the other. Two of his new comrades were quickly freed of this heavy duty. They were elevated to the rank of "immunes" because their superiors had realized that both were gifted craftsmen. This meant not only that they would soon obtain a higher pay, their special skills would also be rewarded insofar as they were freed from heavy and cumbersome services. The Roman system of promotion didn't know so many different ranks as the modern German army.

What was remarkably similar though was that the highest-ranking officer in place, here a centurion, was in fact God.

It had changed little over the centuries.

Volkert sweated like someone poured water over his body. He dropped the shovel and grabbed a log. His hands were already torn by the only roughly cut wood, and as he heaved the pile up, it threatened to slip from his fingers. But then another pair of hands popped up, callous and full of scars, the hands of a man who had made his life using them, through hard work. Together, they set up the trunk, rammed it into the prepared hole next to one already standing, rammed again until he ran deep and held firm, so even the centurion could not do more than utter an affirmative grunt.

Volkert looked gratefully at his fellow recruit. He was about his age, of broad and stocky build, with dark hair spreading wild above the face. His face was flat and broad, the skin tanned and weathered. "I'm Simodes," he introduced himself, and immediately struck Volkert amicably on the shoulder. The German almost lost his balance. "I was a shipyard worker, before I found the recruiters."

"They have pressed you like me? I'm Thomas."

"No, Thomas, I signed up voluntarily." Volkert must have looked surprised because Simodes laughed.

"I'm not a good shipyard worker and have taken the job because my father did it, and the Emperor believes what is good for the father can be only fair for the son." Simodes laughed again, but this time without any real joy. "What nonsense. The only way to escape the endless torment and sadness was to report to the army."

Volkert shook his head. "Take it as you will, but it seems to me that cruelty and sadness are waiting for us here as well."

"Yes, I understand you, Thomas. You're not here by choice. But I have happily exchanged the cries of my foreman against the bellow of the centurions. It may be a philosophical question, but the burden that one chooses by himself is a special kind of freedom. I'm Greek, so forgive me this attitude."

Volkert saw the wicked sparkle in the eyes of Simodes and smiled. The massive man was probably not wrong. To bear all this with a little more composure and humor would probably make everything a lot easier. Volkert sighed. A philosophical view about himself was something new to him. "Anyway, thank you, Simodes."

"Don't thank me, give thanks to the Centurion. Because we were so busy, we get water!"

The Greek was right. A legionary with a big water bag came up and filled a wooden tankard of equally impressive size. Everyone was allowed to take some deep swallows. Volkert was amazed again to find that water and wine have been mixed. The sour taste that rather reminded him of vinegar was even somewhat refreshing.

"Enough laziness!" roared the centurion, as the water carrier moved on. "No more breaks until the camp is ready!"

Simodes and Volkert reached for the shovels.

"Where are you from, Thomas?"

"I'm German," Volkert said simply.

"What did you do before you were put into service?"

"Sailor."

Simodes nodded. "My father loves the sea. Good attitude for a shipyard worker. Likes to assemble triremes for the Emperor. The only water I like is the one in which I bathe. The ocean scares me. I'm glad that I'm far away from the coast."

Volkert said nothing.

"And, Thomas, is there someone waiting for you?"

"My bride," replied the German, his voice suddenly damped. "I hope so."

"So say we all," said the Greek philosophically. "I hope for you that your bride can march quickly. I heard this morning that we get more of our training on the way."

Volkert stopped. "On the way? Where to?"

Simodes shrugged. "Wherever the Emperor may send us. But it is clear that we either go to one of the borders in Germania or the East to pay homage to the dead Valens. Perhaps the high lords still need a bunch of recruits they can feed to the Goths. No matter how, one of us is getting closer to home."

"That's reassuring," Volkert muttered. His gaze wandered over the boundaries of the training site to the actual camp, where they had been given quarters. Out there, somewhere, in one of the

70

villages in the vicinity, he suspected, was Julia. He wasn't allowed to leave the camp. If Simodes was right, and it would fit the tense situation at the borders, the opportunity to leave wouldn't arise too soon. Hopefully, Julia had open eyes and ears to learn when the recruits left. Otherwise, he would be gone one day, and his chances of ever seeing her again would be very, very low.

Simodes saw the storm of emotions that raged through Volkert, easily recognizable on his face. "Do not worry, my friend," he said awkwardly. "It won't be so bad. Gratian has put the Alemanni in their place, and when we go to the East, then they will have already dealt with the Goths. The magicians of the future will take care of this."

Volkert's head snapped up. "The what?"

"Didn't hear about it? Symmachus and the other pagan senators have gathered with the help of their priest mage from the future to save the empire from the outside dangers and to teach the raging Christians reason." Simodes smiled apologetically. "The story goes around everywhere. Interestingly, the priests themselves put that into the world. Anyway, some of my Christian friends are quite sour. They accuse the Emperor of being too soft and not recognizing the threat."

Volkert controlled himself with difficulty. There could be no doubt about whom these rumors referred to. Something was going on that could be extremely dangerous for the *Saarbrücken*! It matched the impression he had gained from his meeting with Petronius.

Something was brewing.

"You don't seem to worry," Volkert said carefully.

"No, no, I don't care. I give nothing to those rumors. Oh yes, I believe in magic and witches, but I do not fear them, and wars have historically been decided by the sword not by magic. They're all hysterical. But yes, if anything of this is for real, let's hope the strange magicians are diligent and secure the borders, so that we have a quiet time, don't you think?"

"Yes ... yes, sure," Volkert said thoughtfully in response.

"Help me with that trunk!" Simodes said.

Volkert didn't really hear him, though.

10

Claudia Lucia Michellus was an impressive woman whether being angry or joyful. When she lifted her mighty bosom and stretched her wide upper arms in wagging movements to convince friend and foe of her superiority, everyone remained silent, waiting for either a curse or a blessing from the lips of the senator's wife. "The Senator" she was called behind closed doors and not unjustly; who exactly was in charge of her husband's policy – she or him? – no one could say with absolute certainty. Her penetrating gaze and piercing voice were among the greatest means of Lucia's power, and her massive shape, surrounded like with a tarpaulin by a wide-cut tunic, commanded awe and respect. As a young wife, Lucia had been an enchanting beauty, and sons of wealthy and respected personalities had applied for her favor in large numbers. Once her father had married her to the young Michellus, who had just become censor, everyone thought of the rising youngsters being a brilliant match. Michellus also had been likewise convinced, at least at the beginning. He had, however, developed one or two doubts over the course of time, especially the more his wife had replaced her charm with body mass and a certain desire for power. The fact that he had taken the opportunity to travel to Sirmium so willingly came surely not by accident.

But now, in the private chambers of the dominatrix, there was no trace of rigidness and rigor visible. It was the soft, caring and understanding Lucia who held her sobbing daughter, returning home, lovingly in her arms.

"Julia, I beg you. Calm down!"

Her thick hand patted her daughter's head which she held pressed to her chest. It was surprising enough that Julia did appear back at home. But it was obvious that she had been faced with a problem she couldn't solve on her own – a problem that was so important to her that she had even decided to humiliate herself before her parents. There was nothing that made Julia more angry, and her mother knew the sacrifice of her daughter.

It was ultimately a quite satisfactory situation.

"But mother," the young woman replied now, raised her head and tried to wipe away the tears. "You should have seen it. There was no way to escape."

"Yes, the empire has to do so many things which might find our displeasure," Lucia agreed. "I can well imagine how you must have felt, my poor little dove."

"I know the camp to which they have brought him. We must act now!"

Lucia looked distressed. "But what am I to do? Your father is with the Emperor, and I myself am just a simple, weak woman."

"Mother, you're anything but that, and your influence with father's friends is considerable. Send a messenger to the other senators in the city. Meet the military prefect! He holds his protective hand over the strangers! He will have great interest to free one of them!"

Lucia made a thoughtful face and absently played with a strand of hair. Julia had given her tearful descriptions of their fate, accompanied by hugs and kisses, and put her hair in disorder along the way.

"Well, I could write one or two letters, of course. Should I go to Ravenna, it could even be that Renna will actually listen to me, yes, there is a chance. Or I write him a letter, too."

"Yes! Mother!" Julia clutched Lucia's arm with both hands, a pleading look in her eyes.

The "Senator" wondered about her daughter quite much. She actually seemed to be aflame with serious love, which was ultimately a rather unbecoming behavior for their stand. Never before has Julia shown such behavior and Lucia had to admit that this kind of passion was rather confusing for her.

"You have to write the letter at once!" Julia insisted. "I want to write for you; you dictate the words to me! If you send the messenger today ..."

"Gently, gently," her mother said softly. "You don't even know if this man is still where you left him. Who knows whether our intervention will even come on time?"

"They will have documentation! Even when he was transferred, they will know where! We must not miss this opportunity."

Lucia looked at her doubtfully. "Should I really demand so many favors to save this man? Julia, he is of highly dubious origin and certainly not of nobility. I really think that he is a poor choice for you. You are called to higher fame! Please consider! It will cause you no joy! What kind a life can he offer you? He has nothing, he is nothing, he will remain to be nothing. In your shoes, I'd try to forget him quickly. And think of the *infamia*!"

Lucia winced. She knew that look, this suddenly petrified expression on her daughter's face. When Julia stared like this, then the gates were closed, and the roads to reason were barricaded. Now any discussion, even entreaties and threats, made no sense. She knew that look well enough, and she knew her limits. Before her daughter would completely quit the conversation, she had to come around, and as quickly as possible.

"Forgive me, Julia. I know that you're serious about this man. I was wrong."

Julia's face turned a bit softer again.

Her mother sighed. That had been a close one.

"You must do everything in your power! It's really an important matter for me, mother! I would kill myself if I had to learn that he got impaled by some barbarian, dying in a foreign country. That would be unbearable. Do you hear, Mother? Unbearable!"

"All right, all's good," Lucia replied soothingly. "I understand you, and you really care for that man. If he is the man for whom you regard him, he will be determined to prove himself. Nothing will happen to him."

Julia sat up.

"No, nothing will happen to him," she confirmed vigorously. With defiant movements she removed the last remnants of moisture from her eye. With one hand she ran over her slightly disheveled hair. "He'll be fine, because you're going to do something about it, Mother."

Lucia knew this determination well enough. She had heard it often. Usually, this kind of approach led to hours of clashes, which ended in mutually enhanced screaming fits. Julia had usually more success with her father, who just reflexively recoiled as such from the authority of his daughter as of his wife. Lucia was not as soft and that was counterproductive.

Normally.

She reached out and stroked the right cheek of her daughter. Her fleshy face radiated love, understanding and confidence. Her smile could melt the hardest heart. It had its effect on Julia.

"I promise you, my daughter, I will do everything to help you. I'll write the letters – to the colleagues of your father, to the Prefect, to anyone who might know something. Leave that to your mother with all confidence. I already know what to do."

Julia's radiant smile let the grief of the last minutes disappear. She hugged her mother and hugged her again.

"Thank you, thank you, thank you," she exclaimed breathlessly. "I knew that you would help me!"

Happy and smiling she ran out as if relieved from all burden.

Lucia looked after her and nodded knowingly.

She wouldn't do anything of the sort.

Absolutely nothing.

11

The journey south on the Via Egnatia was relatively painless. On horseback, they made good progress every day, with the carts and on foot of course not quite so quickly. On a good day and with only short breaks they had always moved for at least twelve hours. The moaning and whining of the infantrymen who were now suddenly made to ride horses faded away with time. None of the men would be a particularly talented horseman in the foreseeable future – but that wasn't necessary anyway. For the kind of battle, Becker had in mind he didn't need mounted machine gunners.

At the height of Masio Scampa, they had reached the Eastern Roman counterpart of the Via Appia. It would now lead them through Edessa to their destination, Thessaloniki, where Flavius Victor was waiting with the remains of the eastern army. The Goths had also moved away from the northeastern Adrianople and reportedly marched toward Thessaloniki as well. Communication improved. Becker himself had been able to send messengers, they would take the sea route over Dyrrachium to Brindisi or sail the Italian east coast northwards to take their message directly to Ravenna. If the *Saarbrücken* could sail to Thessaloniki immediately, they would meet her there upon their arrival. This arduous overland route could have been avoided if information from Flavius would have been forthcoming quicker but until now only sparse messages trickled in from the general and therefore they couldn't wait for developments to unfold, they had to move. Becker also had informed Rheinberg about his advance by messengers and hoped that the captain had succeeded with his negotiations in Sirmium far enough so that he himself could also join the *Saarbrücken* or Becker's troops. The captain had a somewhat uneasy feeling about the fact that Rheinberg was more or less left alone at the court of the Emperor. He knew enough about Roman history to understand that sometimes unforeseen things could happen – and after they had happened, unexpectedly deceased persons were carried away.

He hoped that Rheinberg knew what he was doing.

"We will reach Thessaloniki in a few days," Arbogast interrupted his thoughts.

"Before the Goths?"

The General laughed. "Of course. The Goths drag women and children with them, the aged and the sick. They are a people on the road. This doesn't mean that their warriors would not run ahead of them, but they can never be so far away that they couldn't quickly return for their protection. This limits their mobility significantly. We are not even 600 men, and we have a clear goal we want to achieve. No, don't worry, Legate Becker. We will arrive ahead of them in Thessaloniki, and we will be expected."

Becker nodded. "They won't attack the city directly anyway."

"Certainly not. Fritigern knows that he cannot achieve anything against the fortifications. It is a provincial capital and well protected as such. He will seek battle outside."

"And we will offer that to him," Becker completed the thought. "It's good that the messengers are faster now on the Via Egnatia and we can prepare a lot more before we arrive. Victor could send some additional details, to be honest."

"Victor will be more convinced once he sees us."

Becker gave him a questioning look. "You are superior to him, Arbogast, aren't you?"

"Formally yes, but de facto Victor is the highest surviving officer of the East and my equal. In addition, Theodosius is on the way and will arrive in Sirmium soon, to be appointed by Gratian. Then he is the highest dignitary in the East."

"Before Theodosius makes his first decisions, we have already solved the problem." Becker tried to sound confident, but he was not sure whether he was able to communicate this feeling well with his limited language skills. He got better with each passing day, not least because the officers accompanying the unit gave him, one after the other, evening classes in Latin as well as Greek. The fact that he was forced to constantly speak in foreign tongues made him plunge into the languages like a man dying of thirst throws himself into water. The infantrymen tried honestly as well, albeit with different degrees of success. A number of simpler men would never get more than a gibberish out, but if that was enough to order cervisia in a tavern, to negotiate the price with a whore, and to understand if a Roman drinking buddy wanted to pay a round, then this would be quite sufficient for them.

Unfortunately, the demands on Becker were a bit higher. The fact that he had to learn Latin while Africanus didn't express the slightest interest in German had obviously little to do with arrogance but simply with the basic understanding that the language of civilization was Latin – and with some reservation also Greek, which still enjoyed great popularity. If Becker remembered correctly, the only local who had ever shown serious interest in the German language had been the fisherman's son Marcellus, who was now on duty on the *Saarbrücken* as a ship's boy.

Some anticipated that the German language wouldn't last long here. It would in all likelihood die, along with the crew of *Saarbrücken*, and then made new again in the future. Becker looked at this fact with sober reflection. He knew that people like von Klasewitz, once they realized these consequences, would probably have a very different view.

Becker pushed those thoughts aside. The cultural consequences of their unexpected emergence in the past were to be contemplated later, once he found the necessary leisure.

Whenever that would be. Probably not in Thessaloniki.

"Stop."

Becker heard the command. He had made it a habit not to ride at the front of the column. He straightened up in the saddle – a rather difficult task without stirrups – and saw a mounted scout, one of those Arbogast had sent, come to a halt before them. He reined in his horse whose flanks were trembling with the effort.

"Ave, General," the soldier saluted submissively. "Titus Daecius, my Lord."

"Speak, Titus," Arbogast told him bluntly.

"General, a village seventeen miles north-east of us is looted by a troop of Goths. There are about 900 riders, plus a retinue of ten or fifteen cars to plunder supplies for the main group of barbarians."

"Goths?"

"At least no Huns. Whether Alans are among them, I couldn't see. My comrade Lucius is still close to them and keeps in touch, while I quickly rode back to make a report."

"Have you been discovered?"

Something like hurt professional pride appeared on the brutish man's face. "No, sir. We kept our distance and have been well-hidden from them. But the Goths have also sent scouts."

"Thank you. Fetch a fresh horse and go back to your comrade. He should then return and update your report."

"General!" Titus moved away from the officers.

"They shouldn't stop us, and they shouldn't report us," Becker pointed out forcefully in a low voice. "The car will immediately grab their attention. We can't use any rumors now."

"The farmers in the neighborhood have announced our coming for a long time, Becker," Arbogast snorted. "Don't lie to yourself."

"Nevertheless. We are a seemingly easy prey for an ambitious Gothic leader who wants to cool his temper."

"Are you afraid?" Something was lurking suddenly in the eye of the General.

Becker was unimpressed. "I'm afraid that the news of our arrival and our superior weapons will reach Fritigern's ear too early and he might adjust his plans."

Arbogast seemed to accept the explanation. "Then we have to prevent him from knowing. What we can hardly prevent is that the Goths are aware of us and may possibly attack. We aren't many enough to act as a deterrent for a larger squad – especially after the way the Roman cavalry was slaughtered at Adrianople."

"Can we avoid them? Maybe to the south?"

"We won't get far. There is the coast. And I don't want to bet on whether the scouts of the Goths have not already discovered us."

"So attack is the best defense," Becker concluded.

Arbogast nodded grimly. "That also means that we have to completely destroy the Goths. Nobody is allowed to survive."

"Yes, that's true," Becker muttered and looked around. He narrowed his eyes and pointed to the north. "I see a hill. We can pretend that we want to make camp over there. We sit down well on display. If that doesn't attract the Goths, we have already lost."

"The leader of the group has looted a village and collected his treasures. If he also can add glory to the booty, he won't let the opportunity slip," the officer growled with a pensive undertone. "The hill is good, but is it good enough for your magic weapons?"

"A clear range – but we must do something about the very cautious frontrunners who might flee at the first sign of anything which is amiss and then possibly warn the others."

"How many might that be? A hundred? Two hundred? I will separate two groups of my men and let them look for escaping warriors. If someone moves out of the range of fire of your weapons, we will chase him. There is no guarantee that they won't escape, but –"

"There are never any guarantees," Becker completed. "That's how we do it."

There was no further discussion. The unit changed its direction, and the soldiers made an impressive display in making all unnecessary noises throughout. Commands were shouted like the troop consisted of deaf old men, swords clanged, and the truck was squawking his horn persistently. The choice of the hill proved to be excellent as a dry but well-trodden path, apparently the connection between distant homesteads and the main road led in the right direction and could also be reasonably well managed by the vehicle. Becker threw furtive glances around the area, as if he could make up the Gothic scouts whose attention they sought to consciously attract.

Naturally, they were not to be seen. However, when their own scouts returned and reported that the Goths had become aware of them and apparently developed interest in an attack, this was confirmation enough for the officers.

"It's not just Goths, there's also a division of Huns with them," Arbogast told the infantry captain.

Becker nodded sorrowfully. Among all horse people, the Huns were the ones who inspired the greatest fear and would rightfully demand the greatest respect. Not only that, they were responsible for the *Völkerwanderung* and would produce with their King Attila a historical figure, a man whose reputation would develop into almost mystical proportions. In a few hundred years, the relatives of the Huns, the Mongols, would get ready to build an empire under their powerful leader Genghis Khan that would have no equal. In comparison, Attila wasn't much more than a harbinger of a more devastating fate. Becker had to remind himself that Attila, if he recalled his history lessons well, would be born in about 20 years. Maybe it would belong to his duties, should Rheinberg succeed with his reform plans, to make sure that the "Scourge of God" would never become a problem. No battle of the Catalaunian fields, no glorious Flavius Aetius and no sack of Rome by the Huns. It was possible that all this could be prevented. Becker didn't want to think too much about it, though. He wouldn't bring up the topic with Rheinberg soon enough.

He refocused on the task at hand. They had almost reached the hill. It was covered with numerous rocks and had poorly visible places where the infantry should be able to set up the guns to cover good sections of the plane before them. The problem was the truck who couldn't go up the hill, and ultimately had to be mobile in order to escape if needed, depending on from where the enemy would eventually appear. To repair a dented truck, pierced with arrows, was a task Becker didn't really want to face.

"Your men should be grouped here," suggested Becker, as he explored the terrain with Arbogast and the legate. "Start with the construction of a camp but don't push the men. Post the usual guards, but no more, while my men go for cover and provide your soldiers with covering fire."

The principle of "covering fire" was something the Romans were entirely familiar with, although they used a different word for it. Their tactics knew the concept of entrusting some archers to protect the flanks from unpleasant surprises. That such tactical ideas got an entirely different meaning with the presence of far more accurate and powerful firearms Becker had been able to teach the Roman officers only rather tediously. He hoped the dry runs on paper with the Roman officers would now prove to be sufficient. Most of the legionaries marching with them had heard of the German secret weapons, but only a few had been eyewitnesses of the demonstration in Sirmium. Becker was not sure whether the known iron discipline of the Roman soldiers could endure this quite new experience.

But there was always a first time. And every tactical plan was obsolete at the moment in which they met the enemy.

"The Goths have taken the bait," Secratus reported. The officer seemed unconcerned, as if he didn't care about the prospect that his men might play bait. "They are on their way."

"My soldiers will be in position in a few minutes," Becker said. He had dismounted and led his horse up the hill to obtain the best possible viewing position. "From where do we expect the enemy?"

"East," the Legate said briskly.

"Then our vehicle needs to stay on the western side of the hill," Becker murmured half to himself. "Your men should begin with the construction of the camp."

Secratus pointed to the plane before them. Becker saw that the first tents were already erected. Men worked noisily in a nearby grove of trees to cut down the trunks of barricade. For encouragement, they sang loud and since the accuracy of the axes apparently had suffered under the long march, curses and vituperations by irate decurios were clearly discernible. It was a wonderful spectacle not to be missed and one which couldn't be overlooked by any observer.

Becker looked down the hill after they had reached its gently curved top. Secratus had returned to his men, but Africanus and Arbogast had joined the Germans.

The infantrymen had chosen excellent positions. Lieutenant von Geeren had developed a keen eye for rock formations suitable for the machine gunners. There, the tripods of the heavy weapons would have secure footing. The whole hillside was covered by the unit, from a height of about six meters above the lowlands in front of them upwards. The thick bushes and boulders served as excellent coverage, and as long as the men lay flat on the ground, no one would notice anything of their presence. Becker's only fear was that, despite the wisdom of Secratus, Gothic scouts might have witnessed their placements. Although he wouldn't be able to report more than around hundred men in strange uniforms and armed with equally strange sticks walked up the hill, the fact of their very existence could cause a Gothic leader, if he wasn't totally stupid, to think twice.

Becker cowered down, armed with his binoculars, leaning behind some tall grass tufts and scrutinizing the plane in front of him. The Romans still made a big fuss about the construction of their camp, and only Becker recognized that all workers had the weapons at hand or never stayed further than two or three feet away from them during their work. The guards had been carefully instructed not to notice the approaching enemies too early. Their professional ethos apparently contradicted these orders, as the legate had to insistently repeat this part of the plan several times.

Then Becker straightened the eyepiece further east. The fine line of cautiously approaching Goths jumped into his field of vision. Becker pursed his lips. The enemy was still a good five miles away and thus already quite in range of the guns. But victory was to be absolute. The Goths had to be closer and stay in the field of fire of the entire unit so that something would happen that Becker had paraphrased rather politely in planning: a slaughter.

The captain braced himself. There was little glory in mowing down a completely overpowered and surprised opponent. On the other hand, this was not about honor, it was about survival, and notably also in the long-term.

Becker put the glasses aside and sought the face of von Geeren. The lieutenant, about three meters below him in a similar pose, looked at him expectantly. Becker shook his head. His deputy nodded. The Germans would fire only at the expressed command of their officers.

Crouching next to von Geeren perched artificer Thanfeld. He had his rifle lying beside him, and had buried himself up to his ears. His special services were not needed here. Becker was sure that this might prove to be different once they met the main body of the Gothic army.

But now it was important to win this particular battle.

Again Becker raised the binoculars to his eyes. The dark line of the Goths was now discernible in more detail. Becker found the scouts' estimate conservative. The approaching group consisted certainly of nearly 1,000 riders, although a census was hard to achieve. There was now no turning back anyway – the Goths rode increasingly faster up the hill, and the Roman guards had received permission to openly acknowledge the presence of the enemy – but the chance that someone would escape the carnage had increased significantly because of the higher number of attackers. Becker had no choice but to allow the barbarian riders to get really close.

The Roman troops kept their nerves. While they ran around like excited chickens, Becker realized with a smile that at all important locations a decurion or a centurion was present in order to manage the chaos. It wouldn't be long, and the soldiers would withdraw, seemingly frightened. The timing was important. They had to lure the Goths close enough without remaining in the field of fire of the German weapons. Becker didn't want to imagine what would happen if the first Roman legionaries were struck down by German bullets. He realized with bitter certainty that this kind of incident couldn't be avoided completely in the future, but here and now, as the alliance had not developed sufficient mutual trust, this would have fatal consequences.

"The right time," Becker said, lips curled in silent soliloquy. "The right, the right, the right ..."

It almost seemed to him as if the ground already trembled under the hooves of the onstorming Goths. The muffled rumble that swept over the plain undoubtedly came from the onrushing horsemen. Becker gritted his teeth, never let the eyes from the eyepiece, calculating and observant. He knew von Geeren waited for his command so that the horns of the legionaries would give the agreed signal for disengagement. The thoughts raced in Becker's head, as experience, intelligence and intuition merged into an almost unconscious calculation and decision-making process. Becker had not managed to be promoted to captain in a relatively young age because he was too slow or too stupid.

The Goths had approached. Now the ground was shaking. And their war cry was deafening.

"Now," roared Becker and raised his hand. The horn sounded. The senseless chaos of the Romans ended abruptly, and with their famous precision the legionaries followed their officers to prepared positions. The soldiers melted away like butter in the sun, without paying much attention to the mocking cries of the Goths. No one turned around and attacked the Barbarians, no one wanted to prove his bravery, and no one run away prematurely in wild panic. Becker could not help but nod approvingly. Secratus had his men under control, there was no doubt.

Becker put the binoculars to the side. He didn't need any magnification anymore. Even with the naked eye, everything was now clearly visible. And von Geeren looked at him expectantly.

Becker's reviewed his plans and the reality of their unfolding. The onrushing Goths, howling with triumph, the quietly retreating Romans, the position of his men, those of them squatting behind the machine guns, the thick tubes of their killing machines pointed toward the onrushing bunch – it was like a painting full of deadly presence, and to consider all this seemed to take an endless amount of time for Becker. All components of his tactical design now fell to their places.

A plan that would work.

Becker was surprised at himself.

Then he nodded toward von Geeren.

Commands were shouted.

The storm rose.

12

Strange, Jan Rheinberg thought, as he furtively wiped the damp palms on his toga, *why am I so nervous?*

He was, as so often, almost too often in the last few days, present in the big tent of the Emperor and waited for two men to join him, those because of whom he had been summoned: the Emperor himself, who still supervised the imminent march of his troops to the West, as well as Ambrosius, the bishop of Milan, who had recently arrived. The name in itself filled Rheinberg with respect. The work of the father of the Catholic Church was well known, even for him as a Protestant, and his efforts were an integral part of Roman domestic politics. Nevertheless, the German tried not to let it affect him emotionally, since beyond all historical transfiguration this very Ambrosius had been a politician who had not hesitated to use state violence to enforce his principles and had been ready to sacrifice human lives to do so.

The Catholic Church had canonized him later, but regardless of what they believed or not, the Ambrosius Rheinberg was about to meet was no saint. He was a powerful personality full of energy and without a doubt someone who could convince and wanted to. Rheinberg knew the historical Gratian had listened to him, and even more so his successor Theodosius, with all the disastrous consequences that had followed his advice. The unity of the Church, Ambrosius' biggest goal, hadn't been achieved by the religious laws of Theodosius. But on that way they had driven the empire to the brink of civil war and beyond.

A development that Rheinberg wanted to prevent.

When three men entered, he looked up. The first face he recognized was the tired young likeness of Gratian, who gave Rheinberg a nod like an old acquaintance and sat down with a quiet moan. The indefatigable and almost invisible Elevius immediately came to the fore and brought some refreshments for the visibly exhausted ruler.

The second man as well, Rheinberg had met before: It was Theodosius, who had arrived only yesterday. The future General of the East – and, if Rheinberg could prevent it, hopefully never Emperor of Eastern Rome – had shown restraint and dignity in the face of sudden responsibility. He measured Rheinberg with a keen eye. The captain didn't know how far the Spaniard had already been informed by others about the potential future of the empire, but one thing was clear – Theodosius, a very pious and staunch Trinitarian, was a strong ally of the bishop in this group. There had been no great effort for Ambrosius to convince the future emperor that exaggerated religious tolerance was the wrong remedy. And Theodosius had pursued this belief with great assertiveness in his time.

However, that was Rheinberg's perspective, the foundation stone for doom had been laid by young Gratian and he would begin to make serious mistakes in a few years.

The third man was Ambrosius himself, dressed in a humble monk's robe, his face frozen in a make-belief expression of contemplation, as if the upcoming conversation would be like a game of cards, and therefore it was necessary to leave the other players in the dark about his feelings. He also gave Rheinberg a nod, had previously been introduced to him briefly, and had since then cultivated excellent courtesy. Rheinberg steeled himself.

After all the men sat down and the servants had brought light meals and drinks, Gratian took the floor.

"Gentlemen, as you have all noticed, the camp is disassembling, and we will return to the western heartland. Unpleasant information forces me to turn my attention back my actual domain. Even my planned visit to Ravenna has to be postponed. The German tribes have become restless again, and it is time to step up border security. I leave some troops under the command of Theodosius but must take the main part of the western army with me. The general will, as soon as possible, travel to the East to lead the reconstruction of the eastern forces. He enjoys my full confidence in this regard."

Rheinberg didn't comment on the last sentence. He hadn't stayed long enough at the court to understand the intricacies of political power flows that took place under a polite surface. But he thought he had realized that influential officers and generals as Richomer and Victor had strongly advocated for the appointment of Theodosius, even more so than Gratian had been ready to admit in the meetings which have been attended by Rheinberg. The motivations behind this he couldn't even guess, they showed, however, that the young Emperor was not regarded as someone who had sufficiently proven himself as a military leader and so as a legitimate emperor. This apparent willingness of the Emperor to be influenced was what Rheinberg secretly counted on. But now, at this moment, some forces of a different kind were against him.

"On the other hand, I hear that the men under Legate Becker and General Arbogast are not far from Thessaloniki and there is a plan to attack the Goths with the miraculous weapons and the rest of the Eastern Army in a very early stage and to lure them into a kind of ambush."

"A very daring plan that risks the core of the army, which I am to rebuild," Theodosius commented. He had not been present during the demonstration of Becker's company, and although he was willing to give a certain amount of faith to the numerous accounts of what happened, he lacked to be personally impressed. Rheinberg wouldn't blame him.

"To send our foreign visitors on their way had been my decision," Gratian recalled with mild severity in his voice. "I don't think it will help us a lot if we discuss this in detail. We will see how the outcome of this decision will be, and then we can talk about whether the risk has been unnecessary or worth it."

Theodosius bowed his head as a sign of respect. Everyone in the tent knew that the appointment of the general was a probation and would probably lead to appointment as Augustus of the East. Even the Spaniard wouldn't risk this opportunity with excessive criticism. Rheinberg had even looked up the date. In the former past, Theodosius would post some minor successes and then be made Augustus in January 379, just over two months from then, which would relegate Gratian officially back to be just the ruler of the West.

There wasn't much time. Rheinberg hoped that Becker would have success. It was of absolute importance. Nothing was more convincing than success. A victory over the Goths would greatly strengthen Rheinberg's position at court.

"We should discuss the matter another time – when we have up to date information," the bishop said in a low voice.

Again, Theodosius was almost intimidated, surely humble, and just nodded. Gratian appeared to be grateful for the intervention of Ambrosius, because he relaxed, took a cup of wine and looked both friendly as well as curious at Rheinberg. The German suddenly realized that the Emperor didn't wish any further part in the discussion and wanted to be perceived merely as a spectator. He expected a kind of spectacle. Rheinberg felt like an animal in a zoo.

"Dear guest," the bishop turned abruptly to the captain, "we have not called you here to discuss military matters, although I would like to admit that they are of the utmost urgency. I want to talk to you because of the many issues that have been reported to me, without denying that the superior weapons you have brought into the Empire could turn the tide in the fight against the barbarians. In fact, I will include your Legate Becker and his men in my prayers, because, like all Roman patriots, the safety of the Empire is very close to my heart, and everything that makes the East stable and protected is to find my blessing."

Rheinberg registered that Theodosius imperceptibly curled his lips. He also knew that Ambrosius didn't mention the death of Valens with good reason. Valens had been, in contrast to the far more orthodox thinking of Gratian and Theodosius, quite positively inclined toward the Arian Christian, something the bishop had been enraged about. Regrettable as was the death of the eastern emperor for the safety of the Empire, the more pleasing was this event for Ambrosius' plans to build a state church, and of course one that had the sole authority of definition about what is the right faith and what isn't.

Rheinberg said nothing and let the man continue.

"However, there are other critical developments that may have become even more problematic by your arrival," Ambrosius said. "Should you be successful with your soldiers and your fearsome weapons, you will no doubt be men of great influence in the Empire. For me, this raises the question of how do you position yourself in regard to religious disputes, Rheinberg. You are familiar with the situation in the Empire?"

"I'm aware that there is lack of respect among Christians in regard to different interpretations of some important principles of faith," Rheinberg replied diplomatically. "In addition, I realized that important church officials find the protection of pagan religions by official tolerance outdated and call for a change of government policy on religion."

Ambrosius nodded in satisfaction. "Well said, Rheinberg. I fight as bishop of Milan, an important representative of the Church, so to speak on two fronts – against heresy and against pagans. Preferably to eradicate both as far as this is possible. Here it is my belief that the state has to play a more important role than before. What is your opinion?"

Rheinberg felt the focus of attention resting on him. Theodosius looked at him searchingly, almost hostile. Ambrosius' face still looked as unconcerned as if he had asked only out of polite interest. Gratian, still holding the cup in his hands, made a curious expression. Rheinberg felt that his palms began to get moist. He suppressed the reflex to wipe them. It would have been a clear reference to his emotional state for everyone.

"I understand your worry, Your Eminence," he said cautiously. "Spiritual questions have moved people quite deeply, and they have an important influence on the life and mind of all the Roman citizens. Sure, the state must have an eye on what is going on in this area in order to avoid that any dispute will endanger the security of the Empire. In fact, I think it would be ideal if religion and state would be in a relationship that mutually strengthens and thus promotes the cohesiveness, helping to guarantee the stability of the realm."

Ambrosius' eyes narrowed for a tiny moment, as he didn't know what exactly he could discern from the well-formulated answer. "I see that we understand each other," he replied. "The fact that Christianity and Empire form a unit and thus reinforce each other is one of my highest beliefs, and I am very pleased to be in unison with like-minded people. So we can count on your support in this fight? That objective can indeed undoubtedly be achieved only if all disturbing elements that contradict this unity will be weakened or exterminated."

Rheinberg bowed his head, pretending that he had to consider that. Now it was necessary to show his colors. Ambrosius, he couldn't convince of anything, and Theodosius surely felt his own suspicion against him, if not outright hostility. The actual addressee of his reply therefore had to be someone else. Rheinberg looked at Ambrosius, took a deep breath and thought but only one thing: how he was able to convince young Gratian? He leaned back. "Your Eminence, you have to know that I come from the future."

"So I was told."

"You don't believe it?"

"It would explain a lot, but there are other possibilities."

"Like what?"

"The fact that Satan has sent you to steer orthodox Christians on the wrong track."

"Devil's messengers defeat pirates and assist the Emperor against barbarians?"

"Satan is a master of deception. Why not do good if it leads in the end to an even greater evil?"

"What mischief do you fear the most?"

"The corruption of my soul, a fatal outcome on the Day of Judgment – for myself, my Emperor and my people."

Rheinberg nodded. "A great fear. Shall I tell you what I fear?"

"Gladly."

"I'm afraid that the Empire will fall apart in a few decades. I'm afraid that a Goth will rule in Rome and that the line of Roman emperors comes to an end. I fear that chaos erupts in the West, and a long, dark time of war and uncertainty will arise. I fear that pagan and brutal warriors flock here from the Far East in large numbers and plunder the churches and slaughter the Christians, and I fear that the Empire can't do enough to prevent this, and what it will accomplish won't be more than to alleviate the danger for a short time. I'm afraid that usurpers alternate in rapid succession, that whole cities are wiped out because they are confessing to one or another Christian variation."

"I see Romans against Romans in civil war, and I look at brave legionaries, bitterly needed to defend the borders, as they march against other legionaries who are supposed to be their comrades. I see Roman swords shedding Roman blood, for power, the true faith, the only correct point of view, while the barbarians are just waiting that Rome will exhaust itself on the field of battle, in order to pour in and sweep away the remains. I fear that the Empire will fall in pieces. I fear that lack of tolerance will destroy the unity of the Empire, pitch brothers against brothers, friends against friends, sometimes wives against their husbands, and parents against their children. I fear that this dispute will nourish discord and weaken the power of the Empire, until it is no longer able to fight internal enemies as well as external ones and grinds to a halt on many fronts. I fear that the Persians will take the provinces in the east, I see lost the conquests of Julius Caesar, and I see the grass growing on the Roman baths, the forums and public buildings, see the roads and aqueducts forfeited, the garrisons and forts, everything that has held together Roman civilization. I see the bishop of Milan dream of the unity of the Church and yet this apparent unity is built on the ruins of an Empire that is no longer able to protect this very church, because it was he who allowed it to turn into rubble. That I fear, most honorable Bishop of Milan."

Rheinberg got up, raised his hand before Ambrosius could answer. "In my time, Ambrosius of Milan, you are regarded as the father of the Church, as one who has established a state church. The historians quickly forget that this state church continued to exist longer than the state to which it had belonged, and that development of history indeed saw the victory of the Trinitarians over the Arians, but that this victory was bought with the blood of Christians and made tolerance an insult. And so constantly new spin-offs and sects have been formed, which were subsequently suppressed with an iron hand until that day the Church deeply divided itself from its foundations and a continental civil war was unleashed that caused untold suffering."

Ambrosius stared at Rheinberg, quite pale.

"I fear even more, Ambrosius. I'm afraid to be stranded with my men in this time, alien to us. I fear for all who are entrusted to my leadership. I fear that all we have brought will be washed away by the stream of time and all the knowledge we have will fall victim to ignorance. I fear that the Empire will refuse this unique opportunity to turn the page and to save itself and will shortly meet its demise, exactly how it is written in my history books. I see my ship in flames, or eaten away by rot, our powerful weapons useless, and our advice lost, and nothing I fear more than that I'm afraid, as the Romans will dance on our graves as priests accuse us to be demons, and I fear that the dark period of which I spoke will begin inevitably in the soonest. I have great fear, noble Ambrosius, that in the year 397, when you will die at Easter, a boy named Honorius, led by a Gothic army commander, will rule the Empire, and that ten years later, in 407, the Vandals, Suevi and Alans will cross the Rhine and on the 24th of August 410 conquer the Eternal City and devastate it."

Deadly silence had fallen. Theodosius gazed at Rheinberg, although he hadn't even hinted that the boy Honorius would be the son of the last Roman emperor ruling the whole realm and therefore be his.

Rheinberg took another deep breath. "In my time, it is known that a Roman governor named Magnus Maximus will hunt and kill the young Emperor here. I know that he will have be regarded as orthodox and will enjoy the approval of many Church Fathers, although Gratian will die, betrayed by his own generals and left alone by his own bodyguard, a miserable death he truly didn't deserve. Christians kill Christians. Christian usurpers kill Christian emperors."

He looked intently at Ambrosius. "Trinitarians kill Trinitarians, Bishop. What a shame and what a folly, what a stupidity and how

shortsighted. These are my fears and anxieties, Bishop of Milan."
Rheinberg sat down hard. "And now call me an emissary of Satan!"

In the eyes of the German was a challenge, an almost furious charge, and for the first time something of an emotional reaction was visible in Ambrosius' face. He glanced at Gratian, who looked troubled by the perspective of his own, violent death, although he already had some time to deal with this possibility. It was obvious that the haunting, evocative portrayal of their prospects by the German had moved him deeply. Its effect was also visible with Theodosius as he pressed his lips together and finally was the first who found words for a response.

"I ... I will be the last Roman Emperor ruling all of it?"

"You will be the last person to claim rightfully to be emperor of Rome in its totality, noble Theodosius. But your religious beliefs and your recognition of the moral power of Ambrosius will be fatal, as they will ultimately harm your rule."

The bishop cleared his throat. "I have the best intentions," he murmured.

"Good intentions don't always have good deeds as a consequence," replied Rheinberg. "And it benefits no one in the Empire to solve the dispute between Trinitarians and Arians with sword and fire. It doesn't help to destroy the Victoria altar and to revoke the Edict of Constantine. It isn't helpful to exempt the Church to an ever greater extent from all taxes and fees while the legions are shivering and suffering and have to march too poorly trained against superior enemies. There is no use to squeeze the people, and to take away all their freedom, and it doesn't help the poor not only to take their last possessions but even to throw them in a religious war or to tell them that the faith of their forefathers is a mistaken belief and they should renounce it or die. It may serve your cause to enforce a dominant faith in the realm, Bishop of Milan, but it doesn't serve the cause of the Empire. It will sow the seeds of doom."

Rheinberg's glance wandered about. He tried not to look too intently into the Emperor's face, but even with his limited grasp of the human nature, everything told him that Gratian had been not only persuaded but convinced. Gratian was, not least because of his teacher Ausonius, a great friend of learning and especially the rhetoric art. Under his reign, representatives of these disciplines acquired numerous high positions at court or offices had been created specifically for them. Rheinberg had known that, had prepared himself well, worked for nights on a kind of speech, knowing that this kind of confrontation was imminent. He knew that Ambrosius was a child of his time, as well as the Emperor, but he knew also that Gratian was easily influenced and would have the fear of any mortal about his own existence and health.

Ambrosius pressed his lips together silently. He knew the Emperor and had read in his face like an open book. And he was no fool. He had lost this fight and that was also obvious in regard to Theodosius.

It was the Emperor who finally ended the silence. "Dearest friends, I think we've all heard a lot we need to think about. I'll leave tomorrow morning with the army and make my way back to the West. Theodosius has to perform tasks in the east and my good friend Ambrosius has left his flock deserted for too long."

Rheinberg was careful not to even to begin to mention the religious riots flaring up in Ravenna, of which he had been reported recently. Ambrosius didn't have to be on site to make his influence visible.

"We will continue this conversation as soon as we see the developments of the coming months and the results of our efforts. Ultimately, the strangers will first need to prove that they are ready to shed their blood for Rome, and I will give them the opportunity to do so. For this, we have to await. Until then, the visitors are under my imperial protection, and their ship is inviolable. The crew members are to be treated as guests of honor, and we want to be open for what they teach us. Once we will know what will become of the Goths, there are more decisions to be made. Until then, my orders are clear." Gratian threw Rheinberg a meaningful look.

Ambrosius stood in silence, his face pinched in defeat, no longer so controlled and expressionless as at the beginning of their encounter. Theodosius, however, seemed almost thoughtful, oddly touched, and Rheinberg had a sudden hope that the Spanish nobleman was not lost entirely for his cause. After all, this was Theodosius the Great ... perhaps more greatness was in him than what has been attributed by Christian propaganda who wanted to thank him for his orthodoxy.

Rheinberg followed the men into the open. It was dark, and a fresh wind blew through the camp, where there was still a buzz of activity. Ambrosius and his companions lingered no longer but went away from the Emperor's tent while Rheinberg remained and reviewed what had happened. He had come far. Hopefully, it was sufficient. The most important things were now taken out of his hand. Becker held the key in his.

Rheinberg decided to take advantage of the dissolution of the camp in order to obtain permission to return to the *Saarbrücken*. The reports of unrest had alarmed him. It was time to take command.

13

"Legio II Italica," Volkert read from the piece of clay the centurion had pressed into his hand without a word. He went on, the queue behind him pushed forward, and soon he was lost in the pile of recruits concentrated around those comrades who were able to read like him. Potsherds were quickly presented by those who knew that he could read, and so the ensign was the one who had to disclose to the mostly desperate or unhappy-looking men wherever they were sent "in order to complete the training," as it said. In fact, the staff shortage was so extreme that most of the recruits, once they had reached their units, had to do regular service immediately, and many of them would die before they had ever learned what would have been beneficial for their survival in the Legion.

"Legio II Adiutrix," Volkert read from another shard. "Legio II Parthica ... Legio II Traiana Fortis." More and more hands, expectant, sometimes trembling, sometimes almost shy, stretched out to meet him, and Volkert read almost mechanically whatever was held before his eyes: "Legio III Augusta ... Legio III Cyrenaica ... Legio III Gallica ..." Soon his mouth became dry, and after some time he found himself standing on the edge of the camp, in the midst of a group of legionaries also assigned to the Second Italic Legion. There also stood to Volkert's great joy the Greek Simodes, the only one among his comrades whom he now regarded as a friend.

"So we are not going too far from here," the Greek said. "No patrolling wild barbarian tribes, no garrison work, just some travelers and the need to look good when an official asks for a bodyguard in shimmering armor. This is good duty, there will always be plenty to eat, and the girls in the area have an eye for dashing young legionaries ..."

Simodes paused involuntarily.

"I'm sorry, my friend. That was very thoughtless of me!"

"It's alright," Volkert said. "I don't blame you. I'm also happy with our lot. The farther it would have sent away me from Italy, the lower my chance would have been to see Julia again."

"We are also assigned to a truly illustrious unit, my friend. VII Pia VII Fidelis is the honorary name of the Legion!"

"Seven times faithful, seven times loyal," Volkert translated in his thoughts. "Those have to be the tough guys indeed."

Over time, he learned more about the legion that had been founded in 165 by Marcus Aurelius when the war against the Germans and the Parthians had been in full swing. Later, the unit had been stationed in the province of Noricum. Noricum. Somewhere, Volkert had heard the name before. When they gave him the name of the city in which the permanent camp of his unit was located, it didn't mean anything to him: Lauriacum. Only when he was talking with some comrades who knew the area and finally, tired of all the questions, the officers brought out an old general map to answer the questions of the recruits, Volkert gathered he would be sent to Austria.

He smiled as he felt almost relieved. Noricum had precious little to do with Austria, of which he knew little; as far as he understood it, the name came from an ancient Celtic kingdom that had once been located there. But it was an interesting feeling that he had been put roughly on the way home, so erroneous and misguided that might be. As someone showed him Lauriacum on the large map, he could even assign its modern name to the city, because it also existed in his time – just that it was called Lorch, located close to the Enns, as many old Roman city foundations could be found near a navigable river.

It wasn't a real border garrison; but not far from it. Simodes' optimism could prove to be extremely premature.

As it turned out, the 5,000 recruits they had in their camp were distributed to a total of nine legions, all in the west of the empire. No support of the troops in the East, no forced marches toward the Goths; Volkert was almost grateful for this development. This didn't mean that he would actually have such a quiet duty, as his Greek friend assumed, but at least there was no immediate war on the horizon, although there would always be the occasional barbarian tribe who tried the border fortifications. The Second Italic Legion would be ready when the border garrisons couldn't stop a barbarian attack.

"Most of the soldiers will be with Gratian now," Volkert guessed. "The Emperor has taken almost all parts of the mobile army to the East in order to help Valens."

"The rumor says Gratian is already on the way back and he'd leave Theodosius and the foreign wizards battling the Gothic invasion," the always remarkably well informed Simodes added. "Once we arrive in Noricum, we won't have to wait long for the main body of the army. Whether Gratian is then forced to call upon us again, only the gods know."

Volkert pricked up his ears. Should the Western Roman emperor indeed be on his way back to Trier, then this also meant that Rheinberg had at least achieved a partial success. And it meant that Becker and his men were traveling somewhere in the east and their subsequent actions would ultimately decide on the fate of the Germans in this time.

His personal fate was not at all independent. If the Germans could be sure of the Emperor's favor in the long run, he could reveal his identity and hope to be discharged from the Legion. On the other hand, both in the Navy of the German Empire as well as in the legions, desertion deserved the death penalty, and Volkert didn't even want to dream of a future together with Julia. He felt torn between the possibilities and threats and once again decided to leave it all for the time being and allow the events to drive him until he had the chance to properly explore his options. With the desertion, to stay in a historical context, he had crossed the Rubicon, and he couldn't expect more from Rheinberg than his ultimate interest to foster the crew's discipline. When in doubt, it would be necessary for him to set an example.

For a moment, Volkert looked at the prospect of having to leave for Noricum almost as the best of all possible alternatives.

The time before they left just flew by. A total of some 250 men was assigned to the Legio II Italica, and early morning of the next day centurion Latinus, who would lead them to Noricum, organized the barely trained recruits in something like a marching column. His face showed evidence that to lead a group of unenthusiastic recruits, half of whose would take the first opportunity to escape, hardly pleased him. The fact that he took a good 30 additional, apparently experienced legionaries with him, who performed more like security guards and less like comrades, confirmed this impression. Finally, the whole column transformed in Volkert's view more and more into the character of a transfer of convicts.

Simodes seemed to be inspired by the prospect of a long march. His remarkably good mood was anything but contagious, and when he had been thrown quite a few dark looks by his comrades, Volkert advised him not to make his sunny disposition too obvious. For the ensign, however, the carefree optimism of the Greek was very pleasant, as he could distract him from his own gloomy thoughts.

After a quick breakfast, each freshly minted legionary had strapped a heavy bundle on his back, filled with tools, food, his weapons, a sleeping pad, extra clothes, and all sorts of useful utensils. Volkert already had determined that over the centuries apparently the requirements had changed little in regard to the capacity of soldiers to carry stuff – regardless of the existence either of donkey carts or diesel engines, any ordinary soldier was still obliged to put everything one needed on his own shoulders. Volkert had practiced marching in the camp and also experienced his share of marches during his basic training in Germany, therefore he was fundamentally better prepared than many other recruits. The prospect, however, to travel hundreds of miles by foot, possibly interrupted only by a river trip when weather and availability of ships allowed, pleased him no more than any other of the 250 men who were preparing for the march.

Already at the end of the first day Volkert's feet already were full of blisters. He had to admit that the sandals worn by the Roman soldiers in summer were not poorly suited for marches as at least that the feet's side weren't too much chafed. Of course, lighter stones flew between foot and sole, so the feet were quickly and thoroughly dirty – and now that the weather had been slowly but surely getting wintry, it was probably soon time to try the boots.

The centurion lead with a strong march pace with only very short breaks and seemed to be seriously interested in a new speed record. Everyone complained, and they were studiously ignored by the veterans. Volkert understood why they were flayed like this: When they went to bed for the night, the recruits would all be far too tired to even contemplate desertion.

In the evening as they made camp, Volkert's feet were torn and full of partially bloody calluses. Simodes handed him an ointment that he himself had mixed and gave some relief. The feet of the Greeks had suffered from the almost eight-hour march, yet he showed a friendly smile, joked, and gave generously of his medicine. His comrades had forgiven him for his intolerable good mood when he shared the recipe for the tincture with them and they noticed that the agent in fact helped because it eased the pain and enhanced healing.

Volkert barely remembered the evening he spent with sheer fatigue, without the usual ruminations and with almost automatic movements while erecting the camp. Fortunately, the troop had not built its encampment strictly by the book, as it was located far from enemy territory. It was enough to set up the tents, set up some guards – the centurion mercifully ordered the veterans to be awake during the most unpleasant time after midnight – and then, after a hasty meal, everyone lied down exhausted. Volkert fell asleep at once. He had never felt so tired in his entire life.

Just before dawn, the horn sounded the alarm, and the recruits were all in full attendance. The breakfast, the morning toilet – the centurion reacted to lack in hygiene with painful discipline – and the demolition of the camp lasted an hour and shortly thereafter they found themselves back on the road. Again and again, Volkert thanked the fate that the Romans had been fanatical road builders, or else the march would have become unbearable by then. They marched following the Via Flaminia and would soon reach Narnia, where the road would bifurcate. On one of the forks one could advance further toward Vienna. Volkert actually started to enjoy some aspects of his march as he had the opportunity to admire outstanding Roman monuments. Across the River Nar led the largest bridge ever built by the Romans, spanning in four impressive arches over the water. And close to Narnia one would pass through the large tunnel built by emperor Vespasian to allow fast traffic through the Apennines, the famous Intercisa. Volkert allowed Simodes to describe these Roman exploits in the most dazzling colors. The Greek seemed to have great admiration for the architectural achievements of the Empire. Volkert made a mental note to be righteously impressed once necessary.

On the second day, the centurion allowed them to proceed a bit more slowly and approved an additional break – primarily so that the recruits were able to take care of their wounded feet. When it was late, the men were a little less exhausted, but nevertheless tired and just grateful to be able to lie down.

Volkert was sure that Latinus would increase the pace the next day. They had made a good 20 miles on the first day and the second perhaps a little bit less. If they aspired for more tomorrow, they would have to put in some energy. The total march to Noricum would require a few more weeks, although a part of the journey was continued on riverboats. Volkert was looking forward to this part of the march, safe and leisurely, and couldn't wait.

With this thought, sleep overcame him.

14

"So, Tennberg, who is with us?"

As if this "us" would have a magical effect on the ensign, the upper body of the young man straightened up and a gleam came into his eyes. Von Klasewitz allowed Tennberg to bask for a few moments in the splendor of his own importance before he repeated his question with a slightly urging undertone.

"Well, I'm not sure, Lieutenant Commander. Some of the officers will possibly remain neutral and not interfere in a confrontation. From the crew I see about 40 firmly on our side, maybe four non-commissioned officers. We can be glad that Becker is no longer with us with his men; that makes things much easier."

The nobleman could not help but to agree with Tennberg. With Becker's infantry still on board, he wouldn't allow the venture he planned to start. But now Rheinberg's hazardous travels ultimately turned out to be a blessing. With luck, the Goths and Becker's men would decimate each other, so two birds would have been killed with one stone.

"That will have to be sufficient, because we get support from outside," said von Klasewitz. "I have spoken with Petronius. He not only has some of Renna's guards in his pocket, he also will bring a few dozen of his most fanatical followers secretly in the vicinity of the *Saarbrücken*. We need to plan carefully, Tennberg! It must be done at night, and we have to see that in the guard schedule our people have the majority at that time. We help Petronius' men on board and show them where Rheinberg's loyalist are. I want to avoid too great a bloodshed, but whoever defends himself will suffer the consequences."

Tennberg nodded eagerly. Von Klasewitz had already detected the man's slightly sadistic inclination some time ago when he had unnecessarily harassed enlisted men and had condoned it, if only slightly. The ensign knew that, and he thanked the nobleman for his acceptance of him with loyalty.

Quite helpful had been the fact that von Klasewitz had hinted that after implementation of the action – he avoided the word "mutiny" as much as possible – some field promotions were necessary, and he would need a reliable and disciplined first officer. With that, he Tennberg had finally in his bag.

Von Klasewitz himself was well aware that for most of the 40 men of whom Tennberg had claimed they would participate the only reason for doing so was greed. Tennberg had promised them what they desired most: a life in luxury, large palaces, willing slaves – there was no insane or wet dream that the two officers wouldn't address in order to get the necessary number of mutineers assembled. He had already talked with Petronius in detail about the consequences and had come to the conclusion that it would be a nice gesture to the Rheinberg loyalists afterwards to have the worst of the mutineers executed for their "atrocities" as scapegoats. Then the finer minds would have calmed down and at the same time would be faced with a *fait accompli*. And von Klasewitz had to hurry, because he knew that Rheinberg would eventually return to the *Saarbrücken* in the near future. The nobleman had read the historical works in Rheinberg's cabin and knew that Gratian wouldn't continue his campaign in the East. With Becker's men on their way and with Theodosius as general, there was no reason why that should change – and also Rheinberg had made clear that he preferred no direct involvement of Gratian in military activities in the East. Accordingly, the Emperor would devote to his duties in the West and that would certainly be the occasion for Rheinberg to return.

It was necessary to act quickly and accurately.

"I have the guard plan adapted as far as possible, so nobody else notices something," von Klasewitz said to his loyal assistant. "If all goes well, we will have the right constellation of men in the night guards in three days. I chose the shift from midnight for our action, because the few men who do not belong to us will be quite tired. I briefed Petronius, and he has assured me that his preparations have covered all eventualities."

"Then everything is ready," the young man said visibly happy. He seemed to regard the whole thing as a very exciting and promising adventure. At the appropriate time, quite certain for von Klasewitz, the young man would prove to be very useful.

The nobleman rose. "We must keep the lid on it, Ensign. Everything has to run perfectly normal up until the right moment. That fat walrus Köhler especially has his eyes and ears everywhere! If someone smells something, then it will be him."

Tennberg clucked his tongue. "Köhler is at the top of my hit list once the time comes. The man doesn't know where his place is. He'll have to learn the limits of a senior petty officer."

The nobleman could only agree. When the senior NCO would be among the victims of their small action, he wouldn't shed a tear. NCOs who thought for themselves were one of the absurdities caused by the too liberal regiment of von Krautz and Rheinberg, a tumor in the crew's body von Klasewitz intended to remove with resolution. There would be much to do, once he had taken command.

He nodded to himself as he left Tennberg. Oh yes, very, very much to do.

15

Odotheus was a brave warrior. He had followed Fritigern and Alaric from their old settlement area, as they eventually had to give way to the hordes from the East. Although they had been hopelessly inferior to the agile and ruthless attackers, Odotheus had done his own to protect the retreat of the many hundreds of covered wagons and had watched as his younger brother, Vitigis, dotted by Hunnish arrows, had fallen dead from his horse. Odotheus didn't hate the Huns, because he had fought with too many of them side by side against the Romans; they were apostates, who had renounced the Hunnish king for a variety of reasons.

Odotheus didn't hate the Romans either. What he had seen of Rome, he found impressive. The beautiful estates, the fortified cities with the white walls and all the magnificent buildings, especially churches, and the powerfully preaching of rich Arian bishops, who represented his faith and at the same time the importance of the Church in a way and manner in which no Gothic preacher had ever been able to. He had been with Fritigern, had negotiated a settlement in his empire with the Emperor Valens. Then they had been betrayed.

Odotheus had no problem with the Romans. He had just looted a large country farm, and his pack horse was full of treasures, his cart laden with fabrics and animal skins and in his bag jingled Roman solidi. Rome was a fine thing. Just a pity that the Romans simply couldn't give up.

When the leader of their group, the swashbuckling Fastida, had heard of the Roman troops in their vicinity, it didn't take much convincing to bring the mixed group of Goths and Huns to attack this unit to cement the domination of the Goths in this part of the Eastern Empire. There weren't many Romans in that unit and they were clumsy on their horses, and they built their camp with such reckless noise that one could almost feel sorry for them. A quick attack would allow them to capture their weapons, armor, some gold from the pay office. A few survivors would be allowed to escape, so that they could report this terror to their superiors, who were barricaded behind the beautiful high walls and would fearfully pee in their togas – there was no nicer end to a successful day.

Odotheus winced as Rhima, his oldest friend, struck him on the shoulder. An ugly, fresh red scar ran through the beefy man's face, tore a ford through his bushy beard. There the tip of a Roman sword had touched him decisively, a weapon which now ordained the belt of the warrior with its owner being with his ancestors for some time now; one of the countless victims of that memorable battle at Adrianople, where the Emperor fell.

"Well, my friend, don't dream! The command to attack has come! Ride by my side and maybe, maybe I'll leave you a Roman to deal with!"

"You will leave one for me?" Odotheus cried and spurred his horse. "Rhima, let's treat that scar properly! The wound tarnishes your senses and your mind!"

But his friend could hear him no longer as the roar of the galloping had become deafening, and yet one of the most uplifting sounds Odotheus had ever heard. Dust kicked up, dirt moved by the hooves, and this sound mingled with the encouraging cries of the Goths, the guttural war cries of the Huns, all made a concert of a special kind, a music of war which was throbbing the blood in his temples. He no longer even noticed that he himself tore his mouth open and a war cry escaped, he brandished his sword over his head and became one with the power of the Gothic attack.

He didn't understand what hit them.

He saw how Rhima was torn from his horse just before him, threw his arms backwards, the horse screaming and squirting in a sudden fountain of blood from a devastated neck. Rhima looked as if something had punched through his chest, an invisible force that left him perforated and conjured red, glistening spots on his breastplate. Odotheus looked for a moment, staring in the eyes of his dead friend, which showed surprise, incomprehension, nothing of the former arrogant confidence and joy.

Then he was gone, crushed under the hooves of the horses following him.

Everywhere the animals cried, their powerful chests shredded, a slush of blood and offal. Everywhere the men cried, whose limbs were torn with unexpected, sudden violence, skulls burst, shattered by invisible hammers. Odotheus spurred his horse, as if he could escape the horror.

Before him rode the daring Fastida, face contorted into a grimace, and a moment later a cloud of blood and brain matter seemed to drift toward Odotheus, emerging out of nowhere, where just now the head of their leader had been.

And then the pain, penetrating, hot, without warning. No sword felled the brave Odotheus, no spear pierced his entrails, and yet the invisible force threw life out of his body like a demonic curse.

Odotheus was already dead when he hit the ground, saw nothing more of the hooves trampling his face and crushing his bones.

He didn't see his comrades who shared his fate. He didn't notice the desperate attempts to escape the terrible curse that had haunted them. He didn't see Gothic warriors, who pressed their large hands on gushing wounds and screamed in panic and tried to run. He was spared the whimpering and moaning of the wounded, spared by the Roman soldiers who, with horror on their faces, rode through the battlefield and redeemed the wounded from their suffering. He also didn't hear the awful screams of the surviving horses who beat around them, bleeding, until Roman spears also ended their agony.

He was no aware of the group of seven riders – four Goths, three Huns, who had been riding at the back of the bunch – who had time to turn around their horses and escaped with wide eyes and pale faces, fast, as the devil was about to pursue them.

16

Becker looked at the bodies and tried to guard himself against the horrific images. He stayed in the background, gave precedence to the Roman legionaries, as they walked the field, outwardly cool and in a wide column. Every now and then a blade jerked up or a spear thrusted downwards where a wounded Goth or a suffering animal were redeemed. Becker had to remember the lessons that Rheinberg had given him, especially about the fact that medical care on the battlefield at this time either didn't exist or if the most was concentrated on those who had a certain chance of survival, to carry them to a quiet place and an opportunity to lie down. There were doctors and in the some of the Roman legions even field surgeons who, due to their many years of practice, were able to handle one or the other injury and thus to secure the wounded some chance of survival. But the legionaries here had no surgeons and the casualties weren't Romans but enemies, and even the cautious efforts by Becker to let the paramedics of the infantry go over the battlefield had been rejected by Arbogast with visible contempt. Ultimately, Becker only managed to ask for a prisoner of war to obtain information. This logic the Romans had understood, and Arbogast gave instructions to look for a wounded man who could possibly be saved by the German paramedics to put him through a decent torture afterwards.

The success of the German arms against the completely unprepared Goths and Huns had been overwhelming. When the enemy had been in range and the command given, the bursts of machine guns as well as the well-matched shots from rifles by the infantrymen had mowed the riders from their horses. The Goths hadn't even known what hit them and had reacted totally confused and headless. By their hasty and ill-considered responses, they gave the Germans more than enough time to complete their grisly work. Only a few clever riders at the end of the mass of attackers, who had been able to observe the chaos from a safer distance than the others, had escaped the hail of bullets. But on the field lied hundreds of dead and wounded.

"Cavalry is particularly vulnerable," said a voice beside Becker.

The captain turned and saw Secratus who looked stoically at the actions of his men on the battlefield.

"Horses are great targets and their death causes confusion. They throw the rider off, trample on those who are already on the ground and are no longer controllable. You don't even need to aim at the men; the horses are perfectly adequate. The rest can be done by a normal warrior."

"That's right. But in this case, it wasn't even necessary to target someone particular. The Goths were riding in a tight bunch and wanted to overwhelm your men by the sheer force of their attack. We just aimed into their direction generally. They had no chance."

"My men were very afraid."

"They behaved very disciplined."

"Now they are full of confidence. That was good for morale."

Becker said nothing. His own morals were not quite as good, and he judged the results of this carnage not half as positive as Secratus. His picture of this battle had much in common with a mass execution, a merciless extinction in which the victims had no chance of resistance – or to surrender when no other escape was possible. They had succumbed them like a force of nature.

The captain tried to imagine what would happen if 30,000 Goths came marching toward them. Given sufficient time for preparation, his men would be able to accomplish terrible things. And when after fifteen or twenty minutes of continuous fire, the Roman troops began to take revenge for Adrianople, the completely demoralized Goths would suffer a terrible defeat.

That was the plan.

Why, Becker thought, as he listened without comment to the tactical interpretations of the Roman, did he almost wish that

Fritigern would take the reports of those who had escaped very serious?

"Becker!"

The voice of Arbogast interrupted his thoughts.

"It's getting late, we should establish a real camp now and see that we continue to march in the morning."

"We should leave the immediate vicinity of the battlefield."

The general grinned sympathetically. "Yes, it will start to stink soon. We will call the men to assemble and then march for a few miles. It should be possible to find a more comfortable spot."

Arbogast wanted to turn away, as a centurion with some legionaries climbed up the hill. The men carried a limp form and were accompanied by the medical corporal of the German infantry.

"Lord, we have the desired prisoner," announced the centurion and told the legionaries to let the wounded down to the ground, whereupon the paramedic, shaking his head silently, began to take care of the man. Becker stepped closer and saw that the prisoner had a nasty bullet wound in the right arm but otherwise appeared to be unharmed.

"We have pulled him from under his horse," said the centurion. "The dead animal has protected him from the carnage, but he wasn't able to extricate himself. He refuses to give his name and accuses us to be in an unholy covenant with demons."

The veteran spat contemptuously on the floor. "Barbarians. Cannot differ the invention of modern scholarship from curses and spells."

"How is he, Corporal?" Becker asked and knelt beside the wounded man, who was staring at him warily and somewhat anxious.

"Captain, I've cleaned the wound, stopped the bleeding, applied a proper bandage. The shot has penetrated the arm and has shattered the humerus. Actually, he may have to undergo surgery. It will eventually heal, though not very nicely. He will have complaints in the future, but an infection is obviously not visible. A tough guy who can endure something, he wasn't unconscious for a second."

"Thank you. Can we move him?"

The corporal frowned. "Our Roman friends don't really care, Captain. I'd like to let him rest for 24 hours, but we don't have this option obviously."

"Provide transport on the truck. Make him as comfortable as possible, give him food and wine. When we set up camp, he should get his rest until tomorrow morning. I can't control our Roman friends to put the screws to him for much longer."

"For what did I patch him up again?"

Becker nodded. "Be nice to him. Maybe he realizes that you are not in league with the demons and is ready to tell you something. Then maybe I can prevent them from torturing him."

The Corporal nodded and rose. Two legionaries grabbed the injured and carried him down the hill.

Becker followed them with his eyes, then he sat himself to descend too, in the hope that with increasing distance the still persistent whining and complaining would fade from the battlefield. It wouldn't erase itself from his memory as fast, that he was sure of.

Soon the troop was back on the road. Far and wide, there was no one to see. If there were civilians in the area, they remained fearfully hidden in their homes. The fact that the Romans began, apparently in high spirits, to sing marching songs was certainly not helping to spread a sense of security. Becker was glad when an hour later they had discovered a good camp location, near the walls of a smaller town. When the camp was built, he came back to look after the prisoner. There were things he wanted to know – about the size of the Gothic army, Fritigern's plans, mood and morale among the Gothic warriors. He knew he would probably learn nothing too specific, but every bit of information he could obtain might later prove to be beneficial. When he saw the depressed face of the medical corporal, he already knew that his hopes in this respect could not be fulfilled. "What has happened? Did the Romans already take care of him?"

The young man shook his head.

He was called Brockmann, that much Becker knew about him. Normally, he wouldn't give a paramedic too much attention, but in this century – and after what he had just witnessed on the battlefield – this man was of particularly high importance. Another annotation on Becker's ever growing list.

"The Romans have had us in good view all the time, sir. I don't know exactly what they were talking, but the Goth has obviously listened well to them. I guess they have specially imagined loud and clear what they would do with the prisoner once they get him ready for interrogation. Anyway, the prisoner didn't look very happy."

Becker knew what was coming, but he just nodded to Brockmann.

"I've left him alone only for a brief moment. When I came back, he was already dead. He killed himself. Suicide. That he preferred to torture apparently."

Brockmann swallowed and visibly struggled with his emotions. Becker put a hand on his shoulder.

"How could he kill himself?"

"He had a knife hidden in his boot. We haven't searched him very thoroughly. He brought it out and cut his throat. A fast and precise cut. He must have applied an insane willpower to do this – or he was simply too terrified of what the Romans would do to him."

Brockmann visibly struggled to keep his composure. "It's not your fault, Corporal."

"I would –"

"So far we have only been shortly in this time and still don't know our way around. We learn. Unfortunately, our gaps in knowledge are punished quickly and often brutally. It will not happen a second time. And it wasn't your fault."

Brockmann tried a nod, wiping moisture from the corner of his eyes. His jaws worked silently.

"Go to sleep. I will ask the Romans to clean up the mess. No self-reproach, Brockmann. When one has to be blamed, then it's me and my lack of precautions. Take a rest, drink a cup of wine. We won today. Remember, though, that we do our work here."

The corporal didn't look as if the words of Becker actually had a comforting effect on him. But he saluted, turned on his heel, and disappeared in the direction of the fires, around which the soldiers had gathered. Becker added another item to his shopping list. He had to take care of the mental health of men more than he had hitherto done. No one would come to commit suicide in fear of torture – at least the captain fervently hoped so. But the strain would produce more and more consequences. Becker felt it himself, especially today. He had to take care of this.

Someone handed him a cup of wine. He quickly poured down the thin swill.

He would have to exchange a serious word with Sergeant Behrens. To bring a distillery in motion became quite urgent.

Very much so.

17

Especially at night, one could tell how much Ravenna stank. It was this mixture of excrements – human and animal – and the generally rather dubious hygiene of the city that mingled, close to the harbor, with the stench of less than fresh fish. There were moments in which Seaman Jens Kempner wished to be allowed to stand next to a steel mill or a coal power plant, just to perceive an odor that was not only familiar but reminded him of civilization as he knew it.

But right then, at night, and without a breath of fresh air from the sea, Ravenna stunk. One of the most important cities of the Western Empire smelled like a one-horse town. Kempner had his problems coping with this, and he was glad that the ship's officers did everything to keep the *Saarbrücken* alive because the light cruiser was all the seaman could cling to. The ship, the peace of mind generated by its steel, the powerful guns, the chimneys, the exhalations of oil and coal – everything that Kempner had left many centuries behind him was united here. The fact that the odors that normally exuded the cruiser were now covered by the town was mainly related to the fact that they wanted to save coal and the machine had to be shut down. Until a new source of fuel had been established, they had to use the supplies sparingly, as Kempner knew very well. Nevertheless, he would give a lot to see the smoke rising from the chimneys as soon as possible.

There wasn't much more to do than to indulge in these and similar thoughts, because Kempner had night watch, the worst shift from midnight, and he hated it. One was either too tired or not really awake, and on the quay, Roman legionaries shared his lot with obviously little enthusiasm, and this didn't ensure that Kempner's spirits were awake. He'd have liked to have a coffee, but again the inventories have already been strongly depleted, and the general dismay that the ancient Romans had never heard about this wonderful drink had been great. Kempner had once asked Dr. Neumann if one couldn't something to introduce coffee to the Roman Empire. Neumann had told him that an expedition to Ethiopia was necessary for this purpose and placed the idea promptly on the long, long list. The thought didn't let go of Kempner, and he pictured himself to equip such an expedition as soon as the status of the *Saarbrücken* was secured. He had already informed himself about the Ethiopia of his time, called the Kingdom of Aksum, a Christian state, if he had understood it correctly. The Romans knew that kingdom and stood in a loose contact, so it shouldn't be impossible to travel there. Kempner's plan took shape during every guard shift. He knew he was going to find supporters for this project, and he imagined that with success he could have a coffee roasting, being the one who will introduce the drink to Rome ... the seaman had learned well during the weeks of his stay in this time that a bag of solidi in Rome was at least as a good thing as a bag full of Reichsmark in his own time – of both of it one could basically never have too much.

Oh yes. Kempner smiled softly to himself. It would open a coffee house in Ravenna, and while he still was on duty on the *Saarbrücken*, teach Romans to do the work. To build a coffee roaster should not be so hard, and all he had to do was to ensure the supply of coffee beans. The idea became more attractive with each new planning detail.

"Sailor! Are you asleep?"

The harsh voice interrupted Kempner from his dreams. Involuntarily he snapped to attention, raised his lantern. With horror, he recognized the sight of von Klasewitz, who was looking at him moodily. Kempner got a dry mouth. He hadn't known that the first officer was on night guard! Had not Tennberg been on the bridge when he himself had taken position at the *Saarbrücken's* bow? Perhaps the first officer had been drinking too much coffee, as for him the rationing apparently did not apply.

"Commander! I didn't hear you coming! I was paying attention to the quay!"

"Haven't heard me, ah, yes. Is that your conception of duty during guard service, Sailor? Since everyone could have sneaked up on deck over the railing, you wouldn't have heard that too, huh?"

"Yes, yes, no, I mean ..." Kempner turned red, which thankfully couldn't be seen in the darkness. At least he was now wide awake.

If only for a moment.

What he really didn't hear, as he was focused entirely on von Klasewitz, were the faint footsteps behind him. What he felt was the sharp pain on his skull, and then he collapsed with a groan, unconscious, directly into the officer's outstretched arms.

"Nice work, Schmitt," growled von Klasewitz and lowered the unconscious man to the ground.

Stoker First Class Josef Schmitt, a beefy man, prone to obesity, grinned with his mostly toothless mouth. He pushed a residual chewing tobacco back and forth, weighing a stick in his hairy fist. "The next one?" he asked.

"There is no one else up here. On the bridge with Tennberg, we have to take care of someone, then the deck is ours. The rest of the cruiser is in line once all our men are gathered."

Schmitt spat over the side. A curse on Latin followed. The stoker looked down into the darkness and made a silly face.

"Stop to stare, let the rope ladder down," von Klasewitz said hoarsely. "Then to the bridge, Tennberg will show you who needs your attention. Below, there are our allies!"

Schmitt grunted and did as he was told. He disappeared into the darkness. Von Klasewitz raised his lantern. The first Roman who swung himself over the railing was Petronius. His feverish eyes gleamed in the reflection of the weak light. He said nothing but immediately made room for the following men. The stocky, powerful figures silently climbed on board and filled the bow section. From the bridge Tennberg made a sign – the last deck watch that didn't belong to the mutineers had been rendered harmless. Von Klasewitz raised his lantern in response.

Petronius had gathered his fellow believers, they all wore monks' robes. But their muscular arms with the calloused hands proved that they were used to a different life than just blissful contemplation, and the way one or the other held stick or baton gave room to interpretation what kind of profession these men had pursued before they had dedicated their lives to the church.

Petronius had no doubt chosen people who could be of the most efficient service tonight. The two men nodded at each other. One night before the nobleman had made the conspirators familiar with a floor plan of the *Saarbrücken*. What kind of fear these men might have had in regard to this demonic device, it was undoubtedly outweighed by the willingness to put all effort in this holy and godly deed. And if it was necessary to crush some skulls, this was certainly a sin for which one would find immediate absolution in subsequent penance.

There was no need for further discussion. From the darkness two burly figures emerged, two other crew-members belonging to von Klasewitz's mutineers. They had been commissioned to accompany the monks down.

The group disappeared. Von Klasewitz immediately rushed to the bridge, where Tennberg and Schmitt waited for him. Both received him with a decidedly triumphant smile.

Von Klasewitz held out his open hand. "The keys to the armory," he demanded.

There were three keys for this important room. One he had. One was carried by the second officer. One was in the key box on the bridge, so that the guard on duty could hand out weapons in an emergency. As Tennberg only dropped one into the hand of Klasewitz, the officer wrinkled his forehead.

"Where's the third? I told you that we must avoid at all costs that Langenhagen ..."

Tennberg looked confused at von Klasewitz. "But I thought you had the key! I immediately sent men into the cabin of the Second, but they haven't found it! I thought you had already taken care of him!"

Von Klasewitz cursed. He drew his gun, knew how to handle firearms. It was the first thing his father had taught him on their estate, and it was the only thing he had really understood. "Come with me, Schmitt," the nobleman hissed.

The stoker shrugged. Von Klasewitz overlooked this lax attitude for the moment. Probably the man thought that their shared conspiracy would make them something like equals. The thought alone to be on the level with a creature like Schmitt caused his bile to surge upwards. Schmitt was at the top of the list of scapegoats to be punished in a show trial after he had completely assumed command. Very, very much on the top.

Von Klasewitz rushed down the stairs, Schmitt in tow. Then noises reached his ears, muffled cries and screams. There was a fight! A real fight! That hadn't been planned!

Von Klasewitz stormed through the narrow corridors and stairways in the interior of the *Saarbrücken*. He climbed over unconscious crew members who had been surprised in their sleep by Petronius' people, just as planned. Blood ran from terrible-looking but ultimately harmless lacerations on the face. The men of God were anything but squeamish. The first officer had told them to kill only as a last resort. He needed an operational crew once he had taken command. And martyrs he couldn't afford as well.

Then he met a martyr. The twisted posture and blood-soaked cowl of the priest said it all. Von Klasewitz bent down. A stab wound, right in the chest. Knives were the only weapons that should have been available to the loyalists and someone had the presence of mind to defend himself. This had to be expected. No omelet could be made without breaking eggs.

The din of battle grew louder. Shots were fired. That was unexpected. The nobleman clutched the handle of his weapon. When he climbed through the next bulkhead, he saw a group of his rebels. He tore one around at his shoulders.

"You! What's going on? What are you standing here?"

The man winced and glanced around, seeking help, but all of his comrades were thankful that they were not in the focus of attention.

"The Chief Engineer –"

"What? Speak clearly!"

"The doors to the engine room are closed. Langenhagen and Dahms have weapons, and some enlisted men and officers as well.

119

Köhler is with them, he is also armed. They locked all bulkheads from the inside. We can't enter!"

"Damn!" von Klasewitz exclaimed and let go of the mutineer. He stared at the massive bulkhead in front of him and cursed again, perseveringly, hard. Some men threw themselves meaningful glances. They seemed not to have expected that the posh toff used such a vocabulary.

"Burn!" the first officer finally blurted. "Burn the cursed door!"

No one moved.

"What? Are you deaf?" von Klasewitz shouted.

"All welding torches are in the tool room. And the tool room ..."

The nobleman stared at the bulkhead and reminded himself where he stood. Of course. Dahms was a degenerate idiot, but he knew his craft. He had blocked access to his kingdom, because it was where the tools were stored. No welding torches for them.

The leader of the mutineers thought feverishly. He wasn't left with many options. He could besiege the loyalists and hope their supplies would run out soon. He could even clog the air supplies and ensure that they ran out of the air. Yes, that was an excellent idea! Excellent! He would do just that! This situation would only take a few hours, then the nightmare was over!

A wide grin crossed the face of the nobleman. "We do things differently," he said confidently. "Bring a guard on and erect a barricade in case they want to attack. Then secure the rest of the ship, I don't want any other unpleasant surprises. Leave this problem here to me."

The men hastened to carry out the officer's instructions. The look in the eyes of the nobleman made them almost as fearful as that crazy monk who had stormed the ship.

One or the other began to doubt whether he had done the right thing. But no one dared to show it openly.

18

"Let's see!"

Dahms suppressed a groan as Langenhagen gently but firmly pushed his hand away with whom he had kept the wound on his upper arm covered. The young officer looked critically at the flesh wound.

"I'm not a doctor, Sir ..."

"Johann."

Langenhagen took the first-aid kit and tore off a piece of clean bandages.

"I'm not a doctor, Johann, but that needs to be sewn. I can see the muscle, and it's bleeding like hell. Here, hold this!"

Dahms took the bandage and winced as Langenhagen pressed the wound together to dress the injury firmly with quick, confident movements.

"It will keep the bleeding somewhat under control, but it must be sewn," he repeated. "And keep your arm still. I'm improvising a sling."

Langenhagen proved that he had been observant during the first-aid training. He took care of the wound, and moments later Dahms rested his left arm in a makeshift sling. Fine beads of sweat stood on the engineer's brow.

"Lie down for a moment, feet up. We can't do a lot at this time anyway. We can't get out, they can't come in. We have some weapons, and they have many. They need to take care of prisoners, but we have no more than 18 combat-capable men at our disposal."

Langenhagen's glance fell through the semi-darkness of the engine room. He saw the shining faces of the loyalists in the reflection of the carbide-lamps. In all of them, he read a mixture of determination and despair.

"We have to inform Renna," Dahms groaned. "He's the only one who can still put an end to this outrage!"

"That would be nice, but I don't know how will do that," Langenhagen retorted. "And we will not make it for too long here. If von Klasewitz cuts of the ventilation, it's all over anyway."

"What harm can we wreak?" Dahms asked silently, and let his eyes wander. "We can't just put our hands in our lap ..."

"You will do exactly that!" Langenhagen said forcefully and pushed the engineer gently back, who wanted to sit. It was already a miracle that they had made it this far. Although the mutineers had obviously had a plan, they didn't handle it very professionally. Moreover, the officers who had been filled with suspicion by von Klasewitz fiery speech had become very alert and had made preparations. When the first signs of the uprising had become clear they had armed themselves immediately and tried to organize a defense. Ultimately, this had deteriorated into a decent retreat into the engine room. That von Klasewitz had mustered the support of fanatical monks, allowing them on board even critical officers hadn't thought possible. He had exceeded their worst fears.

But what now? When they had begun to organize themselves, they had been around 30 men. In the engine room remained 18. And the majority of the crew was either overwhelmed or belonged to the mutineers.

A massively built man sat down in front of Dahms and nodded to him. He seemed indifferent, as all of this didn't affect him. He put his paddle-shaped hands on his knees. Just a few minutes ago, he had cracked the skulls of two successive priests with these hands. Fulvius, the Roman blacksmith, had been found on board when the mutiny broke out and immediately took the side of his new friend Dahms. For him, there was no question where his loyalties lay. The world that had opened itself to him in recent days through the teachings of the engineer was fascinating and full of possibilities. He wouldn't trade this for anything and especially not against the fanatical babble of the priests. It might help that the blacksmith was a follower of the ancient Roman gods and had little more than contempt left for the Christians and their focus on what would happen after death.

"Either we wait here until the mutineers think of something, or we risk to break out," Langenhagen finally summed up the situation. "If we just open a bulkhead, they will wait behind it and stifle any attack. We have a few weapons, but they have more, and they have the fanatics of the boarding party. I don't think that all of the crew belong to the mutineers but I'm sure a couple of them are on their side. Against which we can't do much now."

Langenhagen nodded toward Dahms. "What will happen to us if we surrender?"

"Von Klasewitz will spare the normal crew members as well as the NCOs, with the notable exception of Köhler. For both of us he will either conduct a fake trial, or we will experience an unfortunate accident – or we will be handed over to Petronius and his henchmen. For we are demon messengers or something. I think they can imagine an appropriate method of execution, probably involving a lot of firewood."

"Renna will hardly allow that," Langenhagen said.

"When he learns of it in time, certainly not," Dahms admitted. "But where there's a will, there's a way."

"However, I'm out of ideas."

For a moment, all were silent. From outside, no sounds penetrated the door. There was no indication of what would happen next.

Then a voice was audible. It came through the internal communication system. It was von Klasewitz, quite unmistakable. Langenhagen and Dahms immediately recognized the mixture of anger and triumph in the tone of the first officer.

"Gentlemen, may I have your attention! You are trapped below and already have certainly made plans. I can tell you that all your efforts are already doomed. There is no way to escape for you. Therefore, I have an offer – Surrender, put down your weapons and I promise that no one will be hurt. Of course, the officers will be treated differently, but the enlisted men only followed their orders, and I can't blame them for that. I'll give you half an hour to think in peace."

Langenhagen threw Dahms a long look. "That perfidious asshole," he murmured, trying not to look too carefully at the faces of the lower ranks. "He hopes that the guys will overwhelm us and present us on a silver platter. Von Klasewitz is smarter than I thought."

"We all underestimated him."

"So ... what do we do now?"

The answer to this question consisted of silence.

19

Marcellus was afraid of many things, though not really any more than any other twelve year olds. These included sea monsters whose existence was denied by Magister Dahms, but this didn't change the fact that they actually existed. If the Master had not yet seen any, then because the *Saravica* was such a mighty ship that any reasonably minded monster changed its opinion three times before attacking it. On top of that, Marcellus noticed that Dahms, once he thought no one would listen to him, spoke with strong profanity of a hobgoblin[4], who, as it seemed to Marcellus' mind, had to be classified into the category of sea monsters. In any case, he was afraid of them and was usually very happy that thick metal was between them and the sea – and the monsters living in it.

Marcellus had initially also feared Magister Dahms. The man could sometimes be quite grumpy. But he had taken his promise to his father very seriously. Unlike the other oil monkeys with which Marcellus quickly had befriended himself – they were only a little older than himself but had evidently no interest in further education – he was seen as more than just a nimble worker who hurried with the oil can through the machinery and refilled the slow, dark liquid everywhere he was told to. Dahms had drafted a plan for him. The boy had begun to learn the language of the visitors – although his progress so far was rather modest – and the Master had begun to teach him some basic concepts of a science which he called "mechanics." When he had to cut a piece of a paper in hours of painstaking work, previously filled tediously with graphics in as many hours, only to have two circles, one bigger, one smaller, applied with larger and smaller spikes, he certainly had

---

[4]This is a reference to the *Klabautermann*, a traditional irreal entity in German sea-faring folk tales.

doubts about the reasoning behind these tasks. Magister Dahms had been relentless in his lessons, sometimes very strict, sometimes very loud.

He had never raised a hand against him.

He always made sure that he got to eat.

He made sure that he slept enough and wore clean clothes.

Over time, Marcellus had gotten the impression that Magister Dahms' gruffness was not arbitrary, but considered, and when he saw a piece of a black rectangle lying beside his bowl of thick soup one evening that tasted sweet and bitter at the same time – chocolate, the other oil monkeys called it – he knew that to respect Magister Dahms was possibly a good idea, but he actually had no reason to fear him.

At this moment, the son of a Roman fisherman was not afraid of the Magister.

He was afraid *for* him.

And he was afraid of the narrow, dark and stuffy air in the narrow tool cabinet, in which he sat. The tip of a small file he had pressed in such a way against the door frame that the cabinet door was almost closed, but not quite completely, and as long as no one came up with the idea of looking at the gap and to close the door with the latch, he could jump out at any time.

But there the mutineers sat. He had escaped them in the whole mess, had been hiding, had seen, filled with horror, as one of the rebels had mutilated Magister Dahms, had almost cried out and would have run to him, and yet ...

He was not even sure what had inspired him to stay out here. When the swearing first officer had disappeared, two of the mutineers and two monks remained with grim faces. They didn't know anything of the boy in the closet, were focused on the bulkhead, hammered on it every now and then, stared at each other from time to time, half suspicious, half-frustrated, since they couldn't talk with each other.

Marcellus had already resigned to indefinitely remain in this most uncomfortable environment when a fifth man showed up and asked the two Germans to follow him. This left him with the two priests.

When they started to get bored, they did what was their most obvious pastime.

They began to pray.

Very fervently.

They were really good Christians.

And as they sat there on her knees, in a truly demonic environment and begged for the purity of their souls, they didn't notice how Marcellus slowly opened the door, crept out of the closet and slipped with nimble movements through the open bulkhead leading upwards. He pressed himself into a corner when two men marched past him, but either they hadn't seen him or didn't regard the boy as important enough.

It was still very dark once he finally reached the deck. The mutineers hadn't improved the lighting so as not to attract the attention of the loyal harbor guards. Everything seemed to be calm. Most fighting had been inside the ship, barely noticeable from the outside.

Marcellus' heart pounded. He pressed himself against a steel wall, looked hastily left and right. Shadows moved on deck. Under the dim light of a lantern, he recognized one of the mutineers, a baton in his hand. The man looked around vigilantly. Marcellus' gaze wandered to the gangway, about three feet away from him. Directly opposite the ship, there were two guards, standing there as if nothing had happened. He wouldn't be able to pass them.

So only one possibility remained.

Marcellus took a deep breath. The idea of having to jump into the harbor with its cold, brackish water was appalling and frightening. But even more frightening was the prospect of remaining on board with the mutineers and possibly having to witness the death of Magister Dahms. Marcellus had grown up on and around the sea and knew stories of mutiny and piracy. He knew that as a rule no one involved acted squeamishly. He himself might be overlooked and ultimately only sent away, but Magister Dahms would certainly not be treated so friendly.

Marcellus had to act. He narrowed his eyes, looked at the harbor guards who walked back and forth on the quay. Most of them he didn't know, but the broad-shouldered guy with the beard who was standing there with the torch in his hand, staring into the dark harbor water, was well known to him. Rufus was his name, a burly veteran who spent his last years before retirement in the urban service, not particularly bright, but a trustworthy man, a loose acquaintance of Marcellus' father.

If someone would protect and believe him, then Rufus!

Once the idea had formed in Marcellus' head, there was no stopping him. He pulled away from the wall ...

"Stop! Who's there?"

... and passed the few steps to the rail in no time ...

"Stop! Stop immediately!"

... and jumped.

An eternity seemed to pass before he hit the water's surface, and a cold shock ran through his body as he entered the fluid. Almost instinctively he began to swim, pulled upwards, and once his head broke into the open, his eyes fixed on the torches on the quay. The shouting had become noisy, both on the cruiser as well as on land. With powerful strokes Marcellus slipped to one of the landing sites, pulled himself to the bottom step of the stairs carved into the stone, trembling and panting but full of confidence.

Then he heard something popping and whistling as stone splinters rained down on his wet hair. He almost fell back into the water.

They had shot at him!

Marcellus' knees buckled, as he grabbed onto the stairs. They shot at him! They shot! He hadn't thought of that!

But then he heard the angry shouts from the *Saarbrücken* and knew instinctively that there would be no further shooting. And immediately he felt himself pulled up by strong arms. A man had come down the stairs, grabbed the boy's body and threw it over his shoulder. At the top, on the quay, he let Marcellus down again.

It was Rufus.

"What have you done, that the strangers shoot at you?" he barked at Marcellus. The boy stared in disbelief, but rallied himself quickly.

"I have escaped, Rufus! You have to call the Navarch!"

"The Navarch is now Prefect, and why should I wake him? Because a boy has shirked from his duties and has jumped to avoid a deserved beating?"

Marcellus searched for words, while another legionary threw a blanket around his narrow shoulders. "No, Rufus, it isn't like that! Mutiny, there was a mutiny! Priests are on board and have overwhelmed the crew! There are dead and wounded!"

Rufus frowned and glanced over at the *Saarbrücken*, where seemingly peace had returned. Still there was nothing to see from the outside in regard to any change of command on board. "You're serious?"

"Rufus, I don't lie!"

"I'm risking life and limb!"

"Believe me! I don't make it up!"

The legionary exchanged a look with his comrades. "Well, it's certainly unusual for them to shoot in the middle of the night at a little boy who jumps overboard," growled another man. Marcellus saw that others guards suddenly looked very uncomfortable. Of course! Someone had to have looked the other way if anyone sneaked aboard! It was only possible with allies on land! He had to be terribly careful now. "Decurion, what do we do?"

A slim young man raised his head, shrugged. "We don't take any risks and inform the Prefect. We have orders to immediately report anything unusual – and this is definitely unusual."

Murmur of assent rang. Marcellus saw some of the legionaries pale.

The decurion immediately sent a messenger. Then he looked at Marcellus. "You said priests have come on board the *Saravica*?"

The boy nodded eagerly. "They have overwhelmed the men loyal to Trierarch Rheinberg in their sleep. Von Klasewitz has been made the new trierarch, he united himself with those priests."

The eyes of the decurion narrowed to slits. "How will people have come on board? We have –" The young man interrupted himself, raised his head and glanced around. Then three of his men turned around and sprinted off.

"Rufus," the decurion barked.

Marcellus looked wide-eyed as the veteran presented a rope with weighs attached to both ends, took a sense of the situation and hurled it. Hissing, the rope whirled through the air, and then it was wrapped around the legs of the slowest runner, throwing him to the ground.

Rufus trotted leisurely to the man, seized him with one hand and pulled him roughly to his feet. He dragged him mercilessly back to decurion, while the two accomplices disappeared in the darkness.

"Lecius, Lecius, Lecius," Marcellus heard the veteran mutter. "I've always known that no good end awaits you."

"Keep a close eye on him, Rufus!" ordered the decurion and threw the prisoner a cold look. "We will interrogate him alone. Who were the other two?"

"Guido and Oliver, a German and Gaul. I didn't trust them from the beginning," Rufus said and spat on the ground. "I know their whores, and I know their taverns. Give me a few trusted men, and I grab them for you, Decurion."

"No, they will be smarter and leave the city this night. Lecius here is sufficient for us. He will tell us everything we want to know."

"More than that," Rufus growled promising.

Was there sweat visible on the forehead of the prisoner? Marcellus could not quite see.

"Do we want the *Saravica* to talk to us?" asked one of the men.

"We do nothing without Renna's command. Send a messenger. I want to make sure that we get someone with authority here. We keep quiet." The decurion took a deep breath and turned to throw a direct view at the calm cruiser. "I don't want anyone shooting at us."

20

"Prefect?"

"Anything new?"

"No, nothing."

"Then we do it, as discussed."

Centurion Marcus Tullius Salius didn't show how he felt. Renna had known him for ten years, had taken him along with every new posting, and therefore made sure that the man remained in his vicinity. Salius was not just a veteran with his good 15 years of service, he was Renna's man for all seasons, the one he'd send, if there seemed to be no way out. Once Salius had, with his men, hand-picked legionaries, overwhelmed an Alan chieftain, behind the lines of his soldiers, and abducted him from his own camp. He had rescued the wounded Renna from a barbarian ambush without getting much as a scratch himself. He had escaped from Persian slavery and had brought the head of his former lord.

Salius didn't really look like a feared warrior, he was rather lean, almost too slim for the power that resided in him. His harmonious face was close to beautiful, and his curly hair was often a target of good-natured ridicule. Making fun of Salius was no problem, as he seemingly took every humiliation in stride. That was certainly connected to the fact that the centurion knew absolutely what he was worth. Renna had never known him to be other than totally self-controlled, and always of cold, disciplined precision. Sometimes he had the impression that the centurion was absolutely soulless, a killing machine, feeling no joy in his actions. Salius had no great leadership qualities – his promotion to centurion had happened more pro forma; Renna never would have transferred the command of more than 20 or 30 selected men to him. But this centuria, although well below nominal strength, was the private command of the dreaded man, directly responsible to the prefect. No legate or tribune dared give Salius an order. The centurion followed Renna, and he obeyed exactly. If he had any doubts in a matter, he expressed them once and at the beginning but never showed any trace of defiance.

This time there had been no criticism at all. Salius had thrown a look at the quiet *Saravica* from the third floor of the Harbor Master's office and had accepted Renna's order to retake the ship with stoic composure. He knew that he would be left with the details, and from the moment he had been instructed, the precise mechanics of his mind had fallen into gear.

He looked again at Renna, but the prefect had no further instructions. Without a greeting, Salius turned around and walked down the stairs. In a large room 22 selected men waited for him. They had a lot in common, were disciplined, trusted the centurion, all excellent fighters with and without weapons. They all wore nothing but a towel wrapped around the loins. All of them were rubbed with a black paste that would stick to their skin even for weeks, no matter how much they bathed. All wore no more than a thin, long-drawn knife in their hands, Persian style.

And all of them could swim.

"You know everything," Salius said instead of a greeting, while his assistants put away his armor, placed all clothing aside and began methodically and thoroughly to rub him with pitch. Jovius Clavus, his decurion, handed him his knife, a specially manufactured item like all weapons of this team. Clavus was the only one who had not been smeared with pitch, and that because of the fact that his skin was of a natural, deep blackness. When he smiled at his centurion, one saw that he had blackened his teeth as everyone else.

They would have a very bad taste in their mouths for days.

All watched in silence until Salius was ready. The bitter cold didn't seem to bother anyone. Then the diversion began.

The city garrison marched on.

In they marched with discipline, under the noise of the trumpets and pipes, in glittering armor, all armed with glowing torches, the plumes of the officers a red shimmer in the flickering light.

132

A mighty uproar, the good one thousand legionaries taking position and officers barking orders, the harbor filled with warriors. Everywhere, windows opened, and the curious watched what happened down there, only to frantically barricade themselves thereafter.

On the *Saravica*, more and more lights went on, and whistles could be heard. Salius saw men armed with their wondrous weapons in position. He saw one of the large metal pipes threatening, slowly moving toward the marching soldiers.

Renna was taking a horrendous risk. But it was necessary. Salius also risked his life, and he had to get his chance. Even Renna himself appeared in full gear, accompanied by a dozen torchbearers, walking to the wharf and loudly demanding to be allowed on board. Salius and his men had by now left the house and slid through dark alleys, circumventing the fanfare and finally reached the impenetrable blackness of the harbor basin. Here were fishing boats, forming a deep black tangle of bodies in the water, and slowly, using their ropes, without making any waves, the men were in the water.

No word was exchanged. Like fish, the men swam, mostly underwater, only briefly orienting themselves on the surface, and with eyes only opened to slits, to allow no reflection from their otherwise jet-black faces. All 23 men glided toward the *Saravica*, approached the starboard side of the cruiser slowly in an invisible procession. During a brief look out of the water, Salius could see that all men paid attention to the other side of the ship, anxious and ready to fight, observing the parade of the legion, shouting at themselves for courage, their weapons aligned, all pressed to the rail.

Two men stood at the starboard side. But they did nothing else than to look to the wharf through the superstructure of the ship. The noise reached a crescendo because Renna's martial speech was always accompanied by rhythmic beats of the soldiers on their shields. Renna didn't want to talk to von Klasewitz. Once the conspirator they had captured had confessed all and everything under torture, for him there was no doubt that he had to do everything in his power to save Rheinberg's command.

Salius' task.

The centurion didn't consider the two lonely starboard guards with contempt. His strategy for success had a lot to do with the stupidity of his opponents. Stupidity was useful. It should be respected in his opponents.

He was sincerely grateful to them for that and promised them, now that he came closer and closer to the bow of the cruiser, a quick and painless death.

They reached the front starboard anchor chain. Loud noise continued to resound from the shore. Salius was the first who took the metal chain and began to pull himself up. Like all his comrades, he had his hands bandaged well for this purpose. The damp cloth helped him to get a firm grip and avoid injury.

The strangers would have been very surprised if they had witnessed the exercise area of Salius' men. Shortly after the arrival of the ship, the centurion had taken the cruiser thoroughly in inspection from afar and the practice site was redesigned accordingly. There was a long metal chain, which hung in a water-filled basin, at its upper end connected to a rough replica of the bow of the *Saravica* made of wood. Two days after the arrival of the ship, Salius' men had begun to rehearse the boarding of the cruiser.

The centurion appreciated it very much to be properly prepared.

And it paid off once more, as black bodies climbed up the anchor chain in a strange, silent procession.

When Salius swung over the rail, he made no noise with his bare feet. When he had bridged the few steps to the first starboard watch, the man looked up with a slightly bewildered expression. And as the long-drawn dagger went cleanly through the chest in the heart and the man slid with open eyes to the ground, everything continued to proceed in silence.

Jovius killed the second man, who had hardly turned round. He also died a quick and clean death. Salius approvingly nodded at the decurion. The guards had received their deserved reward.

It took a minute, then all his people were on board.

Then a violent bang, a trembling of the ship, many voices shouting. The sudden clutter of arrows on the metal deck of the *Saravica*. Riot, noise, hoarse commands.

Salius allowed himself a glance.

The mutineers had used one of their smaller fire tubes. On the quay, there was aimless chaos. Shredded bodies of a bunch of legionaries who had been directly hit by the powerful cannon were scattered everywhere. Salius caught a glimpse of Renna, who held his bloodied right arm and was carried away by men of his bodyguard. Archers covered the *Saravica* with volleys but then a second blast, a renewed shaking out of the cruiser, and with infernal crash one of the city buildings standing near the pier was hit. The shouted commands of the legionaries mingled with the desperate cries of the residents who fell with the debris on the road, more shattered bodies, helpless wounded, a massive cloud of smoke danced across the flickering torchlight.

A brutal scene, a senseless massacre. The centurion observed it with cold measure.

Salius made the sign.

Twenty-three men slid across the deck of the *Saravica*, everyone of the rebels in sight. The mutineers didn't look behind themselves, laughed at the panic in front of them; only the priests remained serious. But the centurion's men made no difference. Twenty-three blades flashed, twenty-three victims were in their blood and dead yet before they touched the ground. When the remainder turned around, proclaiming surprise, the attackers had already identified the next targets and then the daggers shot forward. This time they met first defense, raised arms, an isolated blade, those smaller fire tubes that the strangers held and directed at the new threat. Salius saw blood spray from the stomach of one of his men when he was felled by an invisible hand, but then the Romans walked about them and their blades had rich harvest.

"The deck is ours!" Jovius reported, the body sprinkled with blood but none of his. Salius saw an imperious movement on the quay. Amid the chaos was his second decurion, Clodius, with twenty other men in full armor. They couldn't swim, but they could run up the now unguarded gangway, with a drawn sword and grim determination to judge those responsible for this massacre. With them was Marcellus, who knew where the crew was and could show them the way. He was wearing a much too large breastplate and a helmet. Two legionaries, including Rufus, went with him alone for his protection.

"Through these doors!" the boy cried in a clear voice. Salius came forward, then Jovius, then other men. Priests who stood in the way became victims of blades, went down, gasping and spitting blood. Marcellus was scared, trembled, observed the carnage with frightened eyes. Rufus picked him up, hugged him to his chest.

"Marcellus," he said loudly to the shocked boy. "Marcellus! Your Master! Let us save him!"

That helped. The eyes of the fisherman's son cleared. Coarse came his instructions. Behind them, they heard the clatter of other legionaries on deck; one tribune must have noticed that something had to be done. Salius grunted. There were actually officers in the Roman army who used their head to more than just to hold the helmet.

Truly a time of miracles and revelations.

Then two of the strangers appeared, with open eyes and fire tubes. The passage was narrow, no more than two men could stand side by side. Jovius threw his head back when a fire tube spoke and tore his throat, the fountain of blood hiding Salius for a moment. A second man went to the ground, and a violent, burning pain shot through the leg of the centurion. He shoved his dagger, cut throats with effortless speed, and the gurgling stifled the cries of pain when the strangers went to the ground.

Salius was bleeding profusely, but he ignored it. He looked behind himself, saw his men climbing over the corpse of the decurion, then he saw Rufus, the boy now on his back, guarding him with his massive upper body and holding a shield in front of him.

"There, down there!" the boy yelled.

Salius plunged ahead. Men with fire tubes turned up, but this time not fast enough. The centurion jumped the last few steps, threw himself forward against to the men who responded like they were attacked by a demon. The centurion didn't hesitate, hurled the helpless defenders to the ground and moments later they were dead.

136

"The bulkhead ... the door! Let me down, they have to open it from the inside!"

Rufus lowered the boy. He ran to the bulkhead, pounding on it, shouted a few words in the language of the strangers. It took only a short time, then the hatch swung open, and fire tubes appeared. But Salius recognized from the facial expression of the boy that these were friends.

"This is Magister Dahms," Marcellus said excitedly. "He's a tribune, at least. He knows his stuff."

Dahms and Salius regarded each other in silence. Langenhagen came out, saw the carnage, then stared at the arm of the centurion. Without many words he reached for bandages, and it took only a few moments until the wound was cared for. Salius eyes fell on a similar application to Dahms' arm, and this was first time he allowed himself something of an emotional expression and smiled.

"We have to overpower the remaining mutineers and free the captives," Marcellus said, and as if he was the trierarch, the men followed his recommendation.

The men of Clodius had swept way the priests. Some of the mutineers had surrendered, and the order was to spare them. As Salius came on deck, Clodius told him that only a small group resisted in the room the stranger called the "bridge".

From there, they had a pretty good field of fire for their fire tubes and the entrances were easy to defend. The oh-so-attentive tribune, whose bloody corpse they had just transported away, experienced that on his own body

"I'm doing this!"

Salius stared at Dahms, who wanted to push him aside. "You are injured."

"You too, Centurion."

Dahms didn't shy away from the Roman's stare. Salius had to accept that this was the territory of the stranger.

"You have a fire-tube?"

"A little one," Dahms said and raised his gun.

"Can you talk to the mutineers?"

"I'll try."

But when the men wanted to approach the bridge, shots whipped at them immediately.

Salius drew Dahms back into cover and looked at him questioningly. "It seems as if the rebels are of the opinion that they have no choice than to fight to the death," the centurion said. "Is that so? In the Roman legion mutiny is punished by death without mercy."

"We commonly do the same, but I would be ready, if you consent, to offer some grace and therefore imprisonment."

"Slavery?" Salius spat. "I would prefer death."

"No slavery. Detention. Prison."

The centurion shrugged. "It should be possible to arrange that – but I don't understand why you want to waste able workers."

Dahms had no interest to explain the fine points of the difference between detention and possibly forced labor and slavery, not least because the politics of the German Empire in the colonies didn't differentiate between those two with much attention. But it was in any case an unbearable thought to think of crew members as Roman slaves.

"Köhler!"

The burly boatswain appeared immediately next to Dahms.

"The megaphone!"

"At once."

Moments later, Dahms had the tube in his hands and led it to his mouth.

"Men of the Navy," his voice boomed over the deck as the legionaries behind him helped freed loyalist up. "I'm Navy Chief Engineer Dahms. Next to me are Lieutenant Langenhagen and Chief Petty Officer Köhler. We have regained command of the *Saarbrücken*. The mutiny failed." He paused for effect. "I call on all mutineers to lay down their weapons. Anything else would be pointless because we are in the majority. Every fight would become a massacre, with most of the victims on your side. I'm ready to give the order to commence attack. But I have another suggestion. I'm also ready, on behalf of the Roman authorities, to assure those who voluntarily surrender now fair treatment, which, I say expressly, excludes the death penalty or any kind of torture. I repeat: Those who give up and lay down their weapons won't die and won't be treated brutally. For that, I give my pledge as an imperial officer."

Dahms paused again. He knew that discussions would now erupt on the bridge. Maybe dispute. Could he sow discord within the mutineers, like von Klasewitz had tried it when they were trapped in the engine room, that would be a success as well.

"Let's give them some time to consider," Dahms said softly to Salius.

The centurion nodded, but then grimaced. "Also, no torture? How do we identify the people behind the uprising?"

Dahms laughed joylessly. "Ask a priest named Petronius about that."

Salius frowned. "The same Petronius I know? The right hand of Liberius?"

"The very same."

"That won't please Renna." Salius looked like Renna's reaction had potential for amusement.

"That's why we take care of it later."

A few minutes elapsed, then the mutineers came out – seven crew members of the *Saarbrücken*, who had laid down their arms, and some remaining priests.

Dahms' men started to round up all the prisoners to the rear deck. Langenhagen gave him a descriptive glance, for he evidently shared some foreboding with the engineer. When they had counted the survivors and the priests were put in a separate group, it became clear – both von Klasewitz and Tennberg were missing. No bodies were found, and they hadn't hidden under the cowls.

In the confusion of the fight, they had seen the tide of events and in all likelihood jumped into the water. Both were known as good swimmers, so that they had used the same path Salius' men had used to enter the cruiser for their escape.

Although Renna immediately ordered a wide search in the city, facilitated by the dawn of the morning, everyone knew that this would be in vain. When it became clear that Petronius as well as some other high-ranking dignitaries had left Ravenna, the search was called off. With the contacts the informant of the bishop most likely had, they were certainly good enough to protect the refugees from the authorities' persecution.

The ringleaders had escaped. The disappointment over this discovery was more than outweighed by the relief that this episode was over. The fight had demanded sacrifice – of the mutineers only few were untouched, the rest dead or seriously injured. Rheinberg would have to sit trials when he came back, and some stations on board were now seriously understaffed.

On the other hand, as Dahms found, once he looked at Marcellus, who after all the excitement had been finally overwhelmed by weariness and had fallen asleep in the arms of a burly legionary, there were now quite good reasons to increase the crew with Roman recruits. That would have been necessary sooner or later anyway.

The reason for "sooner" was a disaster, but the consequence opened the way into the future. Again, Rheinberg would be asked to make decisions fairly quick.

Finally, the worst effects of the nocturnal struggle were eliminated. Even the pungent smell of blood was driven away by a sea breeze. The usual stench of fish and manure, which characterized Ravenna, ultimately retained the upper hand.

When Dahms bid farewell to Centurion Salius, he only nodded solemnly.

"I hope that my services won't be in demand again for some time," the man said. "My prefect wants my report and suggestions soon, so it's better to leave now. You have tend to his injury, I've heard?"

"It's not too serious," Dahms reassured him. "He was bleeding heavily, but will soon be fit again, at least as fast as yourself."

Salius cast a contemptuous look on his bandage. "It's nothing. But your weapons are terrible. I don't want to be a Goth."

"Your work has shown that there are things that are not outweighed by superior weapons."

Salius allowed himself a smile. "We have paid a high price for this knowledge. As I said – may all the gods we believe in make sure that I'll never have to deal in battle with the likes of you."

The centurion sounded sincere and serious.

When he turned and Dahms gazing after him as he walked down the gangway, the engineer couldn't blame the legionary for this attitude.

He turned around, went to the Roman with the sleeping boy in his arms and threw Marcellus a proud look.

"Once he'll be a great legionary!" the strong man boasted proudly.

Dahms nodded. "That may well be."

He waved Köhler, who carefully picked up the boy and carried him to his hammock.

"In fact, I intend to make him an engineer," Dahms said thoughtfully. "Maybe a very brave engineer."

The legionary looked a bit perplexed at him. No idea what that meant. Then he frowned. He'd better continue to look after the boy.

One could never tell.

21

Fritigern looked at the man. He was an embodiment of misery: sweaty, stinking of urine, the hair completely wild, trembling hands. His glance was unsteady, his body shook at irregular intervals, he talked choppy with a lot of fear in his voice. This was not a Hun warrior, who rode mercilessly on his horse against every conceivable enemy, this was a human wreck, a shadow of his former self. The Gothic judge had never before seen a Hun who had so much lost his composure because of any defeat, any desperate situation, any threat. The reports that he got from the survivors of Fastida's group were often confused, contradicted themselves, and were full of religious allusions. There was talk of invisible demons, the wrath of God whose sword had been driven through their ranks. The Hun, a Christian for that matter, spoke of demons or spirits, who tore the horses' skulls and severed them from the shoulders without a sword or an arrow. All six returnees – one had been completely dumbfounded on the way back and had killed himself – had in common that they were the only survivors and that their unit had fallen victim to a terrible, overwhelming opponent. These weren't excuses made by cowards who wanted to explain a lost battle away by describing an overpowering enemy to hide their own failures. Whatever they had experienced, it had confused their senses, triggered deep fear, and transformed them into weeping wrecks.

Fritigern had to take this seriously.

He relieved the babbling Hun. This was the last of the survivors to whom he had spoken. Since the first conversation, he had learned nothing new. Only one thing was certain – whoever accompanied a single Roman cohort on its way to Thessaloniki constituted a new and important force, influencing his strategic considerations and urging the need for additional information.

He sighed. Strategic considerations. As if those have had developed into anything. So far, they had not even been able to agree on what exactly they should do with the totally deranged Eastern Roman emperor, who had at least been nursed back to physical health, and was able to take food in a reasonably well-mannered way and to fuck Gothic women. But whether Valens was actually still an important trump, Fritigern had more and more doubts.

The inability of the allied nations to attack the well-fortified and richly supplied Eastern Roman towns and garrisons, their lack of knowledge of siege engines and their totally inadequate discipline, chaotic hierarchy and large autonomy of a myriad of sub-leaders – all this was not a good basis for a great strategy. Everything Fritigern had ever managed was to keep the great military body in motion to plunder on the way as effectively as possible and to hope that this approach would quickly entice the Romans to concessions and to accept new negotiations.

What was the result? Flavius Victor gathered the rest of the Eastern Roman army in Thessaloniki, and from the West his emperor Gratian sent a bunch of demons who with sorcery transformed good warriors into howling women.

Fritigern had the feeling that the threads of events unfolding slipped away from him.

"So? What do we do?"

The judge had not even noticed that Godegisel had entered the tent. The young nobleman had listened to the reports and seemed to be impressed by what he heard as he looked a little pale around the nose.

"Sit down," Fritigern asked him and served himself plenty of wine. Godegisel did the same. "We need to know more. Choose ten reliable men. Those who are afraid of nothing and no one, who would storm laughing to hell. We need to know more."

Godegisel said nothing, drank his wine. "Do you know what scares me the most at this moment?" he finally asked softly.

"Speak!"

"Would you have given me this order a few days ago, two of the men with whom you have just spoken would have been among those ten, and I would have sworn that they'd met every danger with ice-cold blood."

Fritigern remained silent, then nodded, put down his own cup.

"Then look for the crazies, choose from the madmen. Those who have peculiar tendencies and strange behavior. Take ten of those everyone otherwise avoids, in whose presence everyone sneers or raises children to close their eyes at. Ten in whose heads the long trek and the many battles have infused trouble. Maybe they will be the best for this task."

Godegisel looked at Fritigern searchingly, but the idea seemed to catch him. "But I myself am not one who belongs to the crazies," he pointed out. "You don't seem to worry about me becoming crazy."

"You've heard the stories. Arm yourself. But I need someone with intelligence and excellent powers of observation, Godegisel. Do not disappoint me."

The young man obviously didn't know if he should be pleased with this praise or appalled by its consequences. In any case, he made the decision not to question his leader.

"Ten lunatics, Judge."

"Ten, who can tell me what I need to know."

Godegisel rose.

"I will obey the order. But afterwards you should come to a decision, Judge. I'm tired of wandering, and I'm not the only one. Choose a battle or choose submission. But choose."

Fritigern didn't react. He felt the sudden chill in Godegisel's words and guessed how it was bubbling in the big camp. The doubters became more. The fame of Adrianople faded. Fritigern had to act, better still: to win, if he wanted to remain leader of the Goths.

If even one of his most loyal lieutenants began to warn him, then it was indeed high time to do something.

22

If Julia had learned one thing in her life, then that one could accomplish anything with money. The corruption was widespread in the empire and already for a long time no cause for special concerns: It was a great exception to meet an honest bureaucrat. If one carried a bag of good solidi – not stretched with copper – his concern was taken seriously, found a sympathetic ear and execution was then just a question of the amount to be paid. Julia was not without means because Michellus was one of those progressive fathers who conceded to his daughters a certain amount of control over her own funds. While Julia's sister Drusilla invested her appanage in beautiful clothes, jewelry and all sorts of oils and ointments, and despite the fact that Julia was also not averse to the current fashions, she had due to her permanent disputes always been careful to maintain a "war chest." A part of this sum she had taken when she had run away with Volkert, but it was still more than enough left: a small, real chest full of beautiful golden solidi, some still marked during the reign of Valentinian I, when the empire still had an emperor who knew what to do.

That's what her mother always said.

Julia didn't care, but Gratian's father's minted face was especially helpful in that case to buy favor and services.

When she realized that her mother either didn't intend to keep her word to look for Volkert, or that her influence was not even half as big as she had always claimed, the decision had matured in her to become active herself. She felt more comfortable to take action anyway, instead of waiting for the favors of others. The wait was over, and that alone lifted her spirits considerably.

She decided to seek her luck firstly with an old friend of her father. Senator Lucius Tullius Severus was not only a time-honored and highly respected member of the Senate, he also had a military career behind him, a full 25 years, rising through the ranks to highest offices. Michellus sometimes jokingly called him "our Diocletian," as the career of Severus reminded many to the rise of the great reformist ruler, who had worked his way up from legionary to emperor.

Severus was old as the hills, close to 80, a rare feat in these times. But he had a quick mind and above all contacts in the military, as many young recruits, who had started under him, were now in influential positions. In addition, the old lecher had a weakness for young girls, although a platonic one, without much chance to indulge in them due to his frail condition. Julia intended to exploit this shamelessly.

The dress that she wore under the wide cloak should make a significant contribution. It emphasized a tightly-woven chest area, stylistically modeled like a breastplate of the legion, slit in the middle so that Severus would get a deep insight into promises that he in his age only knew to enjoy in theory. A broad belt clasped her hips, then the fabric fell in soft curves and would reveal slim legs in a most pleasing way with each movement she made. Julia knew exactly which movement would cause the desired effect. When she tried on the dress and had made sure of the correct impression, she sent a slave ahead to announce her arrival. She knew that Severus was in town, and she also knew that he usually received no visitors at this time.

Julia, he would welcome; she was sure that he'd make an exception to the rule for her.

Shortly thereafter, she was on her way. She traveled befitting to her status – litter and bodyguard, led by a strong domestic slave, who saw to it that the carriers had free rein. It was almost noon, and the streets of Ravenna were crowded with pedestrians and the occasional rider.

A remarkable number of legionaries were visible in the city, as since the port incidents security had been strengthened. No one really felt safe, though, as the soldiers themselves stopped people, seemingly to check them, but in fact expecting a few sesterces as bribe. Should one refuse to pay, he was entitled to a very lengthy and very thorough inspection process, in which there was certainly a suspicious circumstance to be found that drove the price one had to pay for an end of the procedure upwards. It was good to look either very poor or ragged – then one was obviously totally innocuous and didn't enjoy any attention – or, as Julia, to sit in a litter. There were limits not even exceeded by legionaries as they could get in serious trouble otherwise.

Julia remained completely undisturbed. The only thing that was intrusive was the inimitable aroma of manure and waste. The beggars who dared to approach the litter were cleared by Julia's slaves. It spoke for the senator's daughter that this clearance didn't consist of a few well-placed blows but of a handful of coins thrown in the right direction.

When they reached the house of Severus, it became clear that they were already expected. The gates opened and the litter could pass unhindered. When the wings closed behind her and Julia got out of the vehicle, it was as if she had arrived in another world. With the beautiful garden of autumn flowers, the clean-cut hedges, and the murmuring fountain, an atmosphere of peace and serenity filled the property of Severus.

The old man waited for them, supported by a slave, who was barely younger than the senator himself. Severus' wife had died three years ago; that it had contributed significantly to the rejuvenation and revitalization of the man was generally considered a fact. His sons and daughters, about whose total number different estimates were traded, lived far away from home, being married or involved in their careers. No wonder that the old senator saw the visit of the enchanting daughter of Michellus to be a highly welcome change.

Very welcome in fact, if one was able to interpret the glances once Julia opened her cape and pretended as if she felt a little too warm. The haste with which he asked her inside, where the underfloor heating of the noble estate probably would support her desire to get rid of all the annoying garment, also spoke of this. Julia's performance was convincing.

"What can I do for the lovely daughter of my good friend Michellus?" Severus finally said, after he had convinced himself long enough of Julia's obvious advantages.

"It is a military matter, dear father."

Severus' eyes flashed. A young woman in a costume that looked like an idealized armor-plate asked him about military affairs. His groans sounded as if he would secretly wish to be at least 30 years younger. Or 20.

By Jupiter, ten years would already help.

"Speak, dear Julia."

The senator's daughter had decided to be open. Her relationship with Volkert had already become the talk of the town, at least in the wider circle of her family. Severus had certainly heard of it, and he probably developed a general understanding of the situation not the least because of his own turbulent past in this regard. So Julia told him everything he should know and ultimately came to the core of her concerns.

"You still have many contacts in high circles. First, I want to find out where Thomas has been posted to, and then it would be good if we could free him from service."

Severus was suddenly serious. "That's not quite that simple, my dove."

"I have money! A large bag full of –"

The old man raised his hand. "It is less about money although coins can never hurt. The point is that if I understand correctly, your lover is incognito. No one knows where he comes from and under which name he has been included in the pay list. Had he given his real identity, he would have already been delivered to the strange visitors. This makes any search very, very difficult. A description alone does not help us. I only know when he was recruited, a date he will ultimately share with many others, as the recruits are all drawn together for training. In addition, he is probably no longer in training camp because the staffing needs are considerable. He will already be on the way to his legion. And that can be anywhere in the West, depending on the development of the military situation in the East."

148

Julia felt her hope sinking. Her determination turned into despair, and she fought against the emerging tears. "There must be something I can do," she said with a choked voice.

"Well, well, my dove," Severus said somewhat helpless. "Don't give up! I promise you that I'll do what I can. I'll use my contacts and try to pick up the trail. An advice I can give you already now: If he was recruited in this area, his first residence has most probably been the camp of my old companion tribune Ercatus. It isn't far from here."

"I have heard of the camp. I was even there, after they had caught Thomas. But no one allowed me inside."

Severus waved. Out of the gloom came a slave, bowed his head before and got a whisper in his ear by the Senator. Moments later, he brought papyrus and something to write. Severus scribbled a long sentence, pulled out his signet ring and some wax. Then he pressed his seal on the note and rolled the papyrus.

"Here, little dove, that will grant you admission. But I don't think your parents will allow you –"

"That's my concern," Julia interrupted and accepted the document.

Severus was wise enough not to pursue the subject any further.

"I'll do my own inquiries. This will take some time to complete. Meet me again in three weeks, then, I'm sure, I know a bit more. In any case, you can travel to the camp and ask yourself, although it will be very hard to figure out something without raising the suspicion that Volkert is one of the foreign visitors. If he wants to remain anonymous, or needs to, this might be not such a good idea. You know what happened recently in the harbor."

"Yes," Julia murmured with a helpless tone. "But I cannot just do nothing."

"I can give you one further advice," Severus said after a moment's thought. "From what I hear, Gratian wants to return to the West. This also means that the leader of the strangers, Rheinberg, will soon be back with his ship. Talk to him. When he is committed to Volkert, the authorities will assist him, should he ask them to."

"He's a deserter," Julia said quietly.

Severus nodded. "Yes, you young people have called big trouble upon you. There is a lack of patience in your age. I didn't behave like that in my time."

Julia abstained from any comment. She had heard other stories about the old man.

"However, this Rheinberg has been described to me as a man of understanding, and he has just nearly lost his ship to mutineers. He might consider clemency because he needs his men more than ever before. You can, dear Julia, be very convincing, so maybe you should talk to him. To save your lover on your own might be an insurmountable task." Severus looked at her sadly. "The time has not yet come for women like you, my dove. You have to go with the flow, meander through it like a fish among the rocks, then you will go far. If you always swim against the water, you might get strong muscles, but will never reach your goal. Whatever you desire you will achieve if you follow the stream, not by fighting yourself to the source. I'm not saying that you should forget what you want. Your will guides you along the stream and help you to overcome the rocks and rapids. If you focus on your will and swim fast with the flow, you'll overtake who'll try to stop you. At the mouth of the lake, your lover is waiting for you. You can reach him that way."

Julia didn't speak, as the words of the old man impressed her. Behind the shell of the lecherous old warhorse was a man who had seen much and lived longer than most of his contemporaries. The young senator's daughter swallowed every contradiction that stirred within her. She decided to devote some more thought to Severus' words before she came to the decision whether his advice was welcome or not.

Severus stood up. "I'm tired, beautiful Julia. I'll do what I can, and I won't tell your parents anything. Come in three weeks."

Julia did the same. "Thank you, I appreciate it a lot, venerable Senator."

Severus laughed and looked at his visitor with an almost youthful intensity. He took her arm and led her out, which due to its frailty rather meant that she led his steps.

She said goodbye to the senator at the gate.

"If you come back, wear this dress."

Julia smiled.

The old man patted her arm. "It helps a lot that I feel immediately less venerable."

23

"I hope that you will be successful with your plan!"

Symmachus looked up from the rear, over the railing right into the Mediterranean Sea. The trip to Ravenna was almost done, and the weather was getting a bit restless. Rheinberg pulled his jacket tighter as the wind picked up. But neither he nor the Senator had the intention to leave the deck, because inside the ship everywhere was dark and stank. It was much more pleasant to endure the cool freshness of the coming winter.

"I'm not sure about Gratian," Rheinberg replied. "Sometimes he seems to open up to my words, then his thoughts are suddenly not traceable for me anymore."

Symmachus sighed. "You have to understand how he grew up. When he was named by his father as his successor, there was loud criticism. The fact that Gratian had predominantly civil and no military training didn't go down well with the legions. We lived for centuries in the belief that the salient quality of any emperor must be to lead his troops and to emerge victorious from the battles against barbarians and other enemies. Anything beyond that is considered a secondary virtue. This has been exacerbated by the reforms of Diocletian, for with the separation of military and civil administration, many new emperors had indeed gained military experience, but none in all the other important matters of administration. In addition, successful men from the non-military sector were more or less without any chance of ever wearing the purple."

"And then we have a heir like Gratian – very young, too young, as some say. Trained in the fine arts, a great friend of rhetoric exercises, taught by a certain excellent teacher, the respected Ausonius. Raised in orthodoxy, and that very early. He learned nothing else than the Trinitarian doctrine in his entire youth – I won't even speak of the traditional religions whose highest representative he actually is supposed to be. His lack of military experience caused two consequences – important generals ignore his orders because they don't regard the Emperor as capable of making the right decisions and Gratian himself has a strong tendency to overly rely on his military chiefs, rather than to gain experience himself and earn the acknowledgement of his troops. It also doesn't help that he invited numbers of rhetoricians and scholars to the court and regarded eloquent speeches with greater importance than military issues." Symmachus sighed again. "Not that I have any objection in principle. A little more subtlety and a little less brutality couldn't harm the empire. But the court doesn't work properly. So Rome isn't working."

"Gratian is not sure of himself?"

"What he is fully sure of is his faith. Ambrosius and Ausonius have done a great job, and this will no longer be reversible. It doesn't need to. As long as Gratian doesn't turn his orthodoxy into fanaticism and bigotry, which leads to intolerance, and as long as he doesn't abuse the state as an instrument to pursue spiritual interests, so shall the Emperor believe in whatever he wants to believe. But by your report, I understand that Gratian is on the way to make exactly that mistake."

Rheinberg looked wistfully at the increasingly wavy sea. On the horizon the coast line of Italy was already visible. He took a deep breath. "I hope he will not make it. Gratian's fickleness in these matters may also develop to our advantage. He must be subjected to the appropriate influence. While he might be sure of his faith, he might on the other side also recognize that it is not necessarily a part of his duties as a ruler to impose his faith on all his subjects. Instead, he'd serve the unity of the Empire by achieving a balance of beliefs. And when he should come to the conclusion not to give the Eastern purple to Theodosius, but to embark on the permanent government of the whole Empire – then the basis for a longer survival of the state would be established, and we might be able to turn to the real problems."

Symmachus looked questioningly at Rheinberg. "What would that be?"

"Keep the Vandals out of Africa and attack the Huns before they have approached the borders of Rome in force. I could still expand the list a bit, but I think these are the two most important points in the medium term."

The senator nodded. "It sounds as if big challenges must be overcome. And what role will play Trierarch Rheinberg in this?"

The question by the senator confronted Rheinberg with the fact that he hadn't given this scenario too much thought so far. His helplessness must have been visible, because Symmachus smiled understandingly.

"Think about it. I suspect that you'd like to bring a lot of your advanced technology in the Empire."

"Oh yes. The Empire has to solve two key problems: transportation and communication. The former can be largely solved by a fleet of steamships, not as well developed as the *Saarbrücken*, but fast, seaworthy and of great carrying capacity. And for communications, I have already some ideas."

"You need an office. Several offices. And actually, you are therefore also a victim of Diocletian's reforms, because you would need both a military as well as civilian office that would allow you to achieve all of this."

Rheinberg thought for a moment but then shook his head. "That will not be necessary. It makes no sense to repeal the reforms. It's not wrong in principle to separate civilian and military careers from each other, which conveys professionalism in both. No, I think, if it actually comes to the question of public office, it'll have to be another solution. I would seek a civilian office to make the necessary changes, if needed at all. As for the military part ... we wait and see how Becker fares against the Goths."

Symmachus nodded. "Now you think. Very wise. Waste some more effort to it."

"A high, important posting for you I would also hold as desirable and possible."

154

The senator laughed and held up his hands. "No office for me! How horrible, just the thought! Strenuous government service brings nerve-wracking obligations! No more time for the finer things of life, the cultural delights! Oh no, Rheinberg, please ask me to take an office only if you want to punish me terribly. I can imagine nothing more horrible than such a prospect! Vade retro!"

Rheinberg heard the speech of Symmachus and smiled. Not because he was mocking him, but because he knew that the senator spoke nothing but the truth.

On Symmachus he couldn't count in this regard.

24

Thessaloniki was impressive. During their ride through the city in which they were admired by the people with big eyes, the Germans could not help but stare back. What was in their time only a ruin, appeared here, as a new building, and the splendor of the city as an imperial residence was clearly visible through both the buzz and the depressing mood in the residents' faces. The Arch of Galerius was one of the first monumental building to be seen, as it was still right on the Via Egnatia. And the Imperial Palace, where they intended to meet General Flavius Victor, had not been completed until about 60 years before, begun by Emperor Galerius, who had raised Thessaloniki to the state of imperial residence. Next to it, the Hippodrome, the great race track, was visible. Becker had to restrain himself to look the citizens of the city in the eyes, because if he made a mistake, many of them would be doomed in the near future.

Theodosius would, crowned as emperor, experience one of his darkest hours in this city, tackling an uprising against him. The emperor, known for its sudden whims, would order the mass execution of 7,000 citizens in that very Hippodrome. Later, he would regret his actions, but too late. Another reason not to elevate the newly appointed general of the East to become the emperor. Nothing cast a clearer light on this ruler the historians would later describe as "the Great."

Flavius Victor, the survivor of the two eastern supreme commanders, expected them at the main entrance of the palace. The whole town was full of soldiers, the remnants of the eastern army had taken refuge here. And the faces of the soldiers showed their mood. The defeat at Adrianople still stuck in their bones. The contrast to the unit that had arrived with the Germans couldn't be greater.

After defeating the Gothic troops a few days ago, the mood was at its peak. For the Romans under Arbogast, one thing was clear – the victory was theirs in any case.

Flavius Victor seemed to be not yet convinced. Nevertheless, his greeting didn't lack in warmth. As the new arrivals had been taken care of, he asked Becker, Arbogast and some of his own lieutenants to a meeting. Becker held back for the time being, leaving the Germanic general to speak, for while he was a blank slate, Victor knew Arbogast well.

The General was aware of the fact that it would be difficult, despite all the information given, to convince Victor of their plans. The situation was complicated by someone who wasn't even present: Theodosius.

"Gratian has appointed a new supreme commander, and I can't make such decisions without having consulted with him," was therefore Victor's greatest objection.

"Gratian ordered this mission; Theodosius has to accept that just like you and me," Arbogast replied. "We learned a few days ago what a striking effect the strangers' arms can have. With their help, we can act immediately and don't have to wait years before we have trained a new army."

"In addition, Theodosius is busy. The Sarmatians threaten the border. He will be primarily concerned with it, using the border garrisons to control the advance of these warriors," Becker said.

Victor measured him with a long look. "How do you know that, Becker? The last thing I heard from Sirmium ..."

"Trust me ...the first mission Theodosius embarks upon after his appointment is the suppression of a Sarmatian attack. Then he will take years to rebuild the army of the East. He is also disturbed by the fact that Gratian will be murdered, and he has to deal with a successful usurper in the West. The Goths will never be defeated, but only pacified and included as *Foederatii* in the empire. Not as subjects but as allies with their own government."

"Foederatii?" Victor echoed with an incredulous tone. "Their own government?"

Becker nodded. "The beginning of the end of the Roman Empire."

Flavius squinted. "If you know the future so well, then tell me what is my fate?"

"No fate that would be worthwhile to report, noble Victor. You are an old man and will not play a military role in the following years. You'll spend the rest of your life with your wife, mostly in Antioch, where you will also die."

If the old officer was affected by this prophecy, he didn't show it. He even seemed to smile almost cheerfully. "Not a bad outlook," he said. "A few quiet years with my wife, to live without war."

"Would it not be much nicer to spend retirement in a safe and well-established East, instead of being busy for years to come with the changing fortunes of war? The eternal question of what would have been if Valens had listened to your advice to wait for Gratian's troops? I offer you this peace and certainty, Flavius Victor. Give me the benefit of the doubt. Ask Arbogast and the other officers about what they have experienced. Maybe this will help you to form an opinion."

The older man said nothing. He looked at Arbogast, who just nodded at him. Flavius Victor appeared to reflect on Becker's words as he rose and walked to the large windows lining the walls of the room. Becker didn't press further. There were moments for quick decisions, but sometimes issues had to be carefully considered. It didn't help if Flavius, whether driven by the orders of Gratian or persuaded by his friend Arbogast, was only half-heartedly behind the project, while Becker wanted to expose the rest of the army of the East to a certain a risk. Flavius had to be at least a bit convinced. This couldn't be accomplished overnight.

"Very well," Victor finally said. "Arbogast, I want to talk to all the officers who were there when you have defeated the Goths. And, of course, I will obey the command of the Emperor. I do not know when Theodosius arrives here, but maybe we really shouldn't wait so long."

"Do you know where the Goths are currently?" Arbogast asked.

"The convoy moves slowly toward our position. Fritigern knows that we gather here. He wants to prepare the second big victory, and if not for you, I would have barricaded myself here and let the Goths walk up and down in front of the city."

Becker frowned. "I would like, noble Victor, that one of your men runs me along the fortifications. I have to gather an accurate picture, so that I can consider setting shooting positions."

"No problem. So do you have the intention to fight the Goths with your secret weapons when they approach Thessaloniki?"

"Only if they attack in great strength and massed. This requires an important prerequisite."

Victor made a sour face. "I can guess what you ask of me. But speak!"

"You have to offer the Goths battle before the gates of the city. We need to provoke them as best we can. Scornful speeches and typical Roman arrogance would be something fine. The Goths have to be so bloodthirsty to run toward your men and their allies with them. They will only do so if they see that their enemies leave the protective walls of the city. Then we have to make an exact series of commands, and it must be clear that your most reliable officers do the right thing at the right time so that we do not fire on Romans, but only on the Goths."

Victor snorted. "Reliable officers. My troops almost exclusively consist of officers."

Becker smiled. "So much the better. When the signal is given, we open the gates of the city and the troops will retreat there. This will make the Goths even more ambitious because they think they have now easy game. And then we can welcome them – our way."

Victor was still not convinced. "You promise me a comprehensive victory, as in your fight a few days ago?"

"I promise nothing, there are too many things that can go wrong. Who knows if Fritigern won't give credence to the survivors of our battle and doesn't fall for our maneuver? But should he fall into our trap, then we will spread great terror among the Gothic troops. We will not quench all – there are too many. But we will break their morale and might stop their pilfering of Greece and the East. And we will be able to negotiate with them."

Becker wondered by himself how naturally this "we" escaped his lips. And at least it didn't seem to offend Arbogast. If Flavius felt differently, he gave no sign.

"Negotiations would be nice. Goths as new subjects. At least allies."

"If they are to agree, we must first break their will and destroy their morale," Arbogast confirmed. "Becker's plan has its risks, but he can succeed."

"Well," murmured Victor. "But if that is so, dear Becker, how can we use your few men in the long term? Sometimes one will die or leave your services, whether he wants to or not. Also, I have my doubts that much of your magical ammunition will remain after such a battle. What awaits us for the time after that?"

This question was a clear indicator for the intelligence of the officer. Becker hadn't expected it, but he'd discussed the issue at length with Rheinberg, and he decided to be as open as possible. "It will be necessary to teach you some of the technological achievements that we have mastered," Becker said. "Many are not directly transferable to the empire, but we can offer improvements that can be adopted with some effort – and certainly a few failures – by your craftsmen. I think that we will provide for an appropriate agreement to give you these technical achievements, and the Roman Empire won't become invincible through them. But we wouldn't experience the rapid collapse in the West as we know it."

Victor nodded. "I can understand that, and I'm very excited about these ideas."

"But there are some other problems that cannot be solved with a new craft alone. Economic problems, religious disputes, public budgets, the corruption in the administration. These are issues where we may be able to give some advice, but there will still be plenty of opportunities to make mistakes. Ultimately, it will depend on whether those in the charge of the Empire will succeed in gaining the right insights and to act appropriately or not."

Victor pressed his lips, exchanged a look with Arbogast, who had had this discussion with Becker several times during their journey here. "I suppose your leader speaks about these things in court."

"I suppose he did that, I'm not sure if he is still with Gratian. Incidentally, this is one of the problems we have to solve: communication."

The military chief inclined his head in agreement. "This is a point at which I would like to agree with you unconditionally. Let us discuss the details of the plan to be implemented against the Goths further once you have an overview of the defenses of the city. I suspect this will be quite important for your planning."

"So it is. Thank you."

"And you, Arbogast, convene a meeting of your officers with mine. I want to know exactly how this fight had been conducted a few days ago, in all the details. I have a feeling that I still cannot fathom correctly the power of these miraculous weapons."

"It shall be done, Victor. How is your injury? The aliens have a medicus with them, who has interesting abilities and medicines. He has done wonders with my own injuries."

Victor waved. "I'm all right. No miracle was needed to recover."

When the three men left the room, Becker had the feeling that Flavius Victor was no threat or danger for the time being. But he would have to convince the old general and couldn't rest forever on the praise that Arbogast had proffered.

As to the coming battle, he looked forward to it with terror.

25

"Go to the Legion! Visits to foreign countries! Meet exotic peoples," Simodes groaned.

"And break their skulls!" Volkert added. Both men were at the end of their strength, lay on their simple beds and looked at the starry sky. The weather had become quite chilly and the campfire gave little heat. Every now and then, when one of the soldiers threw on a piece of wood, and the flames regained some strength, something like a short heat wave rushed over them, fast replaced by the cold of the early winter.

"Cursed be Theodosius, new hero of our great Emperor Gratian," Simodes muttered bitterly and looked suspiciously at the bone in his right hand, on which yesterday enough meat for an evening meal had hung. Today he could not do much more than nibble the rest and suck the marrow.

Volkert didn't contradict his comrade. On their way to Noricum the message came: All recruits had to go to an assembly place, where the new commander of the East had to put their skills to the test. The Sarmatians, a wild mountain people, threatened the borders of the empire, and the garrisons had asked for help. And now everyone marched to Illyricum, where Theodosius was waiting with troops Gratian had left him. Ready to take advantage of the crushing defeat of Valens, the Sarmatians threatened Pannonia, the direct gateway to both the West and the East of the Empire. It would be Theodosius' first test, and as Volkert knew from his history, he would be victorious. After that, Gratian would appoint him Augustus, if Becker wasn't able to forestall this by a convincing action in the East – and if Rheinberg hadn't convinced the young emperor to keep control of the whole empire in his hands.

All this had nothing to do with him. His time on the *Saarbrücken*, his love for Julia ... everything appeared to him in a strange cloud and far away. Almost surprised, he observed himself how he began to put up better and better with his situation. He laughed at the jokes of Simodes, swore like the other legionaries, identified officers with whom one could get along and those who were bad grinders. He came along better and better with his equipment and began more and more to understand the sword and the spear. His sandals and boots fit him, the helmet no longer ached, and he knew how he had to pack the bundle in order to wear it with reasonable comfort on his back. He felt like he enjoyed the small, good things more and more, and the bad things annoyed him less and less. He behaved in such a way that he came through well, and he took care of his surroundings in a way that no one had a reason to actively dislike him. His Latin was better, although consistently vulgar, and the same was true of his Greek, which was supplemented by Simodes through numerous descriptions and vocabulary that Volkert wouldn't have found in any textbook.

Volkert had been initially frightened by this development, but this feeling staled. In the end, he realized how fatalism had overcome him, and he was drifting into acceptance, which was particularly easy in the Legion as in every army: For whoever didn't have to think, it was enough to obey blindly, to submit to the routine, and to simply do only what was expected of one. Volkert remembered a different motivation when he had volunteered to an officer's career, a desire to lead men and to accept responsibility. Here, lying in the mud of northern Italy, with a bad-tempered Simodes at his side, this increasingly seemed like a very distant ideal. Maybe it was a necessary and wholesome repression of feelings that helped him to endure his new life better; maybe it was only the deep fatigue engulfing body and spirit that had led to it. Maybe he would think and feel differently if he had only slept in a real bed and ate decently, a prospect that in the near future would hardly be achievable.

"Sarmatians," Simodes whispered in the night sky. "What are those guys?"

"People with sharp blades that they sink joyfully in Roman legionaries," said Volkert.

"And you think we will be victorious?"

Volkert had allowed himself to deliver a very confident prediction of the course of the war based on his historical foreknowledge. "Oh yes, Rome will be victorious. But whether we ourselves shall be victorious, I don't know. I don't believe that the attackers will be deflected by good words; in fact, there will be fights, and blood will flow. And while I'm very sure that Theodosius will lead the Roman Empire to victory, there also will be almost certainly dead Roman legionaries on the way."

In moments like this the ensign understood what a difference it made to read historical treatises in books and to philosophize about those generals and the advantages of strategy here and there, or, instead, to witness these campaigns themselves. Because then one was quickly confronted with the realization that glorious victories were always fought on the backs of dead soldiers who were also part of the winning side. This contrast forced Volkert to think and when the eyes of his audience shone while he talked of the approaching victory, he wasn't capable of showing the same confidence like them. Instead, he saw himself and Simodes lying in their own blood on the battlefield, while behind them the surviving legionaries cheered the glorious Theodosius.

That was an image he could not scare away from his thoughts even with the greatest effort. Simodes seemed to detect his friend's inner conflict, because he had repeatedly assured him that he'd take "good care of him" during the battle. This sign of sincere friendship touched Volkert and he had thanked the Greek, but the affection of the man hadn't been of great comfort. The fears he carried developed into a jumble of negative feelings, such as wandering a maze from which one couldn't escape anymore.

When Volkert finally stretched himself and felt the cold sneak out of the hard ground into his bones, he knew he would have a short night with little sleep, followed by a long day with many forced marches.

This prospect left him cold as well. The murmur of the comrades was like a lullaby, and then Thomas Volkert slept.

26

"I cannot allow him to serve. But I have to."

This was the third time that Rheinberg had said this sentence. Dahms, Neumann and Joergensen exchanged silent glances. The news of the mutiny, their victims, and the bloody crackdown had left visible traces in the young commander's demeanor. He upheld a disciplined attitude, as was expected of him, but above all, the doctor realized how much was working inside Rheinberg.

"They have to be executed, the whole pack," Dahms insisted. He spoke the words in complete calmness, without ever raising his voice, but his anger and disgust made this controlled reaction particularly haunting. "A court martial, right here, right now, and then legal execution. I want a proper proceeding, without any doubt. But the verdict is clear according to Roman as well as German law. We are here in full compliance and shouldn't shy from it."

Rheinberg looked at Dahms and just as he had repeated one sentence several times, he also reiterated shaking his head.

"Mr. Chief Engineer, I can understand your anger very well. And we had other circumstances, I would have no hesitation to exactly go the way you have just mapped out. But that doesn't work here and now. The promise wasn't only tactically, it was meant to be. It has to be real, and we have to be true to our word."

"Why?" No reproach in Dahms' voice, not even genuine curiosity, only self-control. Rheinberg sighed.

"Because we are here alone, Dahms. Because there is only a finite number of us, us travelers in time. Because we carry unique knowledge within us, each one of us. Because we cannot afford to waste this knowledge by shooting it. Because we are so few and yet all that is left to us from home. This cannot be dismissed, Dahms. When I execute all the men, then their skills are missing one day.

In regard to the machines, in our conversations over a beer, in our memories, and ... just everything. They will be missed, Dahms, very bitterly indeed."

The haunting words of Rheinberg seemed to have their effect on the engineer. He pressed his lips together, seemed almost reluctantly want to understand what he was told, gained a certain amount of insight but could not seal the deal.

"We cannot do that," Rheinberg affirmed. "But we cannot pretend as if nothing happened either. It's fucking crap that von Klasewitz and Tennberg are gone. On them, Dahms, I would've made an example. Von Klasewitz would have jumped over the blade, and Tennberg I would have demoted to a sailor. But ... but so ..."

"I understand well that we cannot just shoot the mutineers," Neumann said. "The Romans have also put to death only a few legionaries, who had been in the employ of Petronius. The imprisoned monks are punished, but out of consideration for the nation's soul, Renna has dispensed executions. It is not as if he wants to react particularly bloodthirsty, and therefore maybe we shouldn't either."

Rheinberg looked gratefully at Neumann. "Then we do it like this: All men are demoted to sailors and are placed on probation for an extended period of time. Whoever behaves decently and does his duty, may be promoted again or is allowed to resign from duty after three years. Whoever gives even the slightest cause for censure, has forfeited his life. I'm going to the officers and non-commissioned officers to instruct them to keep the guys under permanent scrutiny."

"That'll work," Joergensen mused. "The men will be grateful to get a second chance and take good care of their conduct. They know that their life is hanging by a thread. I am committed to make it so. I'll commit myself to the task of monitoring the delinquents particularly diligent."

"Then I charge you to assess the probation," Rheinberg prodded immediately. "I put it in your hands. Have I already told you that you are the new first officer?"

Joergensen grinned like a little boy.

"And I promote you to Lieutenant Commander. We'll make a fine ceremony of it. As a lieutenant, I really cannot give you that much responsibility."

Joergensen grin grew wider.

Rheinberg gaze wandered back to Dahms.

"Are you coming along with this? Some of the mutineers are in your engine room."

"If you command ..."

"No," Rheinberg interrupted him immediately. "I ask you: Do you come along? With your heart? Will you give my decision a chance, Dahms? This is important, we need to jointly represent our decisions before the crew. We have to be convincing."

He looked Dahms straight in the eye. The man avoided his glance for a second, but it wasn't a test of strength, but rather a search for mutual understanding. Finally, the engineer nodded. Briskly, but without further hesitation.

Rheinberg felt relief. He could not afford any new disturbance in his command.

"Then let's talk about other issues that are pending as well. Yes, you've heard the news I brought from Sirmium. We cannot accomplish much here, and I have decided to leave Ravenna and to make sail toward Thessaloniki so that we can stay closer to Becker. I'm now very confident that we are no longer perceived as an immediate threat. Renna is familiar to us; we'll take Africanus along as a liaison officer. Furthermore, we will take another ten Roman sailors who are to serve on the *Saarbrücken* – and therefore, new training needs are ahead of us."

"When they are young, that is no problem," Dahms said. "Once they overcome their fears, they will be ready to digest knowledge. Make sure that they are young guys with some experience on sea, then we'll get along well enough. We need to begin anyway, since we have to compensate for losses already."

"So it is. Gratian has invested a certain confidence in us, and we don't want to squander that trust. It now depends a lot on whether we get the Gothic problem under control. I have exhausted my share of diplomacy and golden speeches until further notice. Now it's Becker's turn, and we'll see where we can still help him, even if the *Saarbrücken* is only used as a floating hospital. Speaking of which ... we definitely need more medical staff." Rheinberg cast a meaningful glance at Neumann.

"I know, and I have already an idea. Ultimately, we'll have to transfer a lot of knowledge if we want to bring some of our Roman friends in. I've been out on a long conversation with Renna, and he hasn't only agreed to send me some of the local doctors for training – preferably those that are still willing to actually learn something – but he found my idea of a medical academy quite interesting."

"An academy? Do you want to become a professor?" Joergensen asked with a smile.

"Each of us will become a teacher," Rheinberg said. "And the idea regarding an academy is excellent – and not only for the medical field."

"But this requires some quiet time for preparation," Neumann remarked. "We need to establish some form of a teaching curriculum, and some relief from normal duty for the most knowledgeable among us. It doesn't look feasible currently."

"Not yet, true. I also fear that we will have to improvise. For me, however, it is of central importance that we begin preparations as early as possible so that we don't lose too much time once the opportunity arises. We have to start somehow."

"Then I have a free hand to take appropriate action?" Neumann wanted to make sure.

"You have, and much more: Don't just think of your area of expertise, but also about other knowledge that we have on board. It's clear for us in theory, but we need a summary of all areas of expertise in our crew, something which goes beyond formal certificates. Each station chief should write up an assessment of his crew members, their skills, any knowledge they have acquired over time, even beyond the diplomas or letters. I also want to know whom can be reasonably expected to do a good job in teaching someone. We have to gain a comprehensive overview. Neumann, I give you the ultimate responsibility for this activity. Report as soon as you have assembled the information."

The doctor took the order without visible reaction. Rheinberg knew this task was in very good hands.

"I've spoken with Renna on some other issues, especially in terms of our collaboration with local craftsmen," the captain continued, "and we have a long-term approach toward a major project. A dry dock."

Dahms woke up again. "This is really needed, Captain. The Mediterranean is poison for our *Saarbrücken*. We eventually need to paint the hull new, clean everything and tackle the rust ... The rust worries me. We always need a dry dock. We need workers and indeed many – to paint and to pump out the water the good old way, with buckets."

"But you know who we talk about when we ask the Romans for a workforce ..." Neumann said vaguely.

"Yes, we are talking about slaves," Rheinberg said. "Of this I'm quite aware. I'm not exactly thrilled about it. But we can influence things only gradually. To ask the Roman Emperor to abolish slavery is totally absurd at this point. But if we should actually succeed in introducing certain production methods and techniques in Rome, things will be done without slaves sooner or later anyway. We can make a first step by making sure that the slaves who work for us are all decently cared for and not subjected to unnecessarily harsh treatment. But we need many hands. No doubt about it."

"We could, of course, and for the time being, do without a dry dock and when an overhaul is necessary move to the Jade Bay in the North and let the *Saarbrücken* fall dry at low tide," Joergensen said.

"Oh yes," Rheinberg said. "There's only one small problem: At this time the Jade Bay doesn't exist."

"Oh," the newly crowned first officer said.

"There was always a strong tidal change at the height of Le Havre," Dahms said thoughtfully. "It should be the same nowadays."

"We can keep the strategy as a fallback safely in mind. But I would prefer for the cruiser to establish a solid base around which we build a ring of workshops, in which we inject our technology, manufacture spare parts, simple tools, and process raw material. A kind of small-scale industry, but focused on keeping the cruiser alive as long as possible," said Rheinberg.

The vision seemed to endear Dahms especially, because his eyes lit up.

"We will make final decisions later, but you, Mr. Engineer, are our man for this project. Let's look at what the Romans can accomplish, what they can learn, and where we may reach our limits. Keep this in mind: To save the Roman Empire and to renew it, we need some technical breakthroughs quite soon. I would like you to start thinking about how we can produce steam engines for deep sea-going ships with local resources, probably made of bronze. Consider powder production, think about cannons and muskets, ideally something more advanced than those of the old mercenary-armies. There are a lot of challenges. We have to restore the absolute supremacy of Rome over the Mediterranean to foreclose the attack of the Vandals in North Africa. And we must be active in the East."

"In the East?"

"We need to catch the Huns before they even come into the vicinity of Rome. I mean the main body of the Hunnic expansion. So far, we've seen only the advance party. It will take a few years until Attila appears. I would prefer that he doesn't appear at all and that we solve the problem beyond the Roman frontiers."

"You think far ahead," Joergensen muttered.

"Maybe," Rheinberg replied. "But if we do it right, Rome will still be safe even once we don't exist anymore. And I have the feeling that we will establish families here, or am I completely wrong?"

He expected and received no rebuttal. Nobody mentioned Volkert. As Rheinberg had learned of his desertion, he had been beside himself for a moment. It didn't occur to him that "starting a family" had been apparently what the ensign had in mind.

"Then that would be clear. Tomorrow I'd like the ship to be ready to set sail. Renna has promised selected Roman sailors for tomorrow as well. We shouldn't waste any time."

170

27

Godegisel looked at Agiwulf. He wished he could say the man would meet his gaze, but it was difficult to be sure. Agiwulf, an otherwise slender, almost thin warrior whose tailor-made skins were extremely rough even for a Goth and hung loosely around his bones, possessed a martial face. One eye was completely lacking, and Agiwulf considered it not necessary to cover the deep, scarred cave. The other eye was shaking and looked permanently in different directions, even if the man's face was turned to the nobleman. Agiwulf was considered completely nuts, at least since he had gotten a good smash on the head in a fight against the advancing Huns several times. He often spoke incoherently, drooling while eating and drinking like a pig, and ran around at night, instead of sleeping, "guarding" the Gothic camp and his people against the "dark spirits" haunting him since. The only reason he had not been released from his suffering was probably the fact that he was absolutely fearless in battle, always rode in the front line, knew exactly where and how he had to carry his sword, and was able to understand and execute commands. Since no one had to feed him, and he was able to defecate without assistance, everyone had come to terms with his condition.

Godegisel looked from Agiwulf to the other men. Some looked as deranged as the one-eyed, others held up better, but what all had in common was that they were considered nuts among the Goths. They were outcasts, all with no family or relatives, or their existence denied by them. No one had a wife or children, at least none that anyone knew. The mighty Bilimer, who seemed to consist only of giant rolls of fat and who wheezed with every movement, had probably never had a woman in his life. He was considered retarded, hardly more than a child, but he possessed an almost overwhelming physical power, and he lacked any understanding of risk or his own vulnerability. Ervig had lost his family during the trek to Rome and was almost broken with grief about it. The muscular warrior wore a simple tunic despite the cold, led an ascetic life, ate only the bare minimum, and didn't talk to anyone. In battle, he was ice cold precision. It was as if seeking death and to take as many as possible with him he thought were responsible for the end of his family. And there was Rechiar, the rider, who seemed to be grown together with his horse, even more than the most fanatical Hun. He lived on his horse, ate and slept there, and there he would beget children, if a woman should ever have come to accept the overgrown, humped shape of his body. He spoke with the horses, more than other horsemen, as if they had a higher intelligence and insight than human beings. Rechiar was educated, could read and write, and when he read from the scripture to his animal, he often found other listeners to his recitation, completely ignored by him. There were people in the camp who considered him a saint, but most considered the twisted, ugly shape as crazy, and that almost automatically qualified him for Godegisel's troop. Rechiar's belief that his life was inviolable so long as he stayed on horseback made him sufficiently fearless and therefore the ideal candidate for this mission.

"You follow my orders. You keep your eyes open. You fight when I say and ran when I say. We need to learn more, and we must not be distracted. Is that clear?"

There were different reactions. Those whose minds were still the clearest and who did not hesitate to utter something once they wanted to, hummed affirmatively. Some others nodded and grinned. Agiwulf drooled. Bilimer bit into an apple. Godegisel deemed that being his consent.

He didn't have much choice.

He moved his horse toward himself, ready to climb it. Each of his men was mounted, but they would not move forward too quickly. Bilimer had an animal that was able to carry him, but it was a bulky, cumbersome horse that resembled its owner in amazing ways. It could move the fat man around, but speed was limited.

Godegisel had to accept that; he was indeed in a hurry but was also under pressure to be successful. Would he return without important information, he was better to stay away from the Gothic camp. Care was more important to him than hurry and Bilimer was not only fearless and strong, he also had excellent eyes. Godegisel didn't want to do without him.

They took their time before they had made their way. They turned their horses toward Thessaloniki, because everyone assumed that the strange powerful reinforcement would go there as it was the rallying point of the rest of the army. To obtain information about the demons was thus most likely to occur in the provincial capital. On the occasion, Godegisel and his men also would form the vanguard of the Gothic main army, which with much slower speed was also to be moved to the city because Fritigern still had the intention to offer battle there. Godegisel didn't expect that the Roman city was impregnable. But the noblemen of the different peoples and tribes grumbled, and the judge was forced to act.

The trip to reach the city would take days for Godegisel's small group. Nevertheless, it was quite possible that they met scouts or patrols of the Romans on the way. They had therefore begun to camouflage the horses, created Roman bridles, made themselves out like rundown merchants. The fact that they had horses made them rich men, but Godegisel wanted to give the impression that this was only the reflection of former prosperity, that they were victims of this war and the Gothic looting. Godegisel himself and Rechiar spoke reasonably good Greek and thought themselves capable of impersonating traders. The nobleman hoped any real test of their cover story would be unnecessary. He would prefer, if possible, to come close to the vicinity of the city without notice.

What to do then would depend on the situation. Godegisel had indeed bothered to think about that multiple times, but concocted no plan. Breaking into the city would probably be the most promising approach, and there were still refugees rushing from anywhere behind the city walls, so it might even succeed to mingle with them once the situation was favorable. Otherwise, he had no choice but to lay in wait and hope that the demons appeared and gave their skills away in public, so that the Gothic scouts would be able to report about it.

Godegisel established himself to expect a tedious and potentially very frustrating mission.

28

Becker was expecting a long and frustrating discussion, but he was pleasantly surprised. As Flavius Victor summoned him, in the General's study he also found Arbogast and some other officers of the Roman army present. He himself was accompanied by von Geeren, although his deputy was still sweating every night on Latin and Greek lessons. At the request of the Romans, Becker had grazed the city for reasonably talented teachers and presented an illustrious group of about 20 men who apparently earned their money with school hours. One Becker had reserved for the officers and the rest released to the troops, which led to almost sheer terror for some school dropouts. When they reassembled to learn languages, those who had prematurely left school first learned the most crude curses to express their feelings properly. But Becker had been merciless. Should they work together with the Romans in future battles effectively, a minimum level of understanding was necessary, and no one knew in what kind of situation some of his soldiers would find themselves. Two hours of language lessons per day he actually regarded as too little, but there was no room for more now.

In recent days, the captain had come to know the fortifications of Thessaloniki quite well, and the Romans had hidden nothing from him. The almost square city, originally built mostly in semi-circular terraces on a slope and then enclosed by a sturdy wall system, was dominated by a magnificent acropolis, in which the headquarters of the armed forces laid in a fortress. Nine gates led outside the city, and the fortifications had been partially built in the Macedonian period but were extensively renovated in recent years. In the middle of the bulwarks was the artificial harbor established by Constantine the Great, with its shipyards and a squadron of the Navy. Then there was one second port outside the fortifications as well as a deep bay where ships could also anchor. Thessaloniki's fame was closely related to its success as a commercial hub.

Once the Romans realized that he wasn't interested in escape routes and catacombs but only in positions from which machine guns and assault rifles would have an optimal range to keep the battlefield under control, the Roman leaders had been even more relaxed. Becker also marched back and forth outside the city walls, climbed endless stairs, walked through narrow corridors and threw countless views from balustrades and towers. Von Geeren as well as some of the sergeants had helped him, and in the evening they had compared their findings and assessments carefully, looked at plans provided by the Romans followed by their own drawings and calculations made. Ultimately, an increasingly clear picture had emerged, and they had come to the agreement that the plain to the west of the city would be the ideal battlefield for their plans. Finally, they approached Victor with their findings and had begun to develop a plan – the approach of the Goths to enter at the plain had to be seemingly free and easy. The remains of the Roman field army had to present themselves to assault, and the enemy would run directly into a fiery cauldron. They had only one chance for the execution of this trap and that essentially for two reasons: The Goths wouldn't be fooled for a second time, and the German would, after this battle, simply lack the ammunition for a repetition. The main weakness of the Germans made itself painfully noticeable in Becker's calculations: All their sophisticated weapons and corresponding tactics availed to nothing if they had no more cartridges left. And to fight with fixed bayonets and sabers drawn certainly held a romantic notion for some, but every shrewd swordsman of this time would without any doubt make short work of the Germans.

He had already discussed with von Geeren the need for all men to undergo an intensive training with the Roman sword and make this the future standard. Even their own officer's sabers were only a poor substitute. Depending on how long they had to wait for the Goths coming, they could start with such a training program soon. Becker had smiled at the thought of how gruff Roman instructors would give the strangers a decent weapons drill. But the idea was good – it would help to alleviate both arrogance as well as superstitious fears.

But that needed further consideration. Flavius Victor would announce his final decision on the plan drawn up by Becker soon. Becker hoped fervently that the General wasn't one of those officers who compulsively "improved" good plans with their own proposals just to prove that they really earned their higher rank. This had already turned many good concepts into disasters, and they couldn't risk that this time.

"Becker, come in!" Victor greeted him in a remarkably good mood. Due to the many meetings lately, some of the formality had faded. Victor had at least recognized that Becker wasn't a demon, but a soldier – a quite strange soldier of quite strange appearance, but these were quite strange times anyway ...

"You are ready, sir?"

"Yes, we have come to a decision. Here, we should sit down."

Becker reined his curiosity and took place as prompted. He tried to read in Arbogast's face, but the demeanor of the old general gave no hint away.

"I will make this brief. We have decided, after careful consideration, to approve of your plans."

Becker controlled a relieved sigh that wanted to slip away. He allowed himself a pleased smile.

"I admit," Victor continued, "that our decision has to do with the fact that the Goths now evidently seem to plan an assault on this city and have increased their marching speed. Our scouts believe that they will be here in a week. They obviously seek a battle before winter comes, and inventories of Thessaloniki would also help them to survive the cold season very well."

Becker nodded. No real news, but that the Goths now apparently acted decisively had apparently been important for Victor's decision.

"I will coordinate the whole operation, but I expect that you and Arbogast will do the actual work. If you require my authority, then you can make use of it, but I think my utter inexperience is likely to be more of a hindrance to proper execution."

Victor's reputation increased in Becker's eyes by a few percentage points, and as did his relief. He exchanged a quick glance with Arbogast, who nodded measuredly.

Flavius Victor's statement was of course an understatement. He had listened not only to the exact descriptions of the first battle against the Goths, Becker's men also had given him a demonstration of what one could achieve with a rifle, a machine gun and a hand grenade. The old military chief had been visibly impressed and had no doubt sufficient imagination to realize what these weapons could do with a massed bulk of Goths and had done so already.

"When shall we start the preparations?" Becker asked.

"Immediately. We begin immediately," was the expected answer. "If everything is supposed to work, we must train rigorously, especially the ..."

"Melting away," Becker helped with a half smile.

"Melting away in front of the Gothic attack in order for your people not to shoot our men."

"Then let's not waste time. May I make a suggestion?"

"Please do!"

"We have to assume that the fleeing Goths have reported our first battle. It also could be assumed that we will soon have to do with an increased number of Gothic scouts. It would be very nice if Fritigern would be informed about as little as possible in regard to the nature of our maneuvers. I want to prevent that they add one to one and then our plan suddenly evaporates."

"So we strengthen our own patrols and secure possible observation points," concluded Victor. "A good suggestion. I will immediately give the appropriate instructions." He rose somewhat slowly and nodded. "Call on me anytime you have something else in your mind. I've just laid the fate of this city into your hands, Becker."

The captain bowed. In reality – and he was painfully aware of it – the fate of the Roman Empire laid in his hands.

When he left the room and von Geeren spoke to him because of his scowl, Becker only grumbled, "Remind me to kick Rheinberg's ass at the next opportunity."

178

Von Geeren didn't muster more than a helpless "Yes, sir!" as a reply.

How fortunate that this answer was always right.

29

The attack came shortly before dawn. How it could have happened that this group of barbarians had succeeded in infiltrating the Roman heartland so far was incomprehensible to everyone, but not many thoughts were lost on the problem. For days they had marched toward the collection point, but they were still a good distance away from the frontier garrisons. The Sarmatians – or to what tribe the attackers actually belonged – probably infiltrated in small groups across the border and had, perhaps with the help of a knowledgeable local ally, reassembled somewhere previously agreed.

And then they had got in the way a column of Roman recruits. Not even 400 legionaries, not even a cohort led by two centurions, both veterans, sure, but …

At least the guards had been attentive. Their shouts tore Volkert and his comrades from the too-short sleep and the roaring NCOs got them on their feet. They knew immediately that this wasn't a frivolous exercise, because in the eyes of the officers the fear of having to fight with a bunch of untrained recruits against a resolute Barbarian battle group was clearly visible.

"Formation! Formation!" Lucius Latinus shouted. "Faster, you fools, or do you want to be slaughtered!"

Hectic activity ensued. Volkert grabbed the sword, spear and shield, and then came the din of battle to their ears and the recruits had to recognize that Latinus had sent the veterans of the cohort, so far used to guard the unreliable draftees, forward in order to buy time – time that was necessary to bring the startled recruits in formation and to give them a slight chance of survival.

Latinus, Volkert recognized, now drunk with adrenaline, was in fact much more than just an annoying training officer. And he was extremely grateful for that.

Moments later, Volkert stood side by side with Simodes in a hastily compiled phalanx. He found himself right in the second row, and the stench of fearful perspiration came from the ranks of men shivering in the morning cold, the smell almost deafening all other senses.

"Shields! Front!" Latinus roared. The first row raised its shields right in front of the body. "Second row! Spears!"

Volkert felt that he reacted like an automaton. The spears of the second row drooped forward, sideways to the front men to meet the onrushing enemy. He could make out the attackers now, wild fellows with long beards, brandishing large battle axes.

"Formation! No one falls back!" the command of the centurion came. He stood, seemingly unfazed by the onslaught of the barbarians, right in front of his hastily erected unit and paid more attention to their discipline than to the deadly mob that approached him.

The barbarians were firing stones with hand loops. The bullets pattered against the shields of the first row.

"The cohort steps forward! One step!"

Like machines, passed through the endless drills, forced by inevitability and the oppressive narrowness of the formation, the recruits made a step forward.

The ground seemed to tremble as the approaching barbarians struck up a great howl. Some brandished the severed heads of the veterans who had bought them time. Volkert felt bad, but then a sudden, cold determination filled him.

"The cohort steps forward! One step!"

Again, the body of the soldiers lurched forward.

"The cohort remains in formation!"

The first barbarians bounced noisily against the phalanx, threw themselves against the outstretched spears, were impaled, others hacked with axes on the recruits, broke the front row. Blood everywhere, screams, falling bodies, the pungent smell of voiding bladders and a deafening noise of cracking bones and the clash of armor.

Volkert screamed and screamed.

"The cohort keeps formation!" the absolutely soulless, cold voice of Latinus pitched through the chaos. "Second row! Shield and sword! Third row! Spears!"

Again, the drill took the conscious control, again Volkert saw his sword moving itself and the tip of the blade drove directly under the rib cage into the body of an attacker, exactly, smoothly, just as they had learned it. A hoarse gurgling sound came from the open mouth of the man, as he breathed his last and fell heavily to the ground. Volkert tried to free his sword from the falling body, saw a shadow rushing an ax on him. Volkert let go of the sword, lifted the shield, knowing that he was too slow, then someone drove a blade into the arm of the axeman, severed bones and tendons, leaving a fountain of blood raining down on him.

Simodes stepped at his side, and then there were two spears from the third row, and the pierced man slumped to the ground. Volkert snatched up his sword, the handle slippery in his bloodied hand.

"The cohort keeps formation." Latinus' command thrust through his momentary dizziness. Volkert saw the centurion severing a barbarian's throat with indifferent composure before he turned back, keeping his recruits in mind. "The cohort marches forward! One step!"

He opened his mouth for another command and the gurgling was only heard at the very front, where Volkert stood. The spear that pierced the neck of the centurion reappeared, colored red, on the other side, tore the skull almost from the neck. Latinus seemed to look directly into the eyes of Volkert, almost regretfully, to plead forgiveness that he let them down in this hour of need. Then the red plume of his helmet fell to the ground.

Volkert looked frantically for the second centurion, but he was nowhere to be seen. Cries of horror went through the recruits. The lines were about to break. Fear gripped the inexperienced warriors, and the effect of the lack of leadership threatened to undermine the iron discipline. Glances were thrown over the shoulders, and everywhere you looked, recruits were in a retreating battle.

Volkert didn't have to be a veteran to recognize the signs of impending disaster. A few more moments and the lines of the legionaries would crumble like dry bread and a hopeless flight would be the beginning of a senseless massacre. Volkert pressed his lips on each other, ran forward, left the column, ignored the astonished exclamations of Simodes.

He knelt beside the dead body of the centurion, grabbed his helmet. Volkert's head would be almost completely covered by the large device, but that was just well.

Volkert knew he had *the* voice. His instructor in Mürwik had certified that, and they had given him enough opportunity to use it. But it was one thing to have the voice. To fill it with authority, that was something else.

He took a deep breath, stretched his body, raised his sword.

Behind him, the ranks broke.

Behind him, rampant panic emerged.

It was now or never.

"Cohort in formation!" he roared with fervor across the battlefield. "Cohort in formation!"

Heads were flying around, pairs of eyes fixed the red plume, ears heard the usual command – the roaring, unmistakable voice, and they felt the authority behind it, allowing no questions and no refusal.

A wave ran through the lines of the Romans. Where the first had turned around, the ranks closed again. Eyes turned forward. Shields went up.

Volkert's sword fell into the thorax of an onrushing Sarmatian and with a movement that looked contemptuously, he wiped the dying man aside.

"The cohort steps forward! One step!"

Groaning, struggling, the recruits made the step forward, and with lifted spears and swords they marched over the prostrate bodies of friend and foe alike.

"Third row! Close ranks! Fourth row, fifth row! Regroup!"

Lost legionaries got a new partner to fight at their sides as the soldiers of the third row closed the gaps in the former second. Still half incredulous, Volkert observed that the endless drills and ruthless disciplining now seemed to be working. A sudden, wild joy came over him. It worked indeed! He had averted the worst of all disasters!

It was absolutely incredible.

The onslaught of attackers faded, but still a few dozen run with fierce determination toward them.

"The cohort steps forward! Two steps! Three! Four! One! Two ..."

Volkert's voice tore all of them along. With hard steps, the phalanx moved toward the barbarians.

"Rome! Rooooooome!" Volkert yelled wildly. His sword flashed high. The phalanx fell into a rut, the spears soared, the blades cut attackers like fillets. The wild cries of the barbarians turned more and more into a howl of rage and fear and everyone felt it: The enemy was broken!

Another five minutes passed before the first attacker turned away from the battle and retreated. Involuntarily, Volkert felt the urge to rush behind the fleeing, and he was not the only one, but then he composed himself, kept a cool head. No squander of the victory.

"The cohort remains in formation! The cohort holds!" His command cut through the ebbing din of battle. As ordered the men came to a halt, breathing heavy, covered with blood. Some sank trembling arms to be subsequently rebuked by a decurion, others stared after the running barbarians who escaped into the misty darkness.

Euphoria, elation, pride. The adrenaline that had whipped up Volkert subsided. He looked at the ground, looking straight into the face of a dead assailant, a man – no, a boy, maybe 16 years of age – with wide eyes and a bloody, mangled torso.

Volkert vomited, writhed over the body of the boy. Someone was holding his shoulder, and no decurion yelled at him, no one said anything.

They had won.

The realization of the passed ordeal came slowly into the consciousness of all. When they returned in the nearly devastated camp, Volkert forced them to stay in formation. He strode among the exhausted and dirty men and nodded at them. Then he looked for someone he could return command to, found an unbelieving decurion, who looked at him with a certain gratitude, and took off the helmet of Latinus.

He was too big for him, in spite of everything.

Not a word, not one. But when the decurion turned away to organize the reconstruction of the camp – an immediate departure was now inconceivable – Volkert saw pride in the faces of many recruits, even among those who, like him, have been pressed into the service. But Volkert also recognized, probably more aware than many of the others who were still drunk with victory, the price they had paid for this triumph. The wounded were brought together, at least those who had a chance of recovery. Comrades helped comrades to dress the injuries. Then Volkert saw with horror as a decurion lowered his sword into the chest of a legionary, who had been lying screaming and coughing on the ground, his hands clenched in front of the bulging intestines from his sliced abdomen. His face was motionless as carved in stone, and Volkert did not know how often he had already provided this last service. Again the sword of the man in front jerked, as he marched over the small battlefield, accompanied by some of the surviving veterans and relieving the seriously injured, whether Roman or barbarian, with fast, targeted strikes from their suffering. This was a cold efficiency, like the battle itself, and again Volkert felt weak with dark clouds circling before his eyes.

The other recruits had now noticed the gruesome spectacle, held in what they do, and many realized that these men relieved them of a work, at least this one time, they themselves would be required to do in the future. Volkert had to think how he would have to kill an injured Simodes, and the thought alone ...

Simodes.

Where was Simodes?

Volkert's last conscious memory was how the blade of the Greeks had rescued him along with two spears from the back row from certain death. He had to thank the comrades and friends for that.

Volkert found himself wandering through the camp, calling Simodes' name. He found himself on the battlefield at the end, and the decurion let him quietly search until he found the horribly scarred body of the Greek, lying under the corpses of two barbarians, his face more astonished in surprise than pain, but nothing left of that serene lightness that had distinguished him during his lifetime.

It became definitely too much for Volkert. Far too much.

He did not even notice as he slumped silently and without further stirring over the broken body of his friend. The darkness that surrounded him he warmly welcomed.

30

Godegisel and his men were lucky. Apparently out of fear of the advancing Goths, the Roman authorities had begun to send away refugees from the city and close the gates. While disappointed Roman citizens with bag and baggage had to make way in order to seek their salvation in another settlement, the camouflage of the Goths as formerly prosperous, but now refuge-seeking traders benefited them. This impression was reinforced by the generosity with which Godegisel distributed solidi among the guards who eyed him and his men suspiciously. But the legionaries here had not been paid for some time. As the supposed refugees asked, clinking Roman coin in hand, for shelter while verbosely lamenting their cruel fate – that is, actually only their spokesman wailed, while the rest sat rather silent on horseback and looked exhausted – there were those who participated in receiving the coins and then opened the way, and all this without any fuss. Once through the city gate, the Goths merged with the population of the overcrowded city. True to their cover story, Godegisel led them to an inn, whose price tag already showed him that only those would find accommodation who had enough cash. Thus, the Goth had sufficiently been stocked with great foresight. A grumpy innkeeper showed them two tight rooms – even this high-class inn was overcrowded – and also found space for the horses. The meal that was proffered to them for a horrendous amount of money was as bad as supply shortages made them expect. Until the Gothic army withdrew – whether victorious or defeated – this situation would only worsen. Bilimer looked particularly frustrated in the face of this perspective.

They were not the only Goths in the city. Such a large metropolis like Thessaloniki housed at this exciting time a variety of nations, and it was also not as if there had previously been no Goths in the Roman Empire. Still, the city was dominated by Greeks and Thracians, and Godegisel gave his men an express order to stay in the hostel as long as possible, not to visit the taverns, and not to touch alcohol.

Then he himself roamed the city. At first he followed the Decumanus Maximus the main street, which was a direct extension of the Via Egnatia up to the central marketplace, the Agora. He didn't hurry, but that was hardly possible anyway, given the jam-packed streets. Thessaloniki already had more than 30,000 inhabitants in peacetime, and the many refugees had surely doubled the population. Although imperial law that forbade the daytime traffic of carts, horses and wagons in cities, the sheer mass of people significantly hindered Godegisel's progress. From the main street he entered the Agora, admired the long shopping street with the Cryptoporticus, the giant warehouse of the city. Here was the center of public life, and for him as a Goth, the impression was overwhelming. Godegisel might still be highly critical of the Romans, but when he strolled down the street toward the impressive theater-stadium, which offered room for up to 20,000 spectators, he had to admit this civilization's great power. He found himself impressed, and yet he felt no awe, only respect.

He stayed close to the taverns and rather consciously sought out those that were frequented by soldiers. Godegisel played the role of melancholic refugee whose difficult fate slowly led him to booze, ready to squander the last of his money in taverns, to perfection. The legionaries took his invitation gladly, treated him decently, and let him sit where he wanted, but otherwise he was increasingly ignored. His solidi were loose in his bag, and therefore many rounds were paid by him. The wine, although poor and acidic, untied the tongues of the legionaries, and once Godegisel called for a decent roast, the soldiers were only too willing to talk about God and the world. The Gothic spy let them talk, didn't steer the conversation, just sat back, made sure that the jars were refilled, and inserted a joke every now and then. He preserved the impression not to be able to speak Greek properly and used the language clumsily when he had to speak. The soldiers grew more and more accustomed to his presence and his appearance became less and less peculiar.

That was exactly what the Goth had wanted to achieve. It took a few days, then he began to collect specific information. An offhand remark here, a few raised eyebrows there, much more wasn't necessary since the arrival of the strangers was talk of the town. But Godegisel wanted to penetrate through the veil of rumors and collect tangible information, and here the legionaries were of great importance.

And so he assembled, in the course of time, a picture. He heard of the secret weapons of the strangers who reportedly came from Germania – a theory that Godegisel held for adventurous. He was careful, however, to express any opinion, and concentrated on refills instead. The descriptions of the weapons and especially their effect corresponded, despite the obvious exaggerations of drunken Romans, with the accounts of the refugees of the recent battle so that the noble came more and more to the conclusion that they had told the truth. Multiple times a cold shiver showered down his spine when he had to imagine what these weapons could do to advancing Gothic army, and even if only half of it became true, how it would shatter the cause of his people. They were actually in very serious danger. His first impulse was to leave the city immediately and warn Fritigern, but then he thought better of it. It was clear to him that he shouldn't give away the advantage of being within the city walls.

This might yet prove to be extremely useful.

When he had collected a first sample of valid information, he commissioned Rechiar to bring them to Fritigern. He took quite a risk, because no one of the remaining men spoke Greek, but on the other hand Rechiar was most likely the one who was able to maneuver through the Roman patrols – besides, he rode like the devil and would therefore arrive fast, *very fast*, at the Gothic troops. With any luck, he would also succeed in making his way back, but Godegisel had emphasized to leave this for him to decide. In his message to Fritigern, he included all the details of which he was reasonably sure and urgently warned him not to underestimate the danger. He knew that the judge had nevertheless no other choice than to attack if he didn't want to lose his authority, but maybe he could do something to move the obvious imbalance in favor of the Goths. In fact, Godegisel's thoughts were about no other problem. He had to find out more about the actual plans of the strangers to get an idea of how they intended to use their superior weaponry. He had the feeling that the Romans would not hide behind the city walls either. The mood was optimistic. There was too much laughing. The legionaries showed too little caution or fear, even fresh recruits, pressed into service, behaved as if the victory over the Gothic threat was now only a matter of time.

He began to understand more of all this two days after Rechiar had left. The Romans had commenced to undergo a hard drill. The taverns, which he had previously visited to entice the bored soldiers to speak, had suddenly been orphaned. Godegisel heard that the Roman troops had begun with exercises before the western gate. It was forbidden for civilians to climb the city walls and to watch the spectacle, and the city gates were closed during the exercises. It was clear that the military leadership had no interest in letting too much information out to the public. But Godegisel felt that since he was here, more knowledge about this development was desperately needed. With the stock of gold in his pockets already diminished considerably, he could not even gather sufficient funds from his companions to take advantage of the Romans' venality. So he found a building near the city walls whose roof ridge was about the same height as the wall itself. This would give him an although limited view of the field before it, and at the same time he was far enough away from the walls so as not to unnecessarily attract attention. The owner of the house, a grim landlord, he was able to convince to give him access with some hard cash. And so the Goth one morning set up for a long day on the cool and windy roof of the building.

He watched as the Roman troops marched out in formation. It looked like the Roman Army he knew: The order of battle was classic and set the troops in the usual units. Godegisel estimated that the Romans mustered about 15,000 able-bodied men and that no significant reinforcements had arrived so far. The 15,000 men were a formidable force but could be beaten, especially since almost all were veterans of Adrianople, where the Romans had mobilized 40,000 soldiers; the sight of the advancing Goths would lower morale. In fact, no reasonably sane Roman general would oppose around 40,000 Gothic warriors with only 15,000 legionaries. Godegisel had heard a lot about General Flavius Victor, and none of the stories hinted even remotely that the old man was crazy. Nevertheless, it really looked as if the Romans had the intention to offer the advancing Goths a battle. For Godegisel, this was incomprehensible, but only at the beginning. Since the foreigners seemed not to partake in the maneuver, their theoretical intervention didn't help him to understand what he observed there.

Once the second part of the maneuver begun, it dawned to him.

A bugle sounded. Godegisel knew it was usually the sign of an attack. But instead of approaching the imaginary enemy with resolute steps, something unexpected happened. With narrowed eyes, the Goth observed as the formerly flawless and impeccable Roman formation suddenly broke up. The apparent chaos turned out to be a well-orchestrated withdrawal movement: The troops were not rushed to the city gates directly. First they ran in a broad front directly to the city wall.

For Godegisel, they were lost from view, but when the soldiers streamed in two columns through the gates into the city, he immediately knew what they had done: Only once they had come up as flat as possible against the city wall, they had moved to the gates. Along with the stories about the strange weapons, that meant only one thing: This was a maneuver to enable these weapons to have a clear shot without the legionaries falling into the danger of being hit by whatever it was the strangers hurled against their enemies.

Godegisel persevered on his observation post. In the hours that followed, the Roman troops repeated the same maneuver four times, each time with greater speed and accuracy. Only then the commander appeared to be satisfied, allowing the end of the exercise. As the Goth marched down the stairs thoughtfully, he was quite clear about in what kind of trap the Romans wanted to capture the advancing Goths and what consequences this would have for his people. If he did nothing, then the attacking Goths would be mowed down like grain on the field, no, even faster, more effective and very bloody. Godegisel could vividly imagine what terrifying effect that would have on the mass of warriors, especially to the survivors. The Goth saw Fritigern already on his knees before the Romans, begging for peace, yes, begging for mercy. A bitter taste rose in the mouth of the nobleman, as he imagined that and while he turned his steps through the evening streets of the city to the hostel, he tried to imagine how he would be able to prevent this disaster.

When he had arrived at the narrow place he shared with three of his comrades, and ignoring the range of expectant to disinterested looks of the men, an outline of a plan had formed in his head already. He was now suddenly happy to be traveling with crazy men, because for what he was about to do, he actually needed absolutely insane comrades.

He took his dinner in silence. Then he sat brooding for a few hours on his bed of straw, with eyes closed, but not asleep. Around midnight he opened his eyes, blinked, lit a tallow candle, and gently woke the men.

Then he gave his orders.

31

"And that's just the beginning," Dahms made clear. He pushed the cap slightly to the side, scratched his head and looked with Rheinberg from the bridge of *Saarbrücken* over the port of Thessaloniki. With gentle slowness, the cruiser glided into the harbor because a vast number of vessels scurried back and forth across the bow of the Germans. The maritime trade had ceased with the onset of winter, so that the harbor build by Emperor Constantine, safely located within the fortifications, was packed. Predominant were the coastal cargo ships of the Navicularii, a mixture of shipowners, traders and captains who supplied the entire coastal region with goods that arrived from other parts of the empire in Thessaloniki or were produced here. These wide boats were rowed, not sailed, and now rested at anchor, as they couldn't navigate the increasingly rough seas of winter.

Spectators lined the quays, and the occasionally visible legionaries seemed to have great trouble to keep the onlookers reasonably under control. On the forehead of the helmsman, a fine film of sweat shimmered, and one could see the attention in his face. Rheinberg didn't interfere. Börnsen was an experienced man and knew exactly what he had to do. His most urgent task was not to sink any of the fishing boats that came quite dangerously close before and alongside them. Many of the boats were overloaded with spectators who stared at the cruiser as a wonder of the world. Rheinberg could hardly blame them – although they had sent a messenger on land to Thessaloniki to inform the city of their arrival. This had probably fired the curiosity up, although it had helped, without doubt, to prevent possible panic.

"We really need to have a proper basis to build on," the Navy Chief Engineer drew Rheinberg's attention back to their conversation.

"We've been here for weeks in this situation. We haven't used a lot of coal, because we were most of the time stationary, but a few tours more and we must re-stash – and I would love to use something better than wood. In addition, the very salty water of the Mediterranean ..."

Rheinberg raised his hand. Dahms was silent.

"I know all that," the captain reassured the man. "And I promise, as soon as this crisis is mastered, we'll take care of it. The top priority. But now we have other worries."

Dahms knew when he had to accept temporary defeat. He nodded curtly and disappeared without further formalities back down. Rheinberg's eyes sought the quay walls.

"There!"

Langenhagen had discovered them first. For a brief moment, Rheinberg felt a lurch. He recalled his long watches with Thomas Volkert and the high hopes he had had for the young man. The ensign had disappeared, and the visit he had received of his bride, the Roman senator's daughter Julia, just before their departure, didn't bode well for his fate. Volkert was a deserter, but he wasn't a mutineer, and he deserved the clemency like those who had opposed the legitimate captain. But where Volkert was staying and whether he was still alive ... Rheinberg had to leave and couldn't promise Julia anymore than Dahms did – first this crisis, then everything else. After all, he had sent a message to Renna, with a request to look into this matter. A response had not reached him.

He would have to punish Volkert but knew that sooner or later members of his crew would wander out of service – and when he forbade them to do so, they would desert. They'd be looking for brides on land, and some would want to start families. Many possessed valuable skills that could quickly turn into hard cash with some ingenuity and adaptation. The plans for building a charcoal-fired Roman Imperial distillery hadn't escaped Rheinberg – and he had already given them, and many other likewise endeavors crafted by the crew, his silent blessing.

But now the matter at hand. Only that.

"It's him!" Langenhagen's voice brought him back to the present. There, in a crowd of legionaries, Captain Becker stood on the wharf, waving at the incoming *Saarbrücken* just as enthusiastically as many of the citizens of Thessaloniki. Next to him, Roman officers stood in ornate armor, including an elderly man Rheinberg assumed to be Flavius Victor, the highest officer of the East. He would keep this post for a while, because Theodosius marched with borrowed troops of the West and new recruits against the Sarmatians. His arrival in Thessaloniki was not expected in the near future.

There was a nice little irony that was so characteristic of the Roman Empire, Rheinberg remembered at that moment. Flavius Victor, the military chief of Valens, was also Sarmatian. How little nationality and origin were ultimately decisive in Rome was one of the experiences that Rheinberg regarded as quite refreshing, especially in contrast with the policy of the German Empire – and that gave him a lot of hope in spite of all pending challenges.

"Börnsen, you are doing very well!" Rheinberg praised the mate, who took it with an imperceptible nod. To close toward the quay without the help of tugs so that they didn't ram the cruiser into the stone wall or damage the ship otherwise – and at the same time thereby preventing a slaughter among the most careless rowing and sailing boats required outstanding skill and foresight.

"Cast the ropes!" Köhler roared on deck, and the sailors at the bow threw the ropes to the waiting German infantrymen who immediately grabbed them and began to pull the cruiser toward the quay.

"Stop the engine," commanded Rheinberg.

The *Saarbrücken* crunched gently against the quay wall. Börnsen twisted his face imperceptibly, but Rheinberg patted him on the shoulder.

"Well done," he muttered.

The rear ropes were thrown and about 20 infantrymen pulled the stern of the cruiser closer. It took five more minutes, and the *Saarbrücken* was firmly moored in the port of Thessaloniki. No sooner the gangway had been lowered than Becker marched over already, accompanied by the older Roman officer, without giving Köhler time to organize a guard of honor.

Rheinberg hastened to meet them. "Captain," he greeted Becker with a broad grin.

"Lord Commander," the officer grinned back and seized the outstretched hand. "May I give you Master Equitum Flavius Victor Tullius, commanding officer of the Eastern Army."

"It's a pleasure and an honor at the same time to get to know you," Rheinberg said truthfully. "I've heard a lot about you."

"In your historical records, I have to believe," Victor said with a smile. "I've heard that there are not too many reprehensible things written about me."

"Mainly known is that you were the general who tried intensively to dissuade his emperor to fight alone against the Goths."

A little sadness clouded Victor's forehead, as he was reminded of the tragedy.

"Also, I read that you served Emperor Julian faithfully and you had a central role in the appointment of Jovian."

"I had a modest share in this."

Rheinberg shook his head, smiling. "Your modesty honors you, General. But let us put historical discussions aside for a moment. I think there are now things before us that are not mentioned in our history books. And because of that, our apparent knowledge doesn't help us anymore."

Victor seemed quite pleased to hear this. Probably the eerie, prophetic statements of the time travelers had him more worried than he had to admit. That they were now like him, without any foreknowledge, made them equal.

Rheinberg didn't have any illusions in this regard. The deeper the Germans intervened in the course of things, the more the historical development removed itself from what they knew from their records. Soon more and more events would occur that would shrink the matches to zero. And this time was certainly not far off, especially if it was possible to finish the Gothic invasion in another and more decisive manner than the historical Theodosius did.

"I suggest that we immediately sit down to a meeting," Becker said. "The Goths are only a few days away from the city, and we don't have much time. In fact, the *Saarbrücken* could be our trump card, so I am extremely grateful for your timely arrival."

Victor agreed immediately, and Rheinberg escorted them to the wardroom. Victor duly admired the surroundings and glanced the image of Wilhelm II, still hanging on the wall. After observing everything in silent astonishment for some moments, he sat directly below the portrait. The fact that the strange time travelers came from an era in which there was also an emperor seemed to have had a calming influence on him.

Rheinberg presented Roman wine, German brandy and coffee, to which Becker attended immediately with shining eyes. Rheinberg observed it with both a laughing and crying eye; except for a small supply the cook watched with diligence, the stock had long been on the decline. Also, black tea was barely to have. It was one point that had to be worked on – and as soon as possible.

There was so much to do.

"Becker, what's your plan?" Rheinberg asked, now relaxed. If Victor was surprised about the confidentiality between the men, he didn't show it. On the contrary, he leaned toward them like a common conspirator.

Becker spread the battle plan before Rheinberg. The captain listened in silence, nodded now and again, but didn't make any comments. Only once Becker had reached the end and looked at Rheinberg expectantly, he voiced his opinion.

"That's a good idea, but it is based on too many uncertainties for my taste."

Victor nodded. "We are aware of that, Trierarch Rheinberg. There are many things that we cannot calculate."

"This unfortunately includes the behavior of the Goths," Becker added. "When in doubt, we will fail, but the only thing that can happen is that the Goths run their heads against the city walls."

"That doesn't help us much," Rheinberg said. "We need victory. A decisive, brutal victory. It should leave such a lasting impression on Fritigern that he becomes willing to conclude any peace with Rome."

"Perhaps he is already!" Becker said. "If he thinks about what his survivors told him …"

"What he thinks is secondary," Victor interrupted him. "He is no emperor; he's temporary leader of the Goths. Alaric and others also have an opinion, although the old man's death certainly is a lot closer than mine. Fritigern is not completely master of the decision-making, and he has enough battle-thirsty lieutenants who would denounce his leadership if he suddenly surrenders after the victory of Adrianople! No! Fritigern himself may be willing to negotiate, I will not deny him sufficient intelligence, but the Goths – the Gothic elite – are not. Yet."

Rheinberg could only agree with the generals.

"It is indeed fortunate that we have arrived here in time," he said. "I think that the *Saarbrücken* can make the small but subtle difference if the plan shouldn't develop as conceived. Do we have a map?"

Becker reached into his bag and pulled out a paper. As it lay spread out on the table, Rheinberg wrinkled his forehead, then he nodded.

"We should take the following precautions …"

Bilimer heartily bit into the pastry, so that the juice from the coked meat ran down his double chin. He didn't mind, and the violence with which he stuffed the massive piece into his mouth was astonishing, while he grunted, smacked his lips and belched, keeping other onlookers away from them. Above all, it distracted from Godegisel, who had watched the entry of the giant iron ship with narrowed eyes. He did not share the joy and euphoria of the citizens of Thessaloniki but concealed his adversity. If anything symbolized the absolute technical superiority of the strangers, then this powerful blend of metal and wood, which seemed to tower with its ominous presence above everything else in the harbor of the Greek provincial capital.

Godegisel was not just impressed, he was troubled. He was scared, really scared. The maneuvers and tactical games of the Roman army, wonder weapons or not, had been ultimately comprehensible for him. This monster of iron was far beyond his imagination. Roman triremes were already mighty ships for the Goths, who knew little more than barges. But the cold presence of this ship that looked like a monster from an ancient Greek saga seemed, despite the fanciful embellishments on the bow, to be something else entirely. Godegisel felt a strange mixture of desire and disgust – desire to possess this powerful instrument, to subdue and break every Roman resistance with it, and disgust, as if he understood instinctively that this ship was in the wrong place and the wrong time, was an abnormality that didn't belong to Thessaloniki or to Rome or to his world. The strangeness that emanated from the monster seemed to be palpable, but the citizens of the city cheered the cruiser as a savior, and once, in addition to the foreign flag of the visitors, ostentatiously a cloth with the inscription "SPQR" was hoisted at the stern of the ship even louder cheers broke out.

Godegisel swallowed his contempt. Strangers who traveled through times like demons said the rumor, and they dared to run their vessel on behalf of the Senate and people of Rome. Gratian had to be very desperate when he allowed this and that reminded the Goth that the cause of this despair was only a few days' march from Thessaloniki.

What distressed the Goth the most were these large structures on the ship from which protruded long dark tubes, stretched apparently harmlessly into the air and yet so full of an indeterminable threat that Godegisel didn't dare imagine how matters would develop with these machinations in action. He had never seen the wonder weapons of the strangers spewing death and only heard vivid descriptions. But in any case there had been descriptions of the metal weapons being carried around by the foreign soldiers, similar to bows or spears. Hand weapons whose concept might be foreign to the Goths but not as alien to them and therefore within the grasp of common knowledge.

But as alien as the elaborate and gigantic siege machines of the Roman army were, whose art to master his people never had been able, looking at the guns of the *Saarbrücken* hardly roused any understanding. Godegisel saw, but he did not realize, how hard he even tried, to imagine what this ship might ultimately have of a military significance.

As Bilimer had devoured his pastry and wiped his thick lips on his sleeve with a satisfied grunt, this was the signal for Godegisel to begin. Dismissing his fat fellow's longing glances toward the sizzling food on the grill, he drew him like a small child through the slow dissolving amount of gawking onlookers toward their hostel.

There were many new things to consider. He would have to send another messenger, as long as one could still leave the city. This would reduce his small force again, but that couldn't be avoided.

Time was pressing. And he didn't know what he should report Fritigern aside from what he had just observed. And about his plan, which suddenly seemed like a wild risk.

Godegisel felt confused and helpless.

He hated it.

32

"That's interesting."

"It is a lie and fantasy!"

Fritigern looked at Alaric. The old man chewed his lower lip like a little girl. For some time, the legendary leader of the Goths had become increasingly frail and sick, yet still far too many listened to him, so that even Fritigern, who had to make the daily decisions, couldn't dismiss his counsel without causing consternation. Alaric was a Goth of old school – wouldn't or couldn't understand what they had experienced so far – and yet he was usually easy to impress. The reports, however, who had been brought by Rechiar and then another one of Godegisel's men, seemed not to convince him at all.

"Godegisel isn't a busybody," Fritigern replied. The young noble was his man, he had to stand up for him. The statements of the spy behind the walls of Thessaloniki were not as unbelievable as Alaric said in his blustering way. In fact, the young man had focused to present a factual narrative of what he had learned. Fritigern could not wish for a better espionage report. But covered by all the objectivity laid the core of the problem: that Godegisel ultimately confirmed the reports of the survivors of Fastida's bunch. There were these miracle weapons, and their effect was catastrophic. And the Romans and their new allies were planning something, a trap for the advancing Goths. Fritigern had this growing, uneasy feeling about the attack and would've liked to cancel the approach toward Thessaloniki. But that was already beyond his power. Rumors among the Goths made the rounds: that there were Gothic spies inside the city, which would in time open the gates; that the Romans fought with the courage of despair but would be hopelessly inferior; that Flavius Victor was seeking death and was willing to sacrifice his entire remaining troops to be with his emperor again; that unbelievable riches have been accumulated in the city and that is why the Romans were so keen to defend it.

Of course, Godegisel would try to help them, but Fritigern had no great hopes. And the other rumors were just that – rumors, many of them probably invented by the Romans themselves to attract the Goths. If that was their plan, they had succeeded, for Fritigern could keep the numerous sub-leaders barely under control. No, to cancel the attack was certainly not a serious option. He had to make the best of the situation, and this was to convince the council of war to assume that Godegisel's warnings were to be taken seriously. It was possible that arrangements could be made to avert the disaster and thus the complete defeat Fritigern saw looming on the horizon. Maybe even with a little luck and God's help, the possible defeat could be turned into a victory.

But his people had to listen to him – and especially the old stubborn Alaric.

"I haven't sent Godegisel because he's a madman who hears voices or someone who doesn't remain calm in battle and can make no decisions."

Fritigern saw the old man in the face. "Or do you want to accuse him of this?"

Alaric made a derogatory gesture. "Godegisel is an acceptable captain and certainly has his qualities. But he was predominantly sent because he belongs to your clients and you wanted to give him the opportunity of probation, so that your own reputation continues to rise in return."

Fritigern smiled thinly.

"If that is so, dear Alaric, then I would have certainly selected him with great care, one who is indeed able to give me reputation and not one from whom I have to think that he invents a fairy tale which might reflect badly on me."

Alaric snorted. "Or did you deliberately pick someone who can tell good stories, so that you both look fine and we swallow these strange descriptions?"

"All this doesn't lead us anywhere!"

The fragile, barely audible voice that interrupted the dispute the room filled faintly. But everyone raised their heads, and an uncomfortable silence spread. Festida the Elder had reached the eightieth year of life this summer according to the general estimate, and it was his son who had been struck down by the same miraculous weapons whose existence seemed to be confirmed by Godegisel's report. The younger Festida had been the only surviving son of his father until that fateful encounter, and the voice of the old man carried weight. Even Alaric had respect for the old man.

"That's silly," continued the elder Festida. Though his voice sounded hoarse, his tone was firm. The frail old man clutched the knob of a cane with both hands, staring with blind eyes on the table to they were all gathered. He did not recognize anyone, yet he saw all. "Godegisel isn't an idiot, Alaric," Festida whispered. "Fritigern has led us to victory at Adrianople. My son died a cruel and unpredictable death and with him hundreds of good warriors. Those who survived, I know well. They are all now in their tents suffering nightmares yet they were experienced warriors who have never lowered their sword against a superior force of legionaries. Each of them fought at Adrianople with the utmost bravery and prudence, and my son thought the world of them." Festida turned his head toward Alaric. "You don't want to bring the memory of my son into disrepute calling his trusted companions crazy, don't you, mighty Alaric?"

The leader cleared his throat. "No, Festida. I will not dishonor the memory of your son. He was a brave man."

"My son was a reckless fool," Festida replied calmly, "but he was brave, that's true. Godegisel has brought us Valens, and he killed the bodyguard of the Emperor. The young man has proven himself, and Fritigern did well to entrust him with this difficult mission."

Approving murmur surged and dried up once Alaric slammed his hand on the table.

"He has brought us Valens, and what do we do with him? Hide him instead to ask the Romans for a ransom and peace on our terms."

"Valens' fate is not our topic," Fritigern retorted a sharp voice. "He is one of our trumps, with which we can wager, if the situation develops to our disadvantage. We will now talk about Godegisel's reports and the question of whether we believe them and want to prepare accordingly."

The leader of the Goths looked around. Thirty-two chieftains of Goths, Alans and Huns had gathered, the elite of the multi-ethnic army, which currently had Eastern Rome under control.

Festida the Elder lifted the cane and slammed it effectively on the ground.

"I believe him. How should we deal with the problem?" he said firmly.

Fritigern nodded. He didn't offer any comment. His gaze wandered, and he saw how cautious agreement surged among the congregation.

Then his look remained at Alaric, who quite obviously felt that he had lost the argument. The old man spat on the ground and nodded grimly.

"Well, Fritigern," he said, as the expectant silence began to become uncomfortable. "So we want to believe these reports. What do we do?"

Fritigern allowed himself a smile, reached for the pitcher in front of him, and took a deep swig of beer. "I have no plan, my friends," he said half apologetically, "but I've read Godegisel's message several times and with great attention. I have ideas, but I need your advice."

He spread out his arms, making sure to include the grumpy-looking Alaric in the gesture.

"Let's discuss it!"

33

Thomas Volkert recognized a powerless speech when he heard one. His Latin was now, just like his Greek, on a level that he could follow any everyday conversation easily. The speech, which had begun to be delivered before the assembled new troops, was no exception, not least because the rhetorician of Theodosius had endeavored to formulate words even the simplest peasant's son was capable to understand. The stupid stuff uttered by the potential future emperor had been of so abysmal primitiveness that even simple peasant sons among the recruits responded with bleary eyes to the uninspired presentation. To underestimate one's own soldiers permanently was nothing that would have happened to a Latinus.

On the way here, since the battle against the scattered pile of barbarians, Volkert had begun to judge the gruff man differently and to look at him with renewed respect. He had to realize to his surprise that the kind of respect that he showed the man was quite different than any he ever had for a German officer or even old Köhler. As a centurion, Latinus was no more than a captain, but above all he was a man who had tried to keep men entrusted to him alive in a most cruel environment and allow them to experience their service's end – because he knew well that most didn't join the legion voluntarily.

And for that Volkert had to realize, the centurion was more than just literally willing to walk over corpses. Oddly enough, it was this new view which drowned any despair Volkert felt. He caught himself daydreaming, where he returned to Ravenna after many battles, as a radiant tribune or even legate and Senator Michellus gave him the hand of his daughter with joy. He woke up in the morning, wrapped firmly in his blankets, and felt the warm stickiness of an extremely wet dream between his legs, a dream in which the senator's daughter whom he had believed never to meet again played an active and memorable role. He found himself carefully looking at his comrades, a scrutiny that had perhaps been restricted by his close friendship with Simodes, and analyzing their qualities as well as shortcomings. He suddenly found himself in the situation to think like an officer.

And when his new decurion, freshly posted from the troops of Western Rome which Gratian had passed to Theodosius, had asked him for the first time if this or that one would probably cause problems and who exactly was probably best qualified for the numerous special tasks that are usually higher paid and meant liberation from bearing service, Volkert had grasped it.

He had emerged from his permanent unconsciousness, his routine, his misery, his emotional bitterness. He looked clearly at the world once more, no longer just drifting, and had, consciously or unconsciously, made the decision to become someone who does something and to make plans.

Without doubt, the death of Simodes had triggered this process. The sudden end of the man who had only recently saved his life had been a great lesson – especially about the value of his own existence and the gift that the Greek had given him, and the debt that he'd never be able to pay it off. He owed it to the fallen not to throw his life away carelessly, but rather take it as an invitation to see it that he made something out of it.

Volkert had regained control. He felt his love for Julia with a new, almost forgotten intensity. Longing and hope, and even the subsequent short bouts of resignation, he felt as almost refreshing and inspiring. The confidence he felt was passed along as he fulfilled his duty. The certainty that this campaign would be successful he gained from his historical knowledge, but this didn't change the fact that he expressed his unshakable belief in a victory during every conversation.

This made him a welcome guest at campfires.

This confidence didn't change much because the speech of Theodosius was anything but enthusiastic. The endless series of platitudes to a generally less motivated, tired and sometimes still inexperienced army had no visible effect, and the prescribed cheers after the end of the speech sounded weak and not very convincing. Especially those of the new recruits as Volkert, who, due to their battle with the Sarmatians, already experienced something "real" legionaries do, didn't get much from the noble and yet so meaningless words of general.

When they were allowed to break the formation, Volkert trotted along with his comrades to their part of the camp. He was scheduled for tomorrow's watchkeeping, so the rest of the day he had basically off. The wet cold of winter had befallen the soldiers in full force, so everyone felt exhausted, frozen and listless. The clothes didn't dry properly, everything was clammy and cold on the body. The mood wasn't good. A few legionaries passed the time with games of chance, two obviously musically talented soldiers had begun to play instruments, the audience grew and listened to very sad-sounding songs. The whole atmosphere in the camp seemed to be more depressed, and that was certainly not helped by the less than inspirational speech of the new general. The prospect of having to confront barbarian invaders in these weather conditions pleased no one, and even the veterans among them showed a rather grim expression.

Just when Volkert wanted to rest at the warming fire, a tribune came up to him. The officer called Vicinio was apparently responsible for the new recruits. A senior centurion accompanied him. It was the tesserarius and therefore corresponded approximately to what Volkert knew from in his time as senior sergeant of a battalion. Without a word, the men sat next to Volkert and held outstretched palms toward the flames. The tribune cleared his throat. The firelight flickered in his hard-lined face, his deep wrinkles expressing the life of a man who had aged too fast and too soon.

"Have you coped with the death of your comrades?" Vicinio finally asked softly.

Volkert, somewhat surprised at the unusual sympathy, nodded hesitantly. He did not know if this answer was ever true, but it seemed appropriate.

"Good," said the tribune, and it sounded almost as if he was glad not to have dealt with this issue any further. "I've been watching you, and I've heard that you have more than a few interesting abilities. Your action in the small battle against the Sarmatians was unusual, but you did the right thing and saved your comrade's life."

"I'm just a simple recruit," Volkert replied politely.

Vicinio waved it away.

"Yeah, let's stop the banter. You have been pressed and have proven yourself anyway. Many are frustrated, and some of your comrades have not coped well. They are full of fear."

"I am not fearless."

"Fearless or not, I have the impression that you can perform your duties even when afraid."

Volkert nodded. What could he say? His assumption of command was well known, and he could hardly take claim to have suddenly gone mad. Did this recommend him for higher tasks? On the other hand, he knew how thin and problematic the staffing of the legions was, and surely men had been promoted for less and comparably fast.

"The newly raised legions need people with your skills, Thomasius. I am looking for those who are to receive posts in the new units. My selection is very limited, the lack begins with very simple problems and doesn't end where soldiers have to be able to command men in battle and keep a cool head."

Volkert nodded cautiously. "I can imagine, sir."

Vicinio grinned in satisfaction. "Good. You are hereby promoted to the rank of a principales and get the post of a decurion. Sign up tomorrow with Egregius here. He will make you familiar with your new responsibilities. Your troop will consist of ten of your comrades whose lives you've saved recently. They will certainly like to follow you. Congratulations on the promotion."

The tribune patted Volkert almost affectionately on the shoulder and stood up. The men looked at the German with a mixture of envy and appreciation. The promotion made him "immune" to watchkeeping as well as simple camp-work because he had been entrusted with a special function. It was this kind of promotion that meant the rise in the ranks of the army, hoped for by each soldier. *Decurion Volkert* – the rank shot through the head of the still surprised man. The sound of it was a suddenly not entirely absurd. Who would have thought that he would embark on a career as a noncommissioned officer? And to collect the higher pay would also cause no great pain to him.

As he wrapped himself in his blankets up at dusk and looked into the crystal-clear night sky, he felt that he had made peace with his fate, at least for the moment. The wild despair and deep depression had given way to a clear will to use his life and to pursue his goals, especially never to lose sight of an eventual return to Julia – to persevere and to achieve this with sufficient patience.

His time would come, he was sure. And with a very different form of certainty that he could not explain rationally or wanted to, he felt his beloved wife-to-be would wait and in turn look for him. The warmth that filled him at the thought was deeper than anything the flickering campfire was able to provide.

34

"They are many."

"But not more than expected."

Flavius Victor didn't say anything, but the lines of worry on his forehead didn't want to give way either. Becker didn't try to spread false confidence, and to have worriers was sometimes invaluable, as they stopped others becoming too cocky or optimistic. In addition, Becker couldn't even blame the old general for his bad mood because from the highest tower of the fortification one could appreciate the impressive military parade with which their enemies presented themselves in front of the city in all their menace. This was, after all, the army that had overcome tens of thousands of Roman legionaries, the flower of the Eastern Roman forces – had swept them away and with them Emperor Valens. Fritigern had not been able to gain a significant strategic advantage from his victory, but ultimately that hadn't been necessary. In his own time line Theodosius, the new Emperor of the East, would give the Goths the status of Foederatii after years of military strife, and thus create the first state in state of the Roman Empire, ultimately putting the cohesion of the whole empire in question. Theodosius had given Rome a breathing space, sure, but ultimately it had been the beginning of the end.

Becker was here to stop the beginning of the end at an early stage and thus to pave the way to a very different development. He didn't want to imagine what consequences it would have for the time travelers if their plan failed. The position of the crew of the light cruiser would be difficult, if not untenable. Their future depended on a gamble of truly epochal proportions. Becker was still giddy every time he thought about it.

"When should we offer them battle?" Africanus wanted to know.

The trierarch had arrived with the *Saarbrücken* at Thessaloniki and continued to fulfill his role as liaison officer. The fact that the mere presence of the dark-skinned man was not only normal but had an almost soothing influence was nothing Becker took notice of consciously. Behind Africanus waited five Roman legionaries without weapons and armor. They were specifically chosen because they were considered fast runners with good stamina. Also, horses waited for them below. These were Africanus' messengers and thus their communication link to the ship. Becker hoped that they wouldn't be needed for more than routine reporting on the progress of the battle. For a moment, Rheinberg had considered himself to leave the cruiser and to follow developments on site but had then taken back his idea.

Becker had noted this with some relief and mock regret. He couldn't use a navy guy interfering in his work. It was hard enough to deal with the suspicious Victor.

But even that would not last much longer.

Because the Goths were ready, there could be no doubt. Since they had arrived in the cold of the Greek winter – which was still very mild and therefore could hardly impress especially the Germans – two days ago, they had put their warriors in position. The convoy with the covered wagons and the women and children had remained about two miles away from the city and was certainly well protected by some units. Becker gave no thought to attacking the civilians. He wanted to break the fighting capacity of the three-peoples-alliance and transform them, according to the plans of Rheinberg, into well-mannered Roman citizens. A slaughter of women and children wasn't one of the measures that would promote this goal.

There was no need to have recourse to so perfidious means of war once their plan developed nicely. The quiet, nagging feeling of doubt that filled Becker during those two days had nothing to do with Victor's forehead crumpled with questions, but it disturbed his concentration. He didn't show – he had to be the confident counterpart of Victor, especially in front of the Roman officers. But it was this kind of intuition that he had learned to use in the past on numerous occasions and to rely on it.

"The time has come," he finally muttered. Africanus looked at him quizzically, as if he wasn't sure if he had heard the answer to his question. Becker stretched, looked in the midday sun and nodded.

"It's time!" he said loudly and firmly. The cornicen next to him had only been waiting for this signal. He raised the horn to his lips and blew a particular signal. The clear sound echoed over the city wall and was recorded and multiplied by other buglers. Becker raised his binoculars to his eyes, saw the leaders of the enemy listening attentively, gesticulating, apparently not aware of the meaning of the signal. That wasn't surprising, because it was new.

Less than five minutes later, a chorus of screams came from the invaders. For now the attackers saw that the city gates were opened and the formations of Roman legionaries began to march to the battlefield. Becker saw with great satisfaction that there was no fault to find in the discipline of the Roman soldiers. With a firm step, the armor and metal parts of their shields polished to a sharp gloss, the cohorts poured out in exact alignment and with no obvious rush. They formed in a classical position, a slightly retracted center, two wings, auxiliaries, cavalry and archers, and with erected signs. Arbogast himself led the troops, their banners bore witness to his high rank and the authority of his position.

A perfect spectacle.

The Goths were properly impressed. Becker watched in amusement as their leaders held back excited warriors who wanted to storm the marching legionaries. No doubt they wanted to give the Romans a chance to move all their troops out of the city to repeat the massacre of Adrianople. Every soldier who remained within the city walls would make the subsequent conquest of Thessaloniki all that more difficult. Thus, the Goths practiced patience and watched as an only half as strong Roman army flowed in a procession from the west gate and positioned itself with provocative composure in front of the hostile troops. The arrogance expressed in the whole maneuver was reflected in many details. The Gothic observers surely saw that Arbogast as well as all other high officers didn't pay attention to them for even one second. Every now and then, it seemed as officers gathered for a cozy chat in the middle of the field, a centurion handed around an amphora, joking with his subordinates. All this was part of the plan, and it didn't miss its effect. The wave of insults and mockery from the Goths grew stronger, but they were not returned as, the Romans brought themselves into position like they were planning a mass picnic, which made it worse for the Goths to watch.

"They're fucking angry," Africanus commented and grinned broadly. Even with the naked eye, the psychological effect was clearly visible. The trierarch obviously enjoyed himself.

"That's what we want," Becker confirmed. "They should become enraged to incandescence. How far are we?"

One of the Roman observers came running and handed a note to Africanus. He took one cursory look and then nodded to Becker.

"The formation is complete. Arbogast is –"

"He's already on his way," Becker interrupted the trierarch and handed him the binoculars he accepted with the greatest self-confidence. In fact, Arbogast, under a flag of truce, and accompanied by several officers, had made his way to the Goths. With measured dignity the Romans trotted to the howling mob of the invaders and moved with straight faces. It was a risky venture, because despite the formal protection enjoyed as negotiators, it was always possible that someone's patience had run out. But Arbogast had specifically asked for this task himself.

This included throwing selected insults, dressed in fine Roman rhetoric, at Fritigern. Among other things, Arbogast would call him for immediate submission, of course in an appropriate tone and with a wrinkled nose. Also, some hints regarding Fritigern's origin and his relationship with the animal kingdom had been pre-formulated.

As much as Fritigern was willing to show reason and insight, he would be urged by his subordinate commanders who waited impatiently for an immediate offensive. Hopefully, they would allow Arbogast to leave unchallenged.

Africanus handed Becker the binoculars. "He has passed the Gothic lines and is now apparently led to the judge. It cannot be long."

Becker took the glass and swung his gaze around, especially along the towers and walls on which he had stationed his gunners. They were not to be seen, which was his intention exactly. They would look tensely at their non-commissioned officers who, at this moment, were in turn waiting for the sign from von Geeren. He stood on a different tower, also with binoculars, and waited patiently for Becker's command. The wait was a nervous ordeal, but choosing the right time was of utmost importance.

"Arbogast has finished," Africanus muttered. In fact, the angry roar of the attackers, now clearly on the verge of losing self-control, resounded up the city walls. The Roman general had apparently done his job well. Accordingly, the return of the delegation was a little hasty, the officers galloped, and the companions of Arbogast shielded the general with their bodies from as close as they could.

But no Goth wanted to give the Romans the satisfaction to brand them as completely dishonorable. Arbogast reached the Roman lines unmolested, and that the insults reaching him from behind would cause serious psychological damage was hardly to be expected.

Becker sighed with relief. He wanted to say something but was interrupted in his effort by the many voices from the Gothic side. And this time the uproar had a different quality. These were not shouts of scorn. This was the prelude to attack, the angry cries of warriors getting ready, reaching for courage. It was the menacing noise of the impending storm. The deep emotionality also took Becker; nobody could shield himself from it. And although the Roman legionaries were still in perfect and completely motionless formation, he imagined that down there many a soldier's heart slipped into his boots.

Even if most of them didn't wear boots.

Becker made a mental note to ask about the corresponding Roman expression, as soon as time and opportunity allowed for it.

This was now definitely not the case right now.

The Goths were ready. And the flood began. Like a black, moving carpet, a good 40,000 Gothic warriors, accompanied by their numerous cavalry, ran toward the stoic wall of the Roman legions. The tramp of feet and hooves on the battlefield accompanied the war cries with a dark, threatening sound. For a second, Becker was very happy to be standing up here. Just for a second.

He nodded to the cornicen. The man pressed the horn to his lips, gave the instrument all the power to drown out the noise. Again, the signal was taken up by the other trumpeters and eventually spilled over to the horn players down, who readied themselves on the battlefield below. What the Goths probably interpreted as a Roman signal to counterattack, as they responded with expectant roar.

The Roman troops melted away, though. It was a remarkable maneuver. The super-strict, precisely calculated formations broke up like ice in the sun. The legionaries threw themselves around and ran as fast as they could toward the city walls. The initially diminishing distance between the front lines became wider again, and the shouts of the Goths turned into sneering because for them it had to look like a headless panic. The Romans, strengthened by their exercises and relieved to get away from the mob, rapidly gained ground, only the Gothic cavalry was able to close fast. Becker observed the maneuvers through his binoculars with cold calculation. There were some running legionaries who stumbled and were swept away by the mass of onrushing Goths, pierced by riders.

It was time.

Becker raised his hand for the agreed sign.

The almost immediate staccato of gunfire was not half as frightening in its effect against the Goths as during their first encounter.

First, nothing remarkable was to be seen.

It was as if no one could stand in the way of the onrushing barbarians, who closed with the city walls.

The Roman legions withdrew already through the gates into the interior of Thessaloniki.

But then one realized it, and the Goths felt it. They saw dozens of their comrades being swept away, they saw whole bunches of bawling warriors as if struck by thunder, their bodies savaged and blood spurting through the air. No sword, no arrow, no spear – and yet collapsing men, screaming horses having their throats torn open by an invisible hand. A man threw his neck back when on his forehead a red mark appeared. Red dots punched on the broad chest of a mighty warrior, pulling him down. Where the magical weapons strafed only, they pierced limbs, torn skin and bones, not always fatal, but causing pain and despair, and others died of shock. Warriors who had fought battle upon battle, beat wildly around, as if to seize and crush invisible spirits. There was fear in the eyes of wild Huns, whose horses went to the ground with opened ribcages, burying their riders more than once. The first, the very superstitious, already turned to flee. Where leaders shouted commands, the such identified officer was killed within seconds. Heedlessness began to spread, sometimes in the truest sense of the word, when a machine-gun burst perforated a skull and left nothing but a bloody mess behind. A half-decapitated fighter, the body cramped on the back of a panicked horse, hurled himself toward the city walls. Senselessly moving, aimlessly expending any strength, they were like a speeding, deadly symbol of futility.

The triumphant, jeering roar turned into screams of fear, pain and panic. Becker closed his eyes, dropped the binoculars, and wished he were deaf, for it was all this that would follow him in his nightmares forever. Not even one hundred assault rifles and a handful of machine guns, and then the few hand grenades some cheeky infantry threw down from the walls and towers to increase the confusion, yet the effect was not to be overlooked. Becker forced himself to open his eyes again.

Not even ten minutes had passed since the Gothic attack commenced, and it already had faltered. It wasn't the amount of dead that was decisive. Becker wasn't able to make a full estimate, but ultimately the shots of Germans couldn't have caused more than maybe 500 or 600 casualties – and with a little good will maybe double the number of wounded. It was, as he had expected, the psychological effect that broke the invaders and dissolved order and discipline.

Becker wanted to raise his hand and thus command the fire to cease, as an unexpected odor penetrated his nose. It smelled of fire, coalified wood, and a fine, dark smoke began to dance before his eyes.

He turned around and stared wide-eyed at the gatehouse of the west gate which was in flames, and he saw the Roman legions, roughly half of them are still outside the walls, as they began to back away from it. The orderly retreat of the Romans came to a halt, followed by a slow reorientation, and then ...

"Becker!" Africanus shouted and tipped the German on his shoulder.

The captain raised his binoculars. An admirable, yes surprisingly disciplined group of Hunnish, Alanic and Gothic cavalry came up from the rear ranks of the invaders. They didn't ride in a bunch but fanned out, with large distances from each other. They rode crouched behind powerful shields, shod with metal. They ignored the panicked compatriots and galloped with precise aim toward the burning gatehouse.

When the Germans directed their fire on them, only a few fell. But Becker saw that lateral incoming shots were deflected by their shields, saw that the falling riders were ignored by their comrades, observed how long sheaves of gunshots partially went into nothingness because of the distances and how the attackers continued their run completely unperturbed to the burning gatehouse, the wide open gate, from which the Romans had already been removed – removed from the outside and the inside.

"Africanus!" Becker cried. "Africanus, whatever happens there, it can only mean one thing!"

The trierarch looked at him half blankly half understanding.

"We were betrayed," Becker said, wiping the cold sweat from his forehead. "They have prepared themselves, and ... they have some of their own within the walls."

Bilimer tripped and fell into the outstretched sword of the legionary. The man, as surprised as the Goth, sank the blade to the hilt into the massive body of the doomed warrior.

Bilimer grunted, got up, took the hand of the soldier who was still holding the handle of the short sword tightly clasped, and yanked. With a smacking sound, the moistly red blade slipped out. With the ease of a man knowing his end has come, Bilimer turned the hand of the Roman who cried when his arm broke and gurgled as his own sword went into his throat. Then Bilimer let go and took another few steps, but his body became heavy and he squatted slowly down to the floor, suddenly breathing very deeply. His eyes lifted, and he looked at the sign of a tavern in front of him, a large wooden board that creaked in the wind. It showed am impaled animal sizzling over a fire.

Bilimer smiled and died.

"Forward!" Godegisel shouted, his own sword arm tired and tense from fighting. His remaining crazies gathered around him, some injured, all splashed red with Roman blood, all caught in various stages of their own madness. For a moment, they had rest because of the increasingly dense smoke from the fire they had laid in several places. Breathing was difficult, and Godegisel coughed, a linen cloth pressed to his mouth. His muffled voice almost failed, but he turned his sword tip at the tavern, and his men understood. All picked themselves up, stumbled forward, pushed the door open, saw a tap room with a few guests who were staring at them horrified.

The Goths ignored the onlookers, rushed to the back side of the building and remained completely undisturbed. No heroes in Thessaloniki who wanted to confront a handful of bloody and wild Gothic barbarians.

The back door led into a courtyard and the court in an alley. No legionaries to see. Godegisel saw the fountain, gesticulated, took a breath. Blades drove into the water, clothing became wet, blood smeared with soot discolored the liquid. It took five minutes, then the blades were covered, the clothes looked dirty, but the all too obvious traces of the fight were hidden from the cursory glance.

"Quiet now! Look like frightened traders! We are poor refugees! No word on your lips! If you have to cry, cry!"

The smoke certainly contributed to letting their tears seem real. Wailing and howling, the Goths wandered into the alley, slowly disappeared in the narrow corners of the city, and the Legion, finally sent by the host of the tavern on their trail, found no one.

And then there were other things to do.

218

The hooves of the riding Goths were suddenly heard by the burning gatehouse. Ahead of them a man in black clothes rode, like a wisp, with a fury that was powered solely by thoughts of revenge for what had just been done to his people.

Fritigern, the judge, had arrived in Thessaloniki.

And he wanted to dispense his judgment.

35

"The Goths are within the walls!"

"Damn!"

Rheinberg stared at the piece of paper which he had been handed over. The noise of the battle could be heard well into the harbor, but Rheinberg had not been sure if something had gone wrong. The message dispelled his doubts. Now was no time to think about the why and how; they had to react.

He looked up, picked up the binoculars and observed the part of the city wall he was supposed to look at. A column of smoke rose in the murky winter day – of red color.

"Are the guns ready?" he asked Langenhagen standing expectantly beside him.

"Loaded and aligned."

"Give fire solution one of the gunners. Execute on my command."

"Fire solution one, Captain!"

It took only a few moments before the 10.5 cm quick-loading cannon on the portside and 15 cm guns at the bow and stern got ready. The mouths jerked slowly upward into position, with the exact degree calculated in cooperation with Becker's people by Rheinberg's gunners.

"Guns in position," Langenhagen reported.

"Give the warning!"

The ship's horn began immediately with a long, plaintive sound. The Romans were prepared for this signal and knew what would happen. Aware legionaries would now avoid certain parts of the city to the west. The civilian population would be driven out of the houses. For all that remained less than a minute, but Rheinberg couldn't permit more time. Others would have fired without any warning. Interestingly, it was the Roman officers themselves who had spoken out against this unnecessary procedure. In their eyes, civilians were, as long as they were not senators and rich men of influence, of little concern.

Rheinberg purposed to set a different tone. He held his clock in his right hand, watching the seconds counting down carefully. Langenhagen, in turn, kept a close eye on Becker's position.

"Still red?" Rheinberg asked to be sure, although the fine column of smoke was clearly visible even with the naked eye.

"Red, Captain!"

"Fire. A volley."

"Fire a volley, yes!"

Seconds later, the *Saarbrücken* shook. The harbor guards flinched, cowered in fear as fire came from the metal tubes and smoke and a deafening roar shot over the harbor basin. Glass splintered where the residents of the adjoining houses could afford it. Fearful cries accompanied the thunder, which so quickly faded as it had occurred.

The effect, however, was almost immediate. Rheinberg had chosen explosive munitions that would detonate on impact. The five projectiles the *Saarbrücken* had fired barely needed a second to reach the western area of the city. They hadn't practiced this, and misses were inevitable, no matter how careful the theoretical preparation had been.

The burning gatehouse was hit by a 15 cm round and turned into an inferno, the bodies of Gothic cavalry, who had never even suspected what tore them into death, were thrown from their horses.

A 15 cm shell hit an adjacent tavern, through which minutes before the Gothic spies had fled in the false security of the city itself, struck the multistory building, exploded with a mighty blast. Guests, host, barmaid, all were merged together with stones, wood and glass into an indefinable mass of blood, guts and building materials. They didn't even have the opportunity to shout out their horror.

Three 10.5 cm projectiles struck outside the city walls, one in the middle of the Gothic hordes, and tore large holes in the already panicking warriors. The new evil out of nowhere, so much more powerful than anything previously experienced, finally broke the invaders' courage. The attack was over, as the Goths ran away.

On the *Saarbrücken*, one saw nothing of all this. Langenhagen and Rheinberg eyed Becker's position. Again smoke.

"Blue, Captain!"

"I confirm blue. Fire solution two, Langenhagen."

"Two it is, Captain."

The mouths of the naval guns were moving to a tiny degree angle upwards and purred a trifle to the left or right.

"Guns aligned, Captain!"

"Fire. A volley."

"A volley, yes!"

Again the guns spoke, again they caused fear and terror. This time all five projectiles went down outside the city wall, and here misses meant nothing because there were enough targets. Five craters formed on the plane in front of the city, filled with dead bodies or injured, with broken and burnt bones, human and animal alike. Warriors were whirled through the air, the pressure wave of the explosion tore legs off, horses lost their balance. Shrapnel cut deep wounds in the mass of the attackers and caused terrible injuries, if they didn't kill right away. Open, utter panic broke out, and the Goths were running as they could, not realizing that the range of the guns of the *Saarbrücken* could still reach kilometers if Rheinberg and Becker wanted it so.

Rheinberg stared through his binoculars.

"That's white smoke, Langenhagen."

"I confirm white smoke, Captain!"

"The guns back to rest. Unloading only on my command. The gunners remain on standby!"

"Resting position and no unloading, readiness for the gunners, yes!"

Rheinberg lowered the glass. He had done it. Becker was apparently satisfied with the result, otherwise he would not have given the signal for termination of the cannonade.

Goths remained in the city, though. To shoot directly into Thessaloniki was no solution. Here the *Saarbrücken* could do very little.

Now this was a problem that had to be solved by the Romans.

"They know exactly what they do," a breathless von Geeren came forth. "And our Roman friends – damn it!"

Another group of Goths had come up the stairs. The few remaining legionaries threw themselves against the attackers, showing contempt of death. From below, the foot of the city walls, screams came up as legionaries tried to fight for access to Becker's position. But the men around Fritigern, who had known exactly where they had to penetrate the defenses, had effectively entrenched themselves – in stark contrast to the Roman legionaries who had defended the access to this part of the city wall very sloppily.

Becker raised his army pistol and choose his target. He cursed himself for not having thought of enough ammunition for himself and von Geeren, but who would have considered this seriously ... he cursed himself again.

A shot whipped and the ball struck directly into the chest of the Goth. The long-haired and bearded man fell down as if struck by lightning, but his comrades pressed on unswervingly. They hadn't lost respect for the wonder weapons, but the superstitious fear receded remarkably quickly. They saw that the strangers in their unfamiliar uniforms looked and acted like ordinary people and made no mistake in assuming that a well-placed sword have the same effect as with a Roman legionary.

"Caution!" Africanus shouted, as he stepped forward with his sword raised, distracting a wild attack of a raging Goth. The man faltered, and then the trierarch hit him powerfully with the flat side of the blade on the back. With a suppressed cry, supported by its own momentum, the Goth stumbled over the balustrade. His long-drawn scream ended abruptly once he hit the ground a good 20 meters later.

Becker stepped back, the gun carelessly tossed aside. The magazine was empty.

Determined, he drew the saber. He knew how to handle the weapon, but he had never used in a real fight – and especially not against opponents who were capable with blades ultimately far better than he was.

"More to come!" Flavius Victor gasped weakly. The old commander was already bleeding from several superficial wounds, and the fact that he had not fully recovered from his injuries since Adrianople didn't help either. Africanus, along with two other legionaries who had survived the previous onslaught of Goths, tried to keep him in the back, but the old veteran urged himself again and again to the forefront.

Another group of Goths rushed up the stairs. It was a wild force, with men who looked as if they were prepared to go through hell. Leading them was a hulking young man with flowing hair, wearing an ornate breastplate over his embroidered shirt. Whoever this man was, he surely was one of those lieutenants who were following Fritigern along, and he radiated an aura of fearlessness and … intelligence. Awareness. Control.

Becker raised his saber. The nobleman stepped resolutely toward him, his sword, shield at the ready, with a metal bracer on his left arm, positioned to repel any attack of Becker. His comrades immediately began to keep Becker's companions busy, and they all had a different, fanatical, disturbing quality in their attacks.

No one could come to Becker's assistance. He parried a powerfully thrust, shuddered as the blow of the enemy's sword almost bounced the saber from his hand. For a moment, his arm felt numb. The Goth took advantage of the momentary weakness and pressed on. His blade wiped Becker's weak opposition aside, and the saber clattered to the ground. The captain reeled back, spread his arms in a gesture of submission, then he felt the hot cold pain with the sword of the Goth plunged into his right lung. Half incredulous, half shocked by the sudden stab, Becker stared down at himself. The Goth, unimpressed, pulled the blade, and it was followed by a gush of Becker's red blood.

The captain fell back, looked in fascination at the lifeblood that spurted from the wide wound before him to the ground, and then he felt a violent jerk. With the flat of the hand, the Goth had pushed his blood-soaked chest.

Becker automatically reached behind him.

There was the balustrade. His hands, weaker, weaker, sought for steadiness, but then another push and shove.

224

The German flew over the wall, fell and fell and fell.

And died.

At the moment as Becker's battered body shattered on the floor in front of Thessaloniki's wall, a Roman relief force had finally stormed the position.

When Godegisel turned, he saw that many blades were directed at him and his comrades were either dead or already in captivity. He dropped his sword and surrendered, without a word, with silent satisfaction in his face. He ignored the heavily bleeding body of Flavius Victor, lying on the ground, ignored the horrified gaze with which the swarthy trierarch and a second stranger rushed to the balustrade and looked down. He felt himself pushed down the stairs by strong fists. There were the remaining Goths, disarmed, and among them Fritigern, the judge who had truly held court, and more than he could measure at this time.

They had lost, in the end, and their act of desperation couldn't change it anymore. Godegisel saw it in Fritigern's eyes, and he saw something like a quiet confidence, a relief. If the Romans were clever, they would now negotiate with the Goths, and the trek of the three peoples through Greece would come to an end. This might ultimately still turn their fate for the best.

A continuation of the fight was already out of the question. Demoralized, the judge and his warriors in captivity, they would not be able to do much. They could continue to be a nuisance, sure, and the Romans might consider offering more than only unconditional surrender.

The Goths would take what they could get.

36

"It's decided!"

The great symbolic importance was that these three words were spoken by Lucia, the wife of Senator Michellus. It showed who ultimately was in charge in the household of the esteemed dignitary. Not always did the other members of the household agree with these decisions. In this particular case, that was true only for one person: The daughter Julia, who was standing with clenched fists in front of their parents and was staring at them half angrily, half desperate.

"Mother ... Father ... you cannot be serious!"

While the gaze of the man, confronted by the plaintive voice of his daughter, began to soften and he hesitated with an answer, the face of his wife showed no signs of doubt or hesitation. She craned her chin and gave her husband a warning and at the same time provocative look, as if to challenge him to be counterproductive so that she could show him what evil he'd call upon himself by that.

Senator Michellus, usually never short of wit and repartee in Senate debates, fell silent before he could say anything. There were fates that shouldn't be conjured, and especially not if Lucia had made the right decision in the end.

"It's decided!" the massively built woman repeated, and this time her tone had something menacing. Julia heard this nuance very well – she was steeled in countless arguments with her mother –, but she had reached an emotional state in which she couldn't care less. No calamity an infuriated mother could provide her with was greater than what has just been declared to her. It couldn't easily get worse.

"I won't do it! I cannot!" Julia said.

"You don't decide! Your father is the one who calls the shots!" That sounded almost comical coming from Lucia's mouth, but it was quite in keeping with the formal rules by which Michellus as pater familiae could actually decide freely about the welfare of all family members. That he exercised this right but only after consultation with his wife – or even by her direct instructions – was another matter. Although Julia was very much aware about the actual power structure, she focused her desperately pleading look on Michellus, who shifted uncomfortably on his stool back and forth.

"Expect no pity from your father!" Lucia said. "We are your parents, and we know exactly what is good for you! Martinus Caius comes from a very reputable house! His father made a lot of money in trade, he maintains cargo ships and caravans in the whole empire! Martinus is about to be raised to the senatorial order and will then be a colleague of your father! Well, not old Roman nobility, but God knows your future groom is rich and will soon be an influential and respected Roman, enjoying the ear of the Emperor! Julia! Please be reasonable! Erase this silly man out of your mind! It is time for you to think about your future. You are not getting any younger!"

In fact, Julia was already at an age in which age-matched women were mostly already married or engaged. Her stubborn nature and the fact that she had previously found each groom that had been presented by her parents unfit, hadn't been conducive to a quick wedding. However, according to the will of their parents, this situation should change now.

"Caius Martinus is an idiot who squanders his father's money and visits the whores regularly," Julia replied.

"He's a tempestuous young man, open to the pleasures of life," Lucia interpreted the fact. "Marriage will mitigate his desires, especially with a wife like you."

"I will not marry that booze bag!"

"Yes, you will. We have already discussed everything with the old Caius. The date is set, there will be wonderful celebrations, and it will be the talk for weeks in Ravenna."

Lucia's face developed a slightly dreamy expression.

"I won't marry him!" Julia repeated firmly.

"Michellus, will you please say something!" Lucia now turned to her husband.

"Yes, Father, please, ask no such sacrifice of your oldest daughter," Julia added with a sudden melting in his voice. Her smile reached a remarkably high level on the sweetness-scale. Michellus slipped even more back and forth on his chair, cleared his throat several times, his gaze wandered from wife to daughter and back. He seemed to consider which agony was easier to bear and closed his eyes for a moment, as if to think. His right hand meanwhile groped toward the small serving table, where a cup of wine was waiting.

"Michellus! I ask you!" Lucia snapped and fixed her husband and lord with a cold stare. The senator sighed, curbing his right hand and then looked at Julia. She immediately knew what was coming, and the smile disappeared from her face. Gloomily she heard her father's reply.

"Julia, we only want the best for you," he began defensively. "You're destroying your life if you continue longing for this man. Let's agree that he would hardly be a befitting husband. He's probably already dead or he has forgotten you."

"I cannot believe it!" Julia said.

"Then you dream like a little girl!" Lucia rebuked. "You're always so insistent to be an adult and make your own decisions! But now you're acting like you're twelve! Julia! Pull yourself together and think of your future! Martinus Caius will take care of you, you will have a prosperous home with all the amenities. With a little gentle pressure, he will change some of his perhaps not quite as desirable habits."

Lucia looked thankfully at the sad and fatalistic expression in her husband's features, who could well imagine what "gentle pressure" actually meant.

"I will not touch him! He will have to take me by force!"

Lucia shrugged ostentatiously. "If that is your will, my child," she said with sudden coldness in her voice. "I don't care how much you like to act like a fool and what kind of adventurous ideas you harbor. You'll marry him and be his faithful wife and servant, as befits a well-bred senator's daughter. You will not bring shame on our family, otherwise your husband will punish you hard. If so, don't expect any help from us."

Again, Michellus seemed to want to add something, but he thought better of it. In some ways, he shared the concerns of his daughter. A major reason that the young Martinus was still available had to do with the fact that his erratic lifestyle was something other parents didn't want to expose their lovely daughters to. Julia, however, was a similarly difficult, although somewhat different case. It appeared, therefore, to their parents as an effective means to intervene now courageously before something worse would happen.

Lucia saw how it worked in her daughter, and an expression of defiant determination was visible on her face.

"Before you say anything, listen to my words," she intoned with a certain theatricality. "I know what you are thinking of! Once you run away, but a second time you will not succeed. Gunter!"

A door opened, and a giant of a man entered. Gunter came from Germania and was a slave in the household of the Senator for ten years. He consisted of a large number of muscles and very little brain, but above all he was his mistress Lucia's faithful servant.

"Lady, you called," the mountain of a man uttered with a submissive tone.

"You will from now on not depart from the side of my daughter. Only in her room she can stay alone! Leaving it, you will accompany her. She may only leave the house to go to church. If she needs something, errands are to be done by a servant. She may not receive any visitor who has not previously registered with me. You will sleep outside her door and keep watch continuously. You will take all meals together with her! The smallest irregularity is reported to me! If she wants to escape and steal away, you have my express permission to forcibly prevent it!" Lucia looked at intently at Gunter, who had endured the cannonade of orders with a straight face. "Did you hear me?"

"I obey, Mistress," the slave confirmed. For a moment, he looked at his new protégé as if to gauge the difficulty of the task. But he said nothing, giving no hint about to the outcome his assessment.

"You can't do that!" Julia exclaimed angrily.

"Yes, I can. I can do much more if you don't obey and do what I say." Lucia rose. "The wedding is in three months. We begin immediately with the preparations. It will be a wonderful festival that everyone involved will long remember."

"I don't doubt it," her daughter replied bitterly. She turned abruptly and left the room.

"Julia!" Lucia thundered. "What is this behavior? I have not ... Julia? Julia!"

Gunter looked confused, remembered his orders, and also turned to follow her.

When they both had left the room, Lucia trembled angrily. Her husband hastily put the cup back on the table and wiped with a cloth over his mouth, his eyes full of guilt.

Lucia sighed.

This family would kill her one day.

37

The small church was like a monastery, although monasteries actually didn't exist yet, as von Klasewitz knew. The first hermit monks lived in Egypt, and Martin of Tours had already set up a settlement near Marmoutiers, and Cassian, founder of the first great Gallic monastery near Marseille, was indeed already born but lived at this time in Palestine and studied local early hermitages. The age of the great orders began to appear on the horizon but had not yet materialized.

The management facilities adjacent to the church building were all newer, and the remoteness of the entire system contributed to the monastic impression. To this place, von Klasewitz and Tennberg escaped in a hectic night-and-dagger operation, on the run from prefect Renna's soldiers who had closed the gates of Ravenna just behind them. Since then, they had persevered here, hidden by Ambrosius and under the direction of Petronius, as Renna had declared a bounty for the capture of the German refugees, and a hefty one.

Their initial bitterness and despair following the failed mutiny had given way to cold fury. The longer they lived in the nameless church and the surrounding buildings, the greater the outrage. Petronius only spurred this, and he understood how to foster the anger especially in the former first officer. Soon he had convinced von Klasewitz that only betrayal could have been the cause for his failure, that his cause was still righteous, and that Rheinberg had to be stopped, no matter what Gratian and his courtiers deigned to decide. They were largely cut off from news, only sporadically a messenger appeared, and so it was all the more surprising that one day a large group of riders, wrapped in hoods, reached the remote location. Petronius hurried and alarmed the German refugees, because the unannounced visit was of high rank and the purpose of some importance.

As he led von Klasewitz and Tennberg in the common room of the farm building, they were amazed at the illustrious group that had gathered in front of their eyes. There was the Bishop of Milan, St. Ambrosius – although not yet put in this exalted state – who had assumed the dignity to sit at the head of the large table. He was accompanied by other high ecclesiastical dignitaries, a blur of names von Klasewitz could hardly remember.

Then there was a different person, a man of handsome physique, with the movements and the habitus of a military. Once von Klasewitz heard his name everything fell into place, and he understood immediately, even smiled, being pleased. They welcomed Magnus Maximus, the Roman military governor of Britain. He knew the man from Rheinberg's historical descriptions. He was the usurper, who in his own time line dared to revolt against Gratian, and his generals would bring the young Emperor, betrayed by his own troops, death. Maximus would for some years rule a large part of Western Rome – almost everything except Italy – and distinguish himself by exceptional piety and zealous orthodoxy, not least in order to gain the pleasure of the Eastern Roman Emperor Theodosius. Theodosius, however, would never recognize the usurper and finally bring him down to assume his role as the last Roman Emperor in history ruling the complete realm all by himself.

In another time.

That was a clear indication for von Klasewitz. The mere fact that the governor met with him here, instead of preparing his rebellion in Britain or Gaul, spoke volumes. The historical events were finally completely changed, the dice newly fallen. With every step they now moved away from the story that they knew. And von Klasewitz knew exactly what was expected of him before even a word had been spoken. Help and advice to the insurgent troops, fueled by the passion of true orthodoxy, to be directed against Gratian and his new allies, to be sent into the field and to help them to overcome the superior technology of the time travelers, or, even better, create new ideas and weapons to use.

The road ahead was clearly drawn, as von Klasewitz suddenly realized with a strange calm. The failed mutiny had just been the beginning of something much bigger. Now he could no longer pick and choose who was friend or foe. And the chance offered him here to wipe out the disgrace of failure and return in triumph on the *Saarbrücken* ...

The first officer didn't notice anymore, as he entangled himself in a web of thoughts and feelings, how he removed himself more and more from reality. He saw himself, again as captain of the *Saarbrücken*, with Rheinberg, nailed to a cross as an inferior criminal. The sudden, savage sense of satisfaction that flowed through him in this imagination washed away any remaining doubt.

"Let us sit down," Ambrosius suggested once the round of introductions as well as an introductory prayer had been completed. Expectantly von Klasewitz took place.

"I think that after the general introduction there is no doubt about the purpose of our meeting today," the bishop immediately began with the basics. "Frightening things have happened in the last few weeks and months, and people have made a lot of mistakes. Including me, if I may say so."

A murmur arose.

The bishop raised a hand. "Yes, including me. I have condemned the foreigners who so unexpectedly arrived on our shores immediately and without consideration. As I had to learn now, that was too hasty a decision. Here among us today is the living proof that the time travelers are not all demons or followers of Satan. Yes, I will admit that even those who follow the teachings of that man Rheinberg may be wrong or simply do not know better and can perhaps be lead to the right path. Unfortunately, an attempt to accomplish this has recently failed."

Ambrosius looked mildly at Petronius, then at von Klasewitz. Should his remark have been meant as a rebuke to their defeat, then he at least it didn't show. The former first officer was very grateful.

"Temporary setbacks should not stop us," the bishop continued. "We know that we are on the right track. The fact that a young and hopeful Gratian can be influenced by both the events as well as the suggestions of strangers is deplorable, but I'm much more concerned than angry. Still, it saddens me, however, that this development and the intransigence of the Emperor now drive me to take steps I myself would never have thought possible. I hope that I'm not going astray, and pray for greater insight and understanding."

The humble habit of the bishop concealed the fact inadequately that he clearly formulated the introduction to a veritable call to rebellion. Von Klasewitz enjoyed the situation. The ritual, formulaic procedure corresponded to the essence of his personality, it meant that he felt at home with these people. That he himself was now one of a group of conspirators who ultimately planned nothing less than the overthrow of the rightful Emperor – and why else should the governor of Britain make the long journey – was then beside the point. Von Klasewitz felt like being part of history, and this flattered his ego to an almost indescribable extent. He had, in many respects, sold his soul and the fact that the buyer was someone who was revered in his time as a saint made it much easier.

"The Emperor is mistaken if he thinks he has to approach not only the heretics in Christendom but also the numerous pagan cults with leniency and exaggerated tolerance. The Emperor is wrong if he thinks that the tax reductions and exemptions for church property and church people are too large and the empire would improve its revenue situation. And he is mistaken if he thinks that a neglect of orthodoxy means that the empire can face the coming dangers – which I don't want to negate! – in a better way. He puts the salvation of all his subjects at risk, and only to obtain questionable and in any case very short-term benefits. The role of the former companions of our friend von Klasewitz here is just as infamous as important, and to end the influence of these men is one of the points with which we must begin."

Ambrosius turned directly to von Klasewitz who stood up immediately and met the eyes of the bishop.

"We especially need the help of our friends from the future who have demonstrated their righteousness for all of us, because we should not suffer the fate of the Goths at Thessaloniki."

234

The events in the eastern part of the empire had made the rounds quickly in the last few weeks. Even von Klasewitz had gained some knowledge in the relative seclusion of his exile. Rheinberg had won. What losses he had sustained wasn't known. But the victory over the Goths had met the nobleman with greater bitterness than it should have. Defeating the barbarians ultimately would have been his destiny if the mutiny would've been successful. However, he probably wouldn't have departed toward the Greek city and would therefore not have been able to turn the tide, he had to admit. Ultimately, it was his envy of Rheinberg's anticipatory behavior that probably hurt him the most.

Von Klasewitz bowed his head in approval, intensifying the recognizable benevolence in Ambrosius' face.

"Come, faithful brethren, let us consider what we can do and when we want to do it," Ambrosius said. "Noble Maximus, you have been invited not least because you have obviously prepared plans of your own. Your ambition is now in great danger, and at any moment Gratian might announce your dismissal. So our time is running out."

The governor of Britain rose, and an aide rolled out maps in front of them on the table. All eyes turned to the future usurper. Implicitly he was the one in the eyes of the conspirators who would take Gratian's position. Up until the young emperor came around with the appointment of Theodosius, he would remain be the only emperor. The price they had to win had become so much bigger, bigger even than what Maximus had originally had set himself as a goal.

Von Klasewitz didn't care much about the details of the plans which they were about to discuss.

All was well, as long as he would play a glorious role in them.

38

"More couldn't be expected."

Fritigern's face spoke volumes, spoke of his feelings, especially his disappointment and humiliation, that he had to suffer. No, the delegation led by General Arbogast hadn't treated him in any way derogatory. He hadn't been tied up or put under a yoke and thus relegated to slavery, as the victorious Romans could have done with him and the completely demoralized Goths. He was still a free man. He didn't have to listen to triumphant eulogies, there were no insults, no offensive language. They had even spoken to him quite honorably, gave him a slave as a servant, and he hadn't been lacking anything. Even his Goths, and with them the Huns and Alans, were treated unexpectedly well – only those who still had resisted, and despite all clear instructions by Fritigern and Alaric, had been attacked. But those who peacefully surrendered and laid down their weapons got to eat out of the Romans' meager supplies. Women and children, the whole entourage, were building a camp under the supervision of the legionaries and remained otherwise completely undisturbed. Here and there, there had been attacks by too high-spirited legionaries, but these had quickly been sanctioned by their leaders with obviously very clear instructions on the matter.

No, on the contrary, in comparison to the time when the Goths were first invited by the Romans to settle, the treatment now was generally decent, almost friendly. That hadn't made Fritigern's negotiating position easier, but on the other hand it had supported his efforts to make the numerous sub-leaders agree to the peace agreement they had finally signed.

This, of course, didn't change the fact that today, weeks after the formal contract had been concluded, the issue was discussed again and again. Especially those of Fritigern's closest confidants, who had sworn allegiance to the former judge and had to deal with the fact that Fritigern now was no more than an ordinary nobleman and no longer the glorious leader of all the Goths, had their problems. Alaric had become very ill and had died two days after the end of the negotiations. In the end, the old man had proved to be remarkably cooperative.

And yet: There had been allegations from many sides. Had the victory of Adrianople actually been so pointless? The great triumph, no more than just an illusion? Many Gothic leaders who had had substantial contribution to the victory over Valens had been less than satisfied. But they were leaders without an army, for the fact that after the carnage at Thessaloniki, after the use of those magical, so destructive, invisible weapons, many warriors had lost any desire for another showdown. Ultimately, they had received what they had come for: land for settlement, status as Roman citizens, a right to limited self-government under Roman civil officials, and relief from any tax for two years in order to put all efforts in the construction of new villages and farms.

These funds were certainly limited, since much of the plunder which they had accumulated since Adrianople had been returned. But even here, the Romans showed an amazing gentleness, yes, great understanding on their part – seeds, agricultural tools, cattle and other livestock had been granted to them as property in order to invigorate the production of food as soon as possible. Of the countless horses, which they had possessed, more than half had been handed over to the Romans, and those they were allowed to keep were primarily used as draft animals. Only a limited group of nobles was allowed to keep horses to ride on or even maintain a small force of fighters under arms as a personal guard in their service, a tiny fraction compared to the powerful army over which they had once commanded.

The Goths had accepted the terms of their surrender relatively quickly. This coincided with the reasons for which they had come here in the first place. They had found a new home and were willing to come to terms with their fate. It could have been worse. Slavery would have been another option.

The Alans and the Huns had been less enthusiastic. The Alans had ultimately agreed to act as auxiliary troops in the service of the Roman army, a tradition that existed for some time anyway. Emperor Gratian preferably surrounded himself with a troop of Alan cavalrymen, quite to the dismay of conservative military circles.

The Huns had been ultimately uncontrollable. Some had followed the example of the Alans and accepted recruitment. None of them had been willing to trade the horse to plow and ox. Already in the course of the negotiations, they had stolen some and once the guard of the legions was finally lifted completely, most of them disappeared. Few in number and without their weapons, which had been collected after the defeat, they had rapidly made their way back northeast to those areas outside the borders of the empire from where they had come. For the Goths and the Romans, they were out of sight and out of mind. Only those strange time travelers of whose existence Godegisel had reported were concerned and continued to be full of suspicion, and they had warned against a return of the Huns – not this small group, but a very great and mighty host under the leadership of a man who was not even born yet.

A too distant, too abstract idea.

"What of Godegisel?" was a question often asked. Godegisel, who struck down one of the leaders of the time travelers, who had ignited the fire in the gatehouse with his men. Godegisel, who had warned them all with such haunting words in regard to the secret weapons of the strangers and triggered so much contempt and disbelief – and scorn, which then turned into silence, unwilling admiration and appreciation. Even the biggest critics had understood that the young nobleman had ultimately prevented the Goths to completely lose face before Thessaloniki. Godegisel had been present when the negotiations with the Romans came to a close, and he had, like all Gothic fighters, been granted amnesty and freedom. Oddly enough, the time travelers had protested only weakly. Fritigern still tried to understand how these people were thinking.

Afterwards, he had sent Godegisel away. A final act of pride, he said to himself, and only very few confidants had been informed. It was an important mission, albeit one whose consequences were ultimately not foreseeable. Some of the crazies who Godegisel had led to Thessaloniki had survived. The young nobleman had asked to be allowed to retain the very strange group of companions as personal retinue, and Fritigern had granted him this. For their trip, they got a wagon and draft horses and some gold. Then Fritigern had sent them on their way. He didn't expect to see the young man ever again, on the other hand one never knew what strange coincidences destiny continued to prepare. Who would have thought that foreign invaders from the east would expel the Goths from their ancestral land? Who would have thought that the Romans who took them in their country would then betray their guests ignominiously? Who would have thought that the three nations would defeat a large Roman army at Adrianople? And who would have thought that they would receive their defeat at the hands of travelers through time, that their weapons would strike down hundreds, even thousands, of them without lifting a sword? Even more improbabilities could be considered, and he considered them well. So much had happened in such a short time, and it was unlikely that anyone would believe any of these tales in the future. He couldn't blame them.

Fritigern, former judge of the Goths, sat calmly on the porch of the small, rural property, which had been given to him by the Romans. Members of his family had begun to inspect the fields and to repair the buildings. The former owner had fallen by the hands of the Goths, and no one had survived who could claim inheritance. This was Fritigern's spoils of war, as he liked to call it, and it was small compared to what had been within reach.

No reason to mourn. Fritigern, the Goth, was now a Roman. Soon the officials of the empire would appear and search among his men for possible recruits for the legion. Soon would be those who had destroyed 40,000 Roman soldiers wear Roman armor themselves and follow the Roman field signs. How ironic, but well considered, not the first time it had ended like this.

And wasn't it ultimately what they had hoped for?

The judge thought so.

39

The weather was wet, cloudy, and rainy, but the days got longer, and hope awoke with the spring. Godegisel slipped back and forth on his horse. Fine rivulets crawled into his neck and further down, and he suppressed a curse. The path through which he led the horses and the wagon was mushy, and the animals were slow. His companions stared as morosely into the weather as he, tired of the day-long ride and last but not least of the uncertainty of that what was waiting for them.

The monotony allowed the young nobleman to look back as he thought about what happened, and he lacked satisfaction in regard to the events of the past. The secret weapons of the time traveler had spoken, and louder than he had expected in his wildest dreams. The small triumph of having killed one of their leaders hadn't lasted for long. It had come as he had feared, and only the relative mildness and the amazing tolerance of the Romans had prevented the worst.

And then this command by Fritigern, one last gesture of resistance, a final seed of defiance. A great irony laid in Godegisel's mission, and he tried to enjoy it in his thoughts again and again and to understand what divine counsel might be behind all this. Surely something was hidden behind all of it, a plan or an intention, but to recognize it exceeded the understanding of the weary traveler. The long journey on winding, little-used paths, full of loneliness, had made him very thoughtful, almost converted him into a philosopher. He felt like a token, which was pushed by larger powers back and forth. Sometimes he had the illusion to make decisions on his own, but then he looked at himself and his deeds from a higher perspective and felt a sudden understanding for the Greek philosophers, the Stoics, of which he had heard. But there was this desire to be able to do something and to have a role to play, to have influence. It was this sudden flash of endeavor that drove him forward, and that made him accept the order of the judge, which had been presented more like a request and less a command.

And although this request was complete madness and the consequences unforeseeable.

Godegisel was on his way to deliver a gift. Fritigern had this trip well prepared, sent messengers, asked sympathizers, but the communication was so difficult that no one could know whether their journey was announced and welcome. A risk, and the nobleman was not one to shy away from it, but it was hiding in the dark, didn't consist of sword and spear, of the random ways of a guard or the flash of the moon behind the clouds at the wrong time.

Sometimes the young Goth wished the judge would've chosen someone else. Someone with the wisdom of age and greater understanding. What did Fritigern see in him? Idle questions he couldn't answer by himself, and their former leader would probably never tell him. He had been selected, and the deep respect that Godegisel still felt for the judge had almost forced him to obey the petition which wasn't an order.

Godegisel let his horse slowly fall back until he was at eye level with the cart. The wagon was closed, and on the box sat a hunched figure, holding the reins. Inside, not to be seen through the weatherproof cover, sat, gently tied up but well gagged, Emperor Valens, the precious prisoner. As Fritigern had noticed that Valens was no longer of value to him, because the Romans had already offered him a gracious peace, he had sent the prisoner to the west. Godegisel's job was to transport Valens surreptitiously and hand him over to people in Gaul who belonged to a group that apparently stood in opposition to the new pan-Roman ruler Gratian.

Godegisel had been thrust directly into the snake pit of Roman rivalries. As the young noblemen also was now formally a Roman, it seemed to be fitting.

What the conspirators wanted to achieve with Valens, Godegisel could only imagine. He would find out soon enough. And perhaps he would also understand which role he was supposed to play.

Whether he himself could make a decision or whether divine intervention pushed him forward on a path laid down and the course of which was unknown to him, Godegisel could only guess.

The young man felt that he was actually not so interested in the answer at all.

The rain became heavier, Godegisel pulled the cloak tighter around and rode back to the top of his column.

No, really, he didn't want to know.

40

"Funny."

"What is funny?"

"How you have changed."

Chief Physician Neumann looked at Rheinberg. Since the death of Becker and the long and quite moving funeral ceremony in a small church near Thessaloniki, the young captain had become calmer and more introverted. Neumann wondered if Rheinberg tormented himself in self-reproach, but if that was so, the captain didn't show any obvious signs. The good thing was that the young man wasn't alone. Many men aboard this ship – and now more and more of their Roman hosts – had become friends. Becker's death had torn a deep and painful gap, but each of them knew that he wasn't the first and wouldn't have been the last. That didn't make things necessarily easier, but it helped to put clarity in their situation.

"We all have been changed by the events," Neumann said, looking down at the construction site. Around 2,000 workers, most of them slaves, lifted earth from what in the not too distant future should become a dry dock. It was these slaves who had just led to a longer conversation between Rheinberg and a delegation from the crew. Although the Roman citizenship had been conferred to the time travelers by Gratian and consequently they all now were called Romans, no one felt right at home yet. If one followed the argument of Köhler, the reason was the terrible beer and the lack of coffee. Neumann knew that there had to be a few more issues moving their minds.

"That was something special right now," the captain said. "Three crew members have asked me if I would allow that thousands of slaves are working for us. I know those three, all convinced socialists.

Do you know how I would have responded months ago, before our time travel, to such notions?"

"Less understanding, I suppose."

"You know the story of my sister and the trouble I had because of her husband?"

"Yes."

"And what have I done now?" Rheinberg made a wide gesture. "I promised them not to forget the issue of slavery. I promised them to give the men the best treatment here. I promised them to ransom whom we can really use for our industrial production and as far as our gold is sufficient. I've even commissioned them to assess the well-being of the slaves, to submit proposals, and to report grievances. I can understand them and their concerns and actually want them to be satisfied and understand that I truly don't want to be a slave owner, and the sight gives me no joy. What have I become now, my friend?"

Neumann smiled. "You've become someone who cares, who wants to hold the crew together, and who has visions he'd like to realize."

"These are big words," muttered Rheinberg. "Far too many of them."

"Oh, Jan, you've never been someone who has been hiding behind big words, then wait and let others do the work. And you've always been someone who was willing to learn. You're not the same person who took off in Wilhelmshaven, and I foresee that there will be so many other changes in the course of the coming years."

"Did you join the prophets?"

"You don't have to be a prophet to predict this. And I don't really tell you anything you don't already know, do I?"

Rheinberg said nothing. The crowd before him worked doggedly on the big construction project. The gates made of huge logs were built in a large joinery that belonged to the pre-industrial complex Rheinberg and his men had begun to build adjacent to the dock. They called it "their base," and the production plant that grew with each passing week and attracted adventurous young Romans willing to learn like light drew moths needed a real name. Once the pit was deep and wide enough, it would be filled with water, and the *Saarbrücken* would be maneuvered inside and the gates closed. Then the bilge pumps of the ship as well as hundreds of slaves armed with buckets would start to siphon off the water and let the cruiser gently run aground. Dahms already worked on a much more effective pumping system that was still operated by muscle power but would be faster and needed only a few dozen instead of hundreds of slaves. Another project on a very long ever growing list.

Rheinberg looked toward Ravenna. The new base was built near the town. Soon it would become a city by itself. The first of the Romans drawn here had already begun to construct houses, provisionally yet, but Rheinberg could well foresee how fast this would change. Renna had jurisdiction – and thus also the "city planning" – given into the hands of the Germans, with imperial blessing. The attractiveness of the new technological center of the Roman Empire was bolstered by the fact that Romans working here enjoyed two years exemption from taxes and duties, including total exemption from service in the legions.

"Captain?"

Unnoticed Dahms had approached them. Rheinberg turned and nodded. "Is it ready?"

"There is time now."

Rheinberg beat Neumann on the shoulder. "Will you come with me? Have you visited our new workshops yet?"

"No, I'm happy to join. I have thrown myself on building our small academy. You will not believe what kind of quack doctors are practicing around here. I have to start all over again in many areas – and on the other hand I am amazed of the knowledge that is already available. Yesterday I met a doctor who performs very excellent eye operations with primitive means! Eye surgery!" Neumann shook his head. "Sometimes I'm learning as much as I teach."

"It's not just you," Dahms added smiling. "If the gentlemen would like to follow me, please?"

The way they had to cover was short. Dahms had ensured that the complex which he had begun to build wasn't too far away from the newly built docking site for the *Saarbrücken*. As a slightly foul smell pierced their noses they reached the first section of the building.

"If I'm not mistaken, we have started tanning," he said. Dahms nodded and pointed to the entrance to tannery. "Want to inspect there?"

"No thanks," murmured Neumann. "What is our product range?"

"On the one hand we started with clothing, especially boots and shoes. Since we could easily teach the local shoemakers, we got that addressed quite fast. We have now a group of twelve well-qualified masters, and although they don't work very fast, we have some products already in stock. We also produce leather for seals. Next over we have built a manufacturing plant in which we experiment with plant juices and resins. That might help us, but until now no convincing results."

"That's been better than nothing," replied Rheinberg and looked very happy. "What's that over there? We wanted –"

"The coking plant, yes. Next week it'll to go into operation. But then really only for emergencies. We produce charcoal; our goal is two tons per day. It's obvious that we need most of it for the machine shop."

As they talked, the men paced further along. It took a few minutes until they passed the not yet functioning cokery and entered an elongated wooden hall with a stone foundation. Dahms shook Fulvius' hand as he came to meet the visitors hastily and with obvious pride.

Rheinberg had not been here since the ground-breaking ceremony that started construction. He had been much too busy with the political realities of the empire. Since his appointment as Magister Militium, he had realized that he had to be more politician than military. But the hard work had helped him to endure the funerals he had to witness. The tragic and totally unnecessary death of Becker was the biggest burden he carried since Thessaloniki. The funeral under German Christian rite had been simple, but had a large amount of attendants. The inhabitants of the city had donated a tomb for the dead captain, with a large marble tablet on which his life and especially his services had been appreciated. An artist had been commissioned to build a statue, modeled after photos that had been found in Becker's belongings. The statue had become a masterpiece and looked very lifelike. The city had made it a point to care for the tomb and accepted the order Theodosius himself had given after his arrival. This included the tomb of Flavius Victor. The old general succumbed to his re-inflicted wounds shortly after Becker's death. His end was the most striking example of the fact of how fundamentally the emergence of *Saarbrücken* had changed history. Many lives had been saved by the premature termination of the Gothic War and Rheinberg regretted not a moment to have intervened. But people like Flavius Victor had died before their time, so amazing that might sound. Whether this also applied to Becker, Rheinberg couldn't tell. Maybe the captain would've been killed in the African colonies in a war that was now removed from the Rheinberg both temporally as well as emotionally.

Dahms tore the contemplating man from his thoughts. "Our steam engine factory ... We are still at the beginning, but we are confident to complete the first prototype of a simple steam engine made of bronze in the next two months. The first Roman steam warship could be in service in half a year."

Rheinberg nodded. The noise in the hall was deafening. In the back bronze was cast and in the front the finer, more mechanical work was done. Molds were ready and Roman smiths and craftsmen listened to the mostly bellowed instructions from Dahms' men. With a steam fleet of simple design, Rome would take back the already fundamentally threatened supremacy in the Mediterranean, quickly move troops along the entire coast – Dahms' blueprints included a troop transport – and could thus respond more quickly to threats.

"All this is only progressing slowly, as we still have to fight very fundamental problems," Dahms said as he led the men. He pointed to a low, long building close to the factory. "Since we have become a part of the scientific academy, our friend Neumann has begun to build here."

The doctor nodded gravely. "I want to be addresses only as *spectabilis!*"

247

"What is taught in that building?" Rheinberg wanted to know. "Medicine? Technology?"

Dahms snorted. "It would be so nice if."

"Now what?"

"Reading and writing." Neumann answered. "Even the most gifted artisans who come to us usually cannot read and write. And mathematics ... they do a lot of estimates and less calculation. If we actually want to create something like an industrial base here, the central problem is illiteracy. However, we have to start somewhere. And before anyone gets in our academy, he has to take a six-month course in literacy. That's not sufficient, and we will continue steadily, but we can't wait forever with the other topics. Look, Jan!"

Neumann pointed to a group of children walking the road under the leadership of a teenager. They waved cheerfully to the Germans and then turned off to one side, obviously heading toward the makeshift living quarters that had been mashed together with the workshops from nothing.

"We have introduced compulsory education for the families of all our employees in factories and workshops. At least six years. And the best will take a preparatory course of our academy. We need to think long-term – because we time travelers won't live forever."

Rheinberg put a hand on Neumann's shoulder. "That's what I hadn't thought of. I'm very glad that I have transferred this task to someone like you. What about our young friend Marcellus?"

At the mention of the name, a big smile slipped on Dahms' face. "As I discussed with his father, I took him under my wing. He can read and write, and that's a real advantage. Now he is learning German, which we'll use as a language of science. He starts with a basic course in mechanics. I'll make him an engineer, the first modern engineer of the Roman Empire."

Rheinberg grinned. "Looks as if you have taken up a real project."

"Dahms is doing right," Neumann said. "We need role models for new recruits. People who've done it. Thus, it becomes attractive to work for us."

"It already is," Rheinberg said. "We've started to send applicants away!"

"We are currently sought after, because we pay in good coin," Dahms said. "But we have to be a magnet for people who want to learn and achieve more than they thought possible. This is by example, and that can't be replaced with all the gold in the world."

Rheinberg nodded. "I see you have it all pretty well under control. I suspect our tour is not yet quite finished?"

"No, I have another project I'm working on," Dahms announced and led the men eventually to a small building in which everything still looked quite unfinished and currently no one seemed to work.

"We have planned a number of other workshops, forges, glass factories and such, partly already under construction," the engineer explained. "But this is something special. You can't see much, and I admit it isn't very high on my priority list, but ultimately I think it is something with which we can score with the Romans. This is, one might say, my department for especially high-class technologies. I have here two projects planned. First, I want to build a functioning arc lamp."

"Arc lamps?" Neumann asked to be sure.

"To be exact, carbon arc lamps," Dahms added. "They could allow us to do various things, such as night shifts in the large factory buildings. But if I imagine that we could also illuminate the Roman Forum at night, then that might make us friends with the urban elite."

"Arc lamps consume electricity," Neumann recalled.

"We build steam engines. One use is likely to establish a power plant. A simple steam power plant should not be that difficult to build as soon as our Roman allies have learned the basics. Copper lines we can produce, and then there only remains the question of the insulation. Of course, the utility will be only used relatively limited, but I think that lighting at night just for the big cities will be very attractive."

Rheinberg scratched his head. Dahms tossed technical visions around in a manner that impressed him greatly. What the engineer was initiating here was no less than an industrial revolution – and in record time.

"What's the second project?" Neumann wanted to know.

"A dry ice machine."

"What?" the other two men asked in unison.

"I've read a lot about the cooling process, according to Carl von Linde, especially his articles on improved refrigeration. Many breweries in our time have used this method. By making ice, we can make the benefits of our technology especially clear. I mean, the Romans already enjoy quite complex air conditioning systems in their villas, which are operated by cool water. It can be damn hot in the summer, and in our effort to provide improved medical care, cold temperatures also plays a big role."

"That's true," Neumann murmured.

"We can pour chilled wine or even make ice cream in midsummer – we need to offer something that makes us popular among the general population, not only for the high and mighty. If we want to survive here, we need acceptance at all levels."

Rheinberg looked at Dahms, as if he saw the engineer suddenly with different eyes. "You think far, and you think right," he finally said. "I'll give you a completely free hand in these projects. Concentrate on things of immediate benefit. I have only one important question: What about weapons technology?"

Dahms nodded gravely.

"This is currently our biggest challenge," he admitted. "First, ammunition for our rifles or for naval guns is unrealistic for the foreseeable future. We can't achieve that. The *Saarbrücken* still has enough in the bunker, which should suffice for a while, but our friends from the infantry have spent theirs pretty before Thessaloniki."

"Alternatives?"

"I sat down with my men, and we have played with different scenarios. We have by now discussed it widely, and it's ample time to think about implementation. What we can manage technically in the foreseeable future are muskets. The problem, however: The benefit to us actually is not so impressive. The range is limited, the loading speed unimpressive, and accuracy a horror. If I were, for example, an observant general of the Huns, I wouldn't be too scared by a company of musketeers, and either ride them down or finish them with my own much more effective archers. Muskets make noise and perhaps frighten the benighted barbarians at the first clash, but after that every military leader with some brain matter would adapt. We have noticed that even against our effective weapons the Gothic leaders have started to adjust properly within their means. I would therefore advise against muskets. The expense would be considerable and the benefits limited."

"So?"

"We can use steam power to build larger pieces – I'm thinking about a steam catapult, which could be good use for sea battles, but also for the defense of cities. The range could be increased and also the cadence, an improvement for sieges and sea battles. I have a few people already designing a prototype. Then there is gunpowder. The ingredients are all known, and we have access to resources. Pyrotechnist Thanfeld provides invaluable help here. We can quickly produce good quantities and simply use it as an explosive or as ammunition for catapults. Booby traps would be readily feasible and could support us in the defense of fortified positions. I'm also thinking of simple hand grenades, with which we could equip the legions. That would certainly have its effect on onrushing barbarians, when they expect only spears and arrows, and especially the cavalry will not like it, because the horse might do something crazy."

"So no firearms?"

Dahms shrugged. "What we manage in any case, are handguns, something like the old dueling pistols – which were often made carefully and are not ineffective at close range. If you wish, I can plan for a workshop, but don't expect great output, if the product is supposed to be of quality."

"Keep it in mind," Rheinberg said.

Dahms nodded, took out a pad and made a note. "What we can produce, of course, are cannons. But this requires, if we want them to endure and to fire relatively quickly, an important substance which is currently not yet available to us: steel. The Romans have a few very clever alloys, but no blast furnaces with which they could manufacture steel. We can't work ourselves around steel. So we need to build blast furnaces. The simplest would be a puddling furnace, something achievable once the coal supply is secured. With steel, we can build more effective steam engines, with boilers withstanding higher pressures. So steel is high on my list."

"And then cannons?"

"And then cannons. First without rolling runs and quite crude, but large pieces with a powerful caliber. If you have a dozen of them that you can move, lengthy sieges would be a thing of the past."

Neumann cleared his throat. "Haven't we make a mistake?"

"How?" Dahms asked.

"Our expected opponent in the future consists of victims and the cause of *Völkerwanderung* – that is, as the name suggests, migratory peoples. They normally break their teeth at Roman fortifications, and they don't build their own. If my historical knowledge does not deceive me, even the dreaded Huns have never built mighty bulwarks that had to be overcome."

Dahms and Rheinberg exchanged glances.

"That's right," Rheinberg finally conceded. "But we have to be honest: Some of the conflicts of the future will have the character of civil wars – Romans against Romans. The fact that Gratian currently supports us and Ambrosius and his friends have for now drawn the short straw is not something we can rely on. The fact that the historical Magnus Maximus has apparently called off his revolt against Gratian in our timeline doesn't mean that there isn't something cooking somewhere – especially when Gratian intends to realize his plan to dismiss Maximus and to summon him back to Ravenna. I'm even sorry to say this, but until further notice we'll probably have to fight on two fronts."

Neumann's expression made obvious that this wasn't a perspective that particularly cheered him. "So cannons," he said dully.

"So it is," Dahms confirmed. "But first steel. I don't want bronze cannons that won't help us much. Well, if we really need them, maybe."

"But they are better than those of iron, especially as long as we don't have standard ammunition," Rheinberg pointed out. "Bronze cannons are more elastic, iron breaks easier."

Dahms looked uncomfortable.

"I want the steel. And that brings us to the last major project."

"And that is?"

"Communication. We have a beautiful radio telegraph system with us. It's not good for much without remote stations and a corresponding network. I think that we can succeed to install wireless telegraph stations in central cities of the empire, where we can build small steam power plants in the future. The advantage that could be gained through lightning-fast communication, especially given the wide frontiers that must be defended, would be of high importance. But this requires a nationwide investment."

"It's an excellent idea," Neumann said. "The fast riders of the present system are not bad, but radio telegrams from east to west, from north to south – that would help the empire tremendously, if only to regroup the troops properly in need."

"This doesn't make the troops themselves faster," Dahms pointed out. "But once we have a steam engine production, we can build simple locomotives."

Neumann looked at Dahms at half aghast, half excited.

"Now you give me the creeps, Mr. Marine Chief Engineer!"

Dahms smiled complacently. "That's good," was his only comment.

"We are continuing this conversation another time," Rheinberg said, raising his hat in order to straighten his hair. "I see that there is currently a lot of work and you have the matter well in hand. I don't know how long the current respite will last – up until somewhere something happens. So we should concentrate on work and achievable progress as long as we still have the rest to do so. I will not bother anyone, as I must soon return to the court because the Emperor asked for me."

"Power politics for fun?" Dahms asked with a grin.

Rheinberg gave him a reproachful look. "Do you want to join me?"

The navy chief engineer made an all engulfing gesture.

"I would like to, Captain, but you can see for yourself ..."

"Yeah ..."

They stepped back into the open. Rheinberg looked in the direction of Ravenna, which loomed on the horizon. About 500 meters away he saw another building that looked like a factory.

"What is it?"

Dahms scratched his head.

"Yes, that's ... that's none of ours."

"Please elaborate."

"Well, it is one of ours in a way ... it's ... well, it's the first private factory, which was initiated by our men. A collaboration with Roman businessmen, to be exact."

Rheinberg smiled appreciatively. "That's not bad! We need to make money anyway, so why not? So much of what we produce here we can later turn into hard cash! Who are the new entrepreneurs?"

"Köhler and Behrens," Neumann answered.

Rheinberg grinned. He had already guessed. The two had been together almost continuously since returning from Greece when time and opportunity arose. "You know about it?" he asked the doctor.

"I get some of the production. For medical reasons."

Rheinberg frowned his face, then understanding loomed.

"For medical reasons, yes?"

Neumann's features remained deadly serious. Only his eyes sparkled with mischief. "For what else, Captain?"

Rheinberg decided to end the conversation at this point.

41

"It works."

"Oh yes, it works."

Köhler and Behrens looked meaningfully into each other's eyes, before they sat back down again and looked at the taproom. The customers were numerous, and the looks of the men who sat at the tables and funneled German-Roman spirits from small cups were glassy. Orders were called across the room, and the barmaid balanced trays of bottles and cups through the crowd.

Lucius Vitellus, the owner of the inn, came up to the two men. He grinned over his unshaven face, wiped his hands on the grease-stained coat, and showed his teeth gaps.

Köhler and Behrens returned the grin. Lucius Vitellus was not just any innkeeper, he was their business partner, along with two other tavern owners in Ravenna. Together, they had raised the necessary capital and technical knowledge in order to build the first distillery of the Roman Empire. The miraculous transformation of mostly cheap wine in high-proof booze and its effect on the revelers who took a strong habituation had Vitellus and his friends quickly convinced. And the clientele of their establishments had understood that they could effectively and efficiently reach the state of drunken bliss they all ultimately strove for. The news of the new stuff had quickly made the rounds, and the first inquiries from Rome and Milan had the business partners enter into a partnership with a haulage contractor. Coopers had been commissioned to prepare suitable drums for trucks, with which the spirits could then be delivered to the surrounding towns. In the tavern itself, the strong drink was, like wine, poured into amphoras before being delivered to the taproom and stayed pleasantly cool. Only the rich could afford to import ice from the Alps to Ravenna in the summer, and before

Dahms' plans with the ice machine did work, they had to use more traditional ways of cooling.

If the demand continued to grow, the capacity of the first distillery close to the industrial center around the newly constructed port of the *Saarbrücken* wouldn't suffice. Behrens and Köhler, whose private income grew steadily through this investment, already laid down plans to build more distilleries in Rome, where they expected the largest market for their product.

"Everything is proceeding quite outstandingly, dear friends!" Vitellus stated in deliberately slower articulation. Once the *solidi* rolled, language problems had suddenly played a large role. Behrens and Köhler devoted themselves with great zeal to Latin, and some of the distillery workers who felt a higher calling apparently began to learn German, which seemed at least so far to obtain the status of a language of science. Since many technical terms were only vaguely translated into Latin – the easiest were medical terms –, in many cases translation wasn't even tried. And even old Vitellus, who was since the beginning of their cooperation of remarkably sunny disposition, had snapped up one or two words of German.

"Sit down, my friend," Köhler said. The innkeeper didn't hesitate. "You're in a good mood!"

"I gave my wife a bag of gold and sent her to Rome, shopping. She was overjoyed and carried the children along. A heavenly peace now reigns in my house! I'm more than just grateful to you!"

Köhler nodded in understanding. Vitellus didn't add the fact in his explanation that he now had the possibility to get warm with the barmaids with complete impunity. Indeed, the efforts of the two officers who insisted on reasonably acceptable and humane working conditions in the distillery and their application also in the associated taverns had not yet proven to be very successful. Once the loans that Vitellus and his friends had given the two Germans were paid off, Köhler and Behrens would be in a stronger negotiating position. Especially the older Köhler felt deep pity for the gaunt barmaids, rushed to exhaustion, of which most were not even slaves – what wouldn't have made the conditions better. In fact, they

256

already planned the opening of their own tavern, with much higher standards on so many levels.

They had muster some patience until then, but the more Vitellus and his family sold, the more the time would come when they would no longer be needed.

"That sounds good," was Köhler's standard answer to Vitellus' euphoria, and also Behrens put up a good face. As the host apparently took advantage of the situation to test the quality of his new product very thoroughly himself, Vitellus was long gone sober. The fact that he still held himself more or less upright and was able to form coherent sentences was amazing. But it also showed apparently what kind of husband the rightly grouchy wife had been punished with.

Vitellus staggered back to the bar. In passing, he slapped a barmaid on the butt, a gesture taken by her with a stony expression in her face.

Behrens and Köhler looked at each other again.

"Soon," the sergeant murmured, "soon we will change some things. By God, in our pub this won't happen. And no slaves, not one. Better: We buy slaves as staff and then let them free immediately, with the offer of proper payment for further services. No slaves, I tell you."

"No slaves," Köhler confirmed.

"Some more things," Behrens added. He looked around. "Quite a lot. We must do what we can."

Köhler smiled. He put a hand on his business partner's arm.

"This is already changing a lot, my friend. And more is to come."

Register of persons

Agiwulf	Gothic warrior
Ambrose of Milan	Roman bishop
Andragathius	Roman general
Arbogast	Roman general
Aurelius Africanus	Roman trierarch
Jonas Becker	infantry officer and company commander
Peter Behrens	infantry sergeant
Bilimer	Gothic warrior
Börnsen	NCO of the *Saarbrücken*
Brockmann	Paramedic of the *Saarbrücken*
Caius Martinus	son of a Roman businessman
Johann Dahms	Chief Engineer of the *Saarbrücken*
Flavius Gratian	Roman Emperor
Flavius Victor	Roman general
Fritigern	leader of the Goths
Godegisel	Gothic nobleman
Dietrich Joergensen	Officer of the *Saarbrücken*
Jovius	Roman decurion
Julia	daughter of Marcus Gaius Michellus
Harald Köhler	NCO of the *Saarbrücken*
Klaus Langenhagen	Officer of the *Saarbrücken*
Latinus	Roman centurion
Lucia	wife of Marcus Gaius Michellus
Lucius Tellius Severus	Roman general in retirement
Magnus Maximus	Governor of Britain

Malobaudes	Roman general
Marcellus	son of Marcus Necius
Marcus Flovius Renna	Roman Navarch
Marcus Gaius Michellus	Roman senator
Marcus Necius	Roman Fischer
Marcus Tullius Salius	Roman centurion
Nannienus	Roman general
Dr. Hans Neumann	ship's doctor of the *Saarbrücken*
Odotheus	Gothic warrior
Petronius	Roman priest
Jan Rheinberg	captain of the *Saarbrücken*
Rechiar	Gothic warrior
Richomer	Roman officer
Rufus	Roman legionary
Joseph Schmitt	crew member of the *Saarbrücken*
Secratus	Roman officer
Simodes	Roman legionary
Quintus Aurelius Symmachus	Roman senator
Theodosius	Roman noblema
Markus Tennberg	Ensign of the *Saarbrücken*
Valens	Roman Emperor
Thomas Volkert	Ensign of the *Saarbrücken*
Klaus von Geeren	infantry officer and deputy company commander
Johann Freiherr von Klasewitz	First Officer of the *Saarbrücken*

Made in the USA
Lexington, KY
16 May 2017